BOMBSHELL

RICHARD RAINE

BOMBSHELL

HARCOURT, BRACE & WORLD, INC.
New York

CONTENTS

PRELUDE

BREMEN BREAKOUT—MARCH

"For God's sake wait, man—it may take all of us to hold him down."

Karl grinned without mirth. "Don't worry, Otto. As long as we don't let him near any high explosive he's as harmless as a kitten."

"Then why have we assembled six men for when he comes out?"

Otto shivered in the bitter German night and looked up to where the asylum walls were silhouetted against the cold moonlight. They waited near the edge of a track inside the wood, and the stone ramparts were just visible through the network of naked branches. It was three o'clock in the morning, and the March wind blew down the River Weser from the direction of Bremen freezing everything in its path. As he listened, Otto could hear the grind and crumble of ice floes on the Weser. He stamped on the iron-hard snow, and

3

the ground hurt his feet through the soles of his shoes. He spoke to forget his nervousness.

"Karl, do you really think they'll get him out?"

"Of course. It is all arranged. We have duplicate keys for the side gate, the inner door, the door to the cell block, and for Bruno's personal cell. The night guard has been bribed to put something in his colleagues' coffee. A perfect operation. He should be coming out any minute now."

Nearer the edge of the wood four more men waited, and Otto heard a brief clink of metal. The handcuffs. He would feel a lot better when they had those clamped over Bruno's wrists. To reassure himself he gripped the short truncheon in his right hand tightly. "Only to be used in extreme emergency," Karl had said. Well, he would treat it as an emergency if Bruno came anywhere near him.

He heard that awful grinding sound again, and the crunch of ice made him feel that the whole world might be breaking up into little pieces. Thank God it had stopped snowing. He felt a compulsion to talk, resisted it, and then gave in.

"Karl, is it because Bruno is a time-bomb specialist that we're bringing him out?"

"I've no idea, and you've more sense than to ask about things like that. Our job is to bring him out, deliver him to the appointed rendezvous, and that's it."

"The truck's engine is bound to have frozen up on a night like this. And why leave it all that way back? We must have a whole kilometer to walk before we reach the truck."

"Exactly one kilometer. That's the idea—then they won't hear the engine start up inside the asylum. We have to take him through Bremen and we must be well clear of the city before it wakes up." He paused to listen. "That's it—the whistle. They've got him. You know what to do?"

"I wait behind this tree next to the trip wire."

"Keep out of sight. You probably won't be needed, but if

4

he breaks loose he'll come down this track. When he goes over the trip wire, hit him—and make sure you get it right the first time. You may not have a second chance."

"I'll get him." Otto clenched the truncheon tighter and slipped behind the tree, being careful not to fall over the trip wire himself. Then he stood against the trunk and waited, his heart pounding, listening to the dreadful groan and rasp of the breaking ice, thinking about Bruno. When he heard voices he peered around the trunk, but the group of men near the edge of the wood was a shadowed blur, a blur that moved shakily. For a brief second of panic fright Otto thought a struggle was going on, and then the shaking stopped and he heard muttered voices. By his side he felt his arm rigid, almost an extension of the rigid truncheon he held as though his life depended on it, which it well might. Then it happened. He heard a brief commotion and the sound of running feet. Bruno was coming!

Otto knew that he would miss the trip wire. By some freak chance his feet would fly over it, and then *he* would have to run after him, deeper into the wood, without a light. Christ! Why hadn't he thought of a . . .

A figure appeared just beyond the trunk, a figure which moved at incredible speed, arms crooked at the elbows, legs racing, racing high, a tall figure, his gaunt face bony in the moonlight. He reached the trip wire, one leg went beyond it, clear. . . . No, he was down! Otto sprang forward, but the figure rolled away from him, over and over, crashing through the dead, snow-encrusted bracken like a self-propelled ninepin. Otto followed, running, half-crazy with fear. He reached the man as he was climbing to his feet. The figure turned to meet Otto's attack, then his foot slipped on the snow and he was down again, flat on his back. Otto stooped, and a clawed hand whipped up, grabbed his throat, and squeezed. For two seconds Otto kept his head, and as the hand squeezed he brought the truncheon down over his

5

shoulder and smashed it on the forehead of the supine figure. The truncheon bounced, left his hand, but the hand at his throat relaxed and then he sensed a flurry of people. As Otto stood up, his knees trembling, he heard the click of handcuffs. A reflex action sent him back to collect the trip wire, and Karl came with him. When Otto straightened up, the men were disappearing down the track carrying the unconscious body. The huge man, a foreigner whose name Otto had never heard, brought up the rear.

"I hope," Karl remarked, "that you haven't hit him too hard."

"Mercy of God!" protested Otto. "That's Bruno Fleischmann, the homicidal maniac."

1 SWITZERLAND: EXPLOSION

1: EXPLOSION—OCTOBER

"Death by high explosive. What a way to go!" Ambrose Cutt dabbed his forehead delicately with a violet silk hand-kerchief and made a face at me.

"When did you hear this?" I asked tightly.

"Our chap in Switzerland phoned me ten minutes ago. Sven Heim's villa on the outskirts of Zurich was blown sky-high and he was inside it at that time. His niece, Else, was with him, I'm afraid. This thing's becoming like guerrilla warfare—that's the fourteenth explosion in Europe since April. The first one was in North Germany, wasn't it, David?"

"Bremen."

We sat in the lounge of Cutt's farmhouse. Beyond the French windows the strong winds of late October were buffeting the bleak stretch of Kent marsh which seemed to go on forever. The afternoon sky was crowded with a sea of gray cloud which stormed its way inland, heading for London, while the old windmill at the bottom of Cutt's garden

9

churned its sails madly. The French windows rattled in their frames as a heavy gust tried to shake them open. Cutt replaced the handkerchief inside the sleeve of his purple smoking jacket and approached his objective with what he would have termed a tactful attitude of mind.

"David, it may appear a trifle unseemly to venture into a business discussion at such a moment, but my clients are still interested in buying Sven Heim's miniaturized jet engine."

"Nikki Kardehay had bought it—you know that, Cutt."

"Ambrose, please. But had the deal actually been consummated?"

Only Ambrose would have used the verb consummated in such a context, and it made me dislike him even more, if that were possible. He sat behind his elegant Queen Anne desk and placed his pudgy hands together as though about to pronounce a benediction. His pink fat face was clean-shaven, his fair hair brushed back over his forehead, his baggy eyes watchful and speculative. A faint aroma of talc drifted across the desk, and there were traces of it on his fleshy nose.

"No," I said. "The contract of sale had been drawn up, and I was flying out to Zurich tomorrow for Sven to sign it."

"Then it's still on the market, and no doubt Mr. David Martini will again negotiate its sale." He leaned forward and smiled persuasively, his voice soft as candlelight. "I stress that we are still most interested. Heim was a clever engineer, and his engine was the most advanced in the world."

"Kardehay outbid you."

"He's a Hungarian billionaire."

"He took out American citizenship papers—you don't make a billion in Hungary these days."

"No, of course not. Quite so. But this time we might reconsider our price. Nothing like thinking you've lost something to make you up the ante." He sniggered gently.

"It's absolutely certain that Sven is dead? When did the explosion take place?"

"At eleven o'clock this morning on the dot."

"And yet your chap only phoned you ten minutes ago?"

"Something like that—there was a delay, apparently. All lines to London were engaged. I do hope you believe me; I wouldn't like to think that when I asked you to call on me I already knew that Heim was dead."

"They found Else's body as well, did they?"

"I don't know any details, but she was certainly inside the villa with Mr. Heim. Rodney had been up to the scene of the explosion, and he said the entire villa had been blown to pieces—literally to pieces. It must have been an enormous bomb. Horrible!" He shuddered and glanced across to where a grandfather clock ticked solemnly, like a time mechanism registering the progression toward an explosion.

"In that case there'll be hardly anything left of either of them. Who the devil can be responsible for these ghastly outrages?"

"I do, of course, fully appreciate that this news is an awful shock," Cutt sympathized smoothly.

"Sven Heim was a very old friend of mine. I just can't imagine why anyone should want to blow up a Finnish engineer. It's out of pattern, too, this one."

"I don't quite follow." Cutt put his head on one side to show me how earnestly he wished to follow. At the bottom of the garden the windmill sails tore around their predetermined circle as though engaging in a wild race.

"Those sails are going to come off," I warned him.

"No, no, you needn't worry. Everything's under control. The wind has to reach a certain force before there's any risk." He pointed to an instrument hanging on the wall. "That little gadget tells me we shall be quite all right, quite all right. You were saying something about a pattern?"

"All the previous explosions have taken place inside West Germany. In each case the victim has been a leading public

11

figure and the time bomb has been placed inside his home. The force of the explosions has varied, but always the house has been wrecked and the police haven't a clue as to who is behind them. It's now taking on the flavor of a campaign of political assassination and is becoming a major political issue in Western Europe. The murder of Sven Heim and his niece completely breaks the pattern for the first time."

"Because he's Finnish?"

"Yes, and because this is the first explosion outside Germany. I find it a very sinister business."

"I do agree, David. Getting back to what we were talking about—I imagine that the well-known international business negotiator Mr. David Martini will be handling the sale of Heim's jet engine on behalf of his heirs now. Hm?"

"Possibly. But I can tell you now that Kardehay will pay the agreed sum, a sum you couldn't meet."

"Supposing this time we did meet it. Yes, let us for a moment suppose that we did." Cutt leaned forward again and smiled engagingly, his head now positioned against the windows so that the tips of the sails raced around behind its silhouette, creating an odd impression of a face in a shooting gallery.

"You'd have to do more than meet it. Kardehay will have first option on that price—you'd have to bid higher."

"I thought you'd say that."

"So you weren't disappointed."

"Maybe we'd creep up a little higher." He moved fat fingers in a crawl over the desk to demonstrate how they might creep. While I said nothing the grandfather clock ticked on, as though counting down the moments toward doomsday. Cutt looked up and beamed. "Just supposing, David."

"I can't discuss it any further now. I'm to take it that you're in the market for a higher bid, is that it?"

"I'd like you to get in touch with me when the propitious moment arrives."

12

"I'd feel more like doing that if you told me why you want to buy. You were cagey enough last time."

"It would make a difference?"

I answered with a look of growing impatience, and Cutt raised a conciliatory palm in a gesture of surrender.

"It might well be used, David, in a new vertical take-off aircraft. Now that's something that's strictly between you, me, and Grandfather." He indicated the clock.

"I'll bear it in mind. And now I'm off. I have some packing to do."

"A long trip?" Cutt came around the side of his desk and rested both hands inside the pockets of his smoking jacket. Standing up, he was short and very plump, and his mandarin slippers made no sound. He helped me on with my coat and turned the collar down. I turned it up again and went around a wooden spinning wheel to reach the front door.

"Not so far. I'm off to Zurich tomorrow."

Cutt clapped his hands together. "I know! You're going to look into the death of your old friend Sven Heim. Am I right?"

"Yes."

He opened the door, and the gale came inside and blew a newspaper to the floor to let us know it had arrived. Cutt picked the paper up and folded it neatly again behind the shelter of the wall, frowning at the wind's impertinence.

"I see," he remarked, "that Egypt is now claiming to have achieved air mastery over the Middle East."

"Really?" I stepped outside, and the wind removed the cloying smell of talc from my nostrils. The front door was painted a tender shade of lavender blue; the gate to the country lane was a highly varnished ship's wheel. Nothing seemed right about the place, nothing except the thatch roof, which Cutt had preserved in its original color. I said good-by, but he followed me to the gate and opened it with

13

a discreet flourish, the wind blowing his flaxen hair all over his head.

"Zurich?" he repeated. "You might just wake up one morning and find me out there."

"That'll be nice."

"Happy landings!"

I got into my parked car, and he retreated inside the farmhouse. As I drove off I glanced down the side of the house where the windmill was performing like a dervish. At that very moment a sail reached its zenith in the perpetual circle and snapped off, cart-wheeling gaily into the marsh beyond. It was the only good thing that happened that day.

2: STOP PRESS

"Think of all the things I've done for you, Madge," I said to the phone.

"Name one," the phone said back to me.

"Just a minute."

I put the receiver down on the table, went over to the window, and closed it against the King's Road traffic. It was dark outside, but there were lights in the darkness, the lights of London's homeward-bound commuter traffic heading for the bridges over the Thames. For a moment I envied Cutt his Kentish farmhouse, and then I remembered the lavender-colored door. I resumed the phone battle. Her voice was aggressive.

"I'm a newspaperwoman and I haven't all night to listen to suspect negotiators chatting me up."

"Will you do it?"

"Print the report?"

"What else?"

"I just wanted to be sure. What's in it for me?"

"A dinner when I get back. Champagne cocktails—you name it, I'll buy it. Within reason," I added.

"All men are misers. And you can keep your lousy dinner, David Martini. Is there a scoop in it for me?"

"If there is, you'll be the first to know, dear."

"Seriously, David, this thing could be very, very big. There are rumors infiltrating London—rumors as to which organization is behind the bomb outrages. If they're true, it will change the whole balance of the Western world."

"Tell me about them."

"Not on your life. You're the one who's going to supply news. Remember? In any case, the rumors may not be true." She paused, and in the background a teleprinter chattered to itself in its own private language. "Come to think of it, David, the rumors are just fantastic enough to be true. If they are, you'd better watch out. Are you sure you want me to do this?"

"Yes. And do try to get a picture of me included. You had some once."

"No problem there, although I can't guarantee they'll print it. What are you doing—setting yourself up as a target?"

"You'll try, then—real hard?"

"Out of the generosity of my great big heart. I'll show you it, sometime. Now"—her voice crisped—"let's check this over. You want a report sent out over the wire service with special reference to Switzerland. . . ."

"Don't forget the London *Telegram*—they airmail it to Zurich."

"All in good time. Now, again, the report is to state that David Martini, international negotiator and long-time friend of Sven Heim, is flying to Zurich to check personally on the bomb explosion that killed Heim and his niece, Else, earlier today. That's the guts of it, but I may tart it up a bit."

15

"Watch it, Madge, I know you. Just the way you said it is fine. And don't forget the picture."

"I'll transmit one to Zurich by radio and speak to the *Telegram* news editor personally. He's a pal. Not that that buys me anything. Is that the lot? I haven't got much time left to get this moving."

"That should sew it up." I spoke casually. "Know anything about Nikki Kardehay?"

"Rich, rich, rich. Ex-Hungarian who came out at the time of the uprising. Took himself off to the States and made enough fortunes for ten millionaires on the stock market. Used some of the loot to become a big industrialist, then transferred his operations back to Europe. Has a large lucrative finger in the armaments pie."

"You're a walking encyclopedia. What I really wanted to know is has he anything to do with manufacturing aircraft?"

"Not as far as I know—in fact, I'm sure he hasn't. The other day I read one of those supplements that list world aircraft manufacturers and he wasn't on the list. Why do you ask?"

"Just something to do with a negotiation I may be handling. I thought I'd ask while I had you hanging breathless on the other end of a phone."

"Is that all, Mr. Martini?" she asked ironically.

"Perhaps it had better be. Do your best for me."

"I don't know why, but I will, even if you only rate a stop press."

3: ROMY

The plane was losing height rapidly as we approached Zurich Airport, and now my fellow passengers seemed lost for topics of conversation while each grappled with his own

16

personal moment of truth. I signaled to the Swiss hostess, who was coming down the aisle, pausing to check a safety belt. My voice was a whisper in the hush of waiting.

"That gray-haired man four seats ahead—I'm sure I know the face but I just can't place it."

"It's Hans Feuring, the German cabinet minister. . . ."

"Thanks, I've got him now. He's the most pro-American politician in West Germany. I should have recognized him."

"It's probably his spectacles, sir." She rested a hand on my chair arm, glad to talk to someone during the minutes before taking her seat for the landing. "He always takes them off in public, before he's photographed. You'll see when he leaves the aircraft. You've enjoyed the trip, I hope, sir?"

"Hardly a tremor all the way." I winked at her. "Gone quiet all of a sudden, hasn't it?"

"It usually does at this point. People are thinking of what they'll be doing when they've alighted," she replied diplomatically.

I nodded as the plane went down into its final dive, the only sound the muted scream of the jets. Then the machine gently bumped the runway, and we were in Switzerland. Somewhere behind me I thought I heard a sigh of relief, and a series of clicks recorded the release of safety belts. A few minutes later we were disembarking, dead on time.

Hans Feuring was immediately in front of me as we left the plane, and the stewardess was right—he put his glasses away just before he stepped out to face the news photographers. I guessed I would be in the picture, too, and as we walked toward the reception hall one reporter left the group around Feuring to speak to me.

"Mr. Martini?"

"That's right."

"You've come to Zurich to investigate the bomb explosions?"

17

"No comment."

"There's a report that . . ."

We chatted all the way to the reception building, and I made careful noncommittal replies, which aroused his curiosity and probably guaranteed another story in the papers. Because of the Feuring group ahead of us, we walked slowly in the brilliant Swiss sunshine, our leisurely pace reflecting the peaceful atmosphere, and then we were held up while the Feuring group began to enter the building. So I glanced back at the plane which had brought us all the way from London.

A crocodile of passengers trailed behind us, the tail of it well clear of the plane. Mechanics were beginning to fuss about the aircraft, and the sunlight reflected . . .

The explosion came as a flash of incandescent light, a searing flash, which blotted out the airplane. Then the shock wave hit me, and I was blown flat, sprawling across someone . . . Feuring. The world was a slow-rolling boom of explosive power, and fragments spattered the building wall. I was lifting myself to my feet when hands came down, closed around Feuring, and helped him upright. He was dazed but unhurt. Blinking, he fumbled for the spectacles and put them on automatically. Security men hustled him inside the building as I looked back.

The crocodile of passengers was in disarray, some lying sprawled on the ground, others climbing to their feet. One man put a cigarette in his mouth and then forgot to light it. The machine was a shatter of twisted metal, and there was no sign of the mechanics who had been working on what once had been a plane. Behind a dense cloud of black smoke, flames crackled in the afternoon, and then the sound was lost as fire engines screamed across the airfield, their sirens a mournful dirge. If we had been only a few minutes behind schedule, the time bomb would have gone off in midair. Hans Feuring would have been added to the list of prominent Germans blown up, and his fellow passengers

18

would have been registered as anonymous statistics in the records of airline casualties.

"I'm Romy Silber, Mr. Martini, and this, I believe, is you?"

I took the airmail edition of the London *Telegram* from the girl and accepted my room key from the receptionist of the Hotel Schweizerhof. The headline and my own picture leaped at me. BRITISH LAWYER FLYING TO ZURICH TO INVESTIGATE EUROPEAN BOMB OUTRAGES.

"Yes, it's me," I said quietly.

"I represent the Nord-Deutscher News Agency of Frankfurt and I'd appreciate a few minutes of your time. We have a regular profile feature we send out, and it's been suggested we include you in it."

I stared at Romy Silber. An inch or two less than six feet tall, her slim figure was dressed in a short camel's hair coat, and on her long jet-black hair she wore a pale-brown Robin Hood hat which gave an impression of severity. The impression was heightened by large horn-rims perched on the bridge of her Roman nose, and her lips combined fullness with will power. While she waited for my reply she fiddled impatiently with the horn-rims. I watched the Zurich traffic beyond the plate-glass entrance doors, where cars with lights on edged their way past the Hauptbahnhof opposite. It was nighttime now, and I had just got back to my hotel and found her waiting for me.

"You don't waste much time," I remarked.

"I was at the airport this afternoon when your plane was blown up. I suppose the bomb *was* intended for Hans Feuring?"

"The police seem to think so. From what I could gather," I added.

"Quite a coincidence that you should be on the same plane."

Her expression was businesslike, the whiteness of her

19

smooth skin glacial, and she spoke English with American undertones. Beneath the undertones lay a faint trace of accent which betrayed her German nationality.

"Would that be a question or a statement?" I inquired.

"Do I get the interview?"

"There's a seat over there. . . ."

"I'd prefer somewhere quieter." She spoke abruptly. "An interview calls for privacy."

"You'd better come up then."

She entered my room on the first floor confidently, heading for a particular chair. "Do you mind if I disrobe?" she asked, and took off her hat and coat. I ordered coffee from room service, and when I turned around she was sitting down with a notebook on her lap. Her camel's-hair skirt rested high above the knees, and her legs were long, slim, and well shaped.

"You've come to Europe to investigate all the bomb explosions," she stated.

"I didn't say that."

"The papers are saying it for you."

"You shouldn't believe all you read in the press—and I thought you were after a profile."

Her black sweater was cashmere, and from the manner in which it fitted her, it appeared to be one size too small. Without the hat she seemed a great deal less severe, and I wondered what she looked like without those horn-rims. She pulled them higher up her nose and spoke crisply.

"The newspaper report said you used to be a lawyer. Why give up that?"

"I got bored with the stuffy courtroom atmosphere—standing on my hind legs all day long pleading the case of someone I didn't believe in before a judge too old to remember what it was all about. One afternoon I had a picture of myself thirty years hence—still standing in the same courtrooms pleading the same old arguments. I'd just finished a case, so I hung up my wig and gown and never went back."

"Just like that?" She snapped her fingers. "A profession like the law?" She sounded amazed.

"Just like that. I set up as a business negotiator and lived happily ever after. Good—here's the coffee."

While we drank our first cup I didn't say anything. She took off the horn-rims, and her eyes were large and deep-blue, with a hint of mockery. Then she pulled her sweater tautly down over her breasts, put on the horn-rims, as though now dressed for business, and resumed the interview.

"Do you speak any languages, Mr. Martini?"

"German, French, Italian, and some Spanish."

"Oh, we can talk in German then!" Her manner relaxed, and she began speaking rapidly in her own tongue. Inside fifteen minutes she had as much of my background as I was prepared to give her, including the fact that my father had been an Italian who emigrated to Britain in 1921 and married a Scots girl. And that I was still a bachelor. Then she turned to the present.

"You really are investigating the murder of Sven Heim and his niece?"

"That's right. Sven was a very old friend."

"Have you any theory yet as to who is behind these bomb explosions?"

"Explosion—singular. I'm only interested in who killed Sven. I thought I'd made that clear."

"But it's only the latest in a chain. There have been thirteen other outrages inside Germany since April."

"What's your theory, Miss Silber?"

She hesitated. "There's a terrible rumor sweeping through Europe like wildfire. Well-informed circles . . ." She trailed off.

"How do you define your well-informed circles?"

"Chatter in the chancelleries, gossip at cocktail parties. Don't underestimate those sources either. They often know."

"Tell me about the rumor." I leaned over to refill her cup.

"I'm not sure I want to at the moment. It's as explosive as the bombs themselves. For a long time the German police thought they knew who was planting the time bombs. The first explosion killed Horst Kramer, the metallurgical specialist, in Bremen. A few weeks earlier, Bruno Fleischmann, a criminal lunatic, escaped from an asylum near Bremen—so it looked like him."

"Why?"

"He used to be a time-bomb expert when he was in the army. It all seemed to fit—the place, the fact that a time bomb was used to blow up Kramer. Then the explosions went on all over Germany, and the police never came up with the ghost of a clue. Gradually, the theory grew that there must be a terrorist group behind them. There have been too many for one man to be responsible without leaving a trace behind."

"What about Fleischmann?"

"That's the creepy thing—he's still at large."

"How did he escape—just climbed over a wall?"

"No, that's odd, too. A group of men organized the escape. A bloodstained truncheon was found in a wood, but none of the asylum guards was attacked. They'd just been put to sleep with dope."

"What was Fleischmann's history?"

"He was apprenticed to a Bremen watchmaker before he entered the army. Because of his previous job he was attached to a secret 'retreat-and-destroy' unit—one of those formations you never hear about—and his function was the planting of time bombs to delay an enemy advance."

"He couldn't have been mad then."

"No. He went over the edge while he was in the army. One night he attacked two officers and strangled them with his bare hands. A medical inquiry found he was suffering from a persecution complex, so he was discharged and sent to the asylum near Bremen."

22

"And now the police have written off Fleischmann?"

"No. Not publicly, anyway. And the press still heads a new explosion with the words 'New Fleischmann Outrage.' But I don't think that's going on much longer."

"Because of the rumors you mentioned?"

She hesitated. "That's right. Am I being of any help?"

I never did reply, because at that moment the phone rang. There was a call on the line for me, and when the name was given it was the last person in the world I would have expected to get in contact with me in Zurich.

4: BILLIONAIRE

It seemed to be a very public place for a private meeting, even though night had fallen. The Quaibrücke is the main bridge over the River Limmat, and it spans the water at its lowest point just before the Limmat merges into the Lake of Zurich. At five-thirty in the evening the wide span of bridge was alive with traffic; an avalanche of cars stormed over the river, headlights glaring, engines roaring. Upriver behind the bridge, the needle spires of Zurich lanced the moonlit sky, while far away down the lake a tumble of peaks was capped with snow, the first traces of the coming winter.

I pulled in close to the tram stop, where Zurichers were boarding several vehicles as though they were refugees fleeing a burning city. Then I sat in my parked car and watched the meeting point, a railed walk under dark trees by the lakeside. Several men stood there, and I thought I recognized one of them, a tall slim figure dressed in a black coat and wearing a Russian-style fur hat. A shadow blotted out the street lamp beside me, and I looked up into a huge slab face.

Even sitting inside the hired Citroën I knew he was one

of the biggest men I had ever seen. His immense body was clad in a windbreaker with a fur collar, and perched on top of grizzled black hair was a small forage cap which had more fur around the base. He stood with his hands tucked high up inside the pockets of his windbreaker. I rolled down the window and peered out. His green slacks were pushed down inside black knee-high boots, and his body leaned against my car. He spoke in broken German.

"Martini?"

"Yes."

"He's waiting for you over there. And he's catching cold. You're late, so hurry it up."

"Who is?"

"The man you've come to meet—Mr. Kardehay. He doesn't like to be kept waiting."

"Pity. And I'm not late. While you're in Zurich treat yourself to a Swiss watch. I didn't get your name either."

"Josip. You're wasting time."

"Josip? Yugoslav?"

"I said Mr. Kardehay was waiting." He spoke German very badly, and the words came out as an ominous purr. I looked at him pointedly.

"Kindly remove your great body from my car."

He stood back as I climbed out and locked the door. When I turned around he had taken his hands out of the pockets, and they were big enough to strangle an ox. He watched me as though I might be the ox he was looking for. I tipped my hand in a pleasant little salute and walked over under the trees where the raw foehn wind came off the lake like a knife. The group of six men parted, and Nikki Kardehay was the man with the fur hat. He grinned and shook ash off his cigar. It blew onto the lapel of one of the waiting men. The man left it on his lapel.

"Welcome to Zurich, David! You are now staying in the richest city in the world. The Bahnhofstrasse may not be

24

paved with gold, but the vaults beneath it certainly are! Doesn't it make you feel wealthier just to take one breath of this expensive air?" Kardehay went on grinning sardonically. "Take a good deep breath and you will reek of money the way a whore reeks of perfume."

I lit a cigarette by turning my back on the foehn and cupping my hand around the match. My change of position put the glow of a street lamp straight onto Kardehay's face. His cheekbones were high and pronounced, his eyes hooded under deep lids, his face clean-shaven and sharp-featured, and his expression still suggested a touch of mocking amusement, as though he found the whole world inexpressibly absurd. He was facing the wind now and seemed to enjoy its raking thrust. I blew out smoke and asked my question.

"Why meet in this Godforsaken spot when it's so much more comfortable in the Schweizerhof bar?"

"Because it is also so much more public. I said on the phone that I wanted a private meeting." He waved a slim white hand. "That fleet of cars over there is waiting to take us to Lugano. We start as soon as you and I have talked."

"What about?"

"Sven Heim's engine, of course." He laid a bare hand gently on my shoulder. "David, I know it may seem heartless, and I enormously regret the death of Heim, but I still wish to buy the engine. I will negotiate with the heirs, and I'm sure you will act on their behalf just as you did for poor Sven. It would be simplest, of course, if we could use the existing contract—then all we have to do is to change a name."

"It may not be as straightforward as that, Nikki."

"Why not? What is the problem?"

The group of men had stepped well back from us, but their bodies still formed a circle which masked my parked car. I couldn't see Josip either.

"The problem, Nikki, is that so far we don't know who the

25

heir is. It was Else Heim, but since she also died in the explosion, we may have to dig to find the new next of kin. That's the first part of the problem. The second part is that the heir, when found, may not want to sell to you."

Nikki's eyebrows were wedges of dark hair well apart from each other, and he used these expressively to demonstrate his meaning. Now the eyebrows shot up in mock astonishment.

"But who is going to want a jet engine when he can have all that money instead? And by using the existing contract he can save negotiation fees." He grinned ironically. "I am sure you would be willing to charge only half your normal fee for no work at all!"

"I never got my fee from Sven—not that it matters. When did you last see him, Nikki?"

"During our dinner in Basel to celebrate the agreement in principle—the dinner you attended. So, it is agreed then, once you contact the heir we do business again? The sooner the better—time is important. I'd like to be kept in touch with all developments."

Another surge of the twentieth century swept over the Quaibrücke, and I stepped closer to Kardehay to hear what he was saying. The fur hat affected his personality, giving him an imperial air, but his dark-brown eyes, almost an opaque brown, flitted swiftly as he spoke English with a strong American accent. There were only faint undertones of his Hungarian origins. His lean face and swift-moving eyes again reminded me of the billionaire's enormous energy. I was still wondering about the oddness of the meeting place.

"You said the Schweizerhof was too public, Nikki. Why all the secrecy?"

"You are publicly branded now as the man investigating the criminal behind the bomb outrages. I am a public figure and have no wish to have my name attached to international assassinations. I might as well hire a theater and appear on the stage as meet you at the Schweizerhof." He lit a fresh cigar, and for a moment watched the crowd piling aboard a tram. "Is it true, David, that you are here to conduct an investigation into the bomb outrages?"

"Just one—the one that killed Sven and Else."

"I never met his daughter. An appalling tragedy."

"Else wasn't his daughter; she was his niece. Her parents died several years ago during a fire in Helsinki."

"So you are here to find out who killed Sven Heim?"

"That's right."

"Rather far afield from your normal activities, isn't it?"

"A fair way off."

"You're co-operating with the police—because you knew Sven Heim, that is?"

"I'd co-operate with the devil himself to find out who killed Sven and Else."

Kardehay pulled up his collar and smiled slowly, his expression wry and amused.

"I haven't overlooked the fact that you didn't answer my question. You weren't a lawyer once for nothing, and"—he looked at me directly, his eyes still—"that's a lesson I learned while we were negotiating. I hope I don't have to emphasize the importance for discretion as regards my dealings with Heim. I repeat—I don't want my name dragged into this horrible business."

"No one rates discretion at a time like this."

He took the cigar out of his mouth and studied me with some care. Tram wheels ground along their tracks, the wind moaned in from the lake, and the traffic roared. He replied while he looked down to tap ash off the cigar with his little finger.

"David, I'm fairly sure I must be misreading you, but that last remark almost has the distinct undertone of a hostile statement."

"It's a statement neither friendly nor hostile—just a neutral statement. I don't care too much for the priority you put

27

on your own good name as compared with the murder of Sven Heim."

"Discretion within reason I was suggesting."

"Which is what you'll get—and that's something you should have learned also while we were negotiating. And if you want to keep me in a really good temper, it might be best not to send bully boys like Josip to collect me for meetings on windy bridges. Who is he, anyway?"

"Josip Riz is my chauffeur—a Yugoslav. I'll speak to him. I didn't ask you here to ruffle your feelings, David. You probably resent my going after the engine again so soon after Heim's death, but"—he extended a half-opened hand toward me—"I want that jet engine, and it's an offer you may be glad to accept on behalf of the heirs when all this"— he waved a hand beyond Zurich—"is just a sad memory."

"It's a sad memory now, Nikki. I'll bear the offer in mind. Is that all you wanted to see me about?"

"I think so, David. Next time we'll have dinner together in warmer surroundings. Go back to the Schweizerhof now and drink my health in brandy!"

He nodded, turned to go, glanced sideways at me quickly, and then walked away with his entourage. I watched them go, climb into their several Mercedes cars, and drive away over the Quaibrücke. As I went back to my own car I wondered what had happened to Josip Riz, chauffeur. Because of one thing I was certain: he hadn't driven off with them.

5: FIZZ

"I'm drunk," said Romy. "I'm never drunk," she said in contradiction. "You've made me drunk," she accused.

"You've made yourself drunk, dear. All through the dinner you were swallowing gin fizzes like tonic water."

28

"And now you've brought me up to your bedroom. I shall hold you responsible for everything," she announced.

"Steady. And in case you've forgotten, this is a suite, and at the moment you're in the living room."

"That wasn't quite the reaction I expected, David." She thought about it and stared across at me owlishly. "You never react the way you should. You receive highly mysterious phone calls, make a date to take me out to dinner later, go off on your own for an hour, never say where you've been, and then feed me on gin fizzes so I'll tell you about the rumors. Well, I haven't—so there!" She looked superior and smug and rambled on. "I think girls are fools to go out with ex-lawyers—they no longer have a public reputation to restrain them."

"That's what really made me give it up—didn't I tell you?"

"Men never tell girls the things that really matter until it's late at night. It is late at night, isn't it?"

"All of nine o'clock. And you'll have to get out of here soon, before the management invites you to."

"I'll go when I'm ready and I'm not going to be pushed. You know something? I have absolutely no recollection of coming up here after dinner. I hope I shan't do anything else tonight and then forget all about it."

"You won't—forget it, I mean."

She smiled dangerously. "I thought that's what you meant."

Standing in front of a wall mirror, she studied her reflection. She had changed for dinner and wore a tight black off-the-shoulder dress without any fussy jewels. From behind I watched her jet-black hair flopping over cold white bare shoulders. They were beautiful shoulders, and her arms gleamed in the light of the wall lamps.

"Just the wall lights," she had said when we came in. "The main lights would kill me—all those gin fizzes."

29

She straightened up before the mirror and smoothed her dress over her slim hips. "That's better, Romy," she told her image. "Who would think you were a newspaperwoman now? David, can I ask you a question?"

"Go ahead."

"Why did you bring me back here?"

"I thought you might want to lie down . . ."

"I'll bet!"

". . . to recover from your gin fizzes."

"I'm recovered, David. Look! Fully recovered!" She stretched her bare arms wide and stretched her dress over her full breasts. Above the dress top the shadow gulch between them expanded and then contracted again as she rested her hands on her upper arms. "You see—I didn't even wobble."

"Not all of you."

"I think you could be wicked. Ex-lawyers are all very wicked—otherwise they'd still be real lawyers." She huddled her body. "I'm chilly. I need warming up." She began padding around the room in her stocking feet, crooning gently to herself. "Romy needs warming up. It must be here somewhere—it *was* here when we went out, here on this sideboard." She began opening cupboards.

"If you tell me what you're looking for, I might be able to help."

"Cognac. Your customs-free bottle . . . Lovely, warm, soothing cognac."

"You'll go out like a light."

"Not with you around, Romy won't. Romy is going to be very, very careful with her ex-lawyer escort. *Wunderbar!*"

She took the bottle of Bisquit out of the cupboard, then found two glasses, poured, handed me my drink with a steady hand, and clinked glasses.

"Here's to Romy not going out like a light." She smiled conspiratorially. "And you have to drink up, too!"

30

Lifting her glass with both hands, she quietly drank the entire contents. Putting the glass down, she gazed at me coldly.

"You look like a boiled lobster. That tie must be choking you."

With deft easy movements she undid the tie, frowning at a point below my chin. I put my hands behind her and encircled her narrow waist. She pouted at me. "You see—I didn't go out like a light."

"Lights are going out in a minute," I assured her.

Stooping down, I wrapped one arm around her legs and lifted. She looped her arms around my neck and sagged contentedly. As I carried her, she guided me and reached out and pressed the wall switches so that the lights went out, leaving only a small table lamp on. I dumped her over the back of the couch next to the table. Spreading her legs along the couch, she wriggled her toes and then plumped up cushions behind her back. As I came around the couch I tripped over her shoes lying on the floor. She nodded with satisfaction.

"You are drunk. I should never have come up here."

Producing her handbag from under a cushion she extracted the horn-rims and put them on.

"That's better. Now I can see what's going on. What is going on?"

"Shut up and move over."

She moved over, and I sat down beside her. Our mouths met savagely, and she pressed her chest against me. I had a mouthful of hair when she whispered solemnly, "My light's still on, too!" As we unlocked, her horn-rims reflected back the light, masking her expression. I reached up, took them off, and placed them on the table.

"You won't want those on."

"I do like to see what's happening. No! Please leave the lamp on. For a few minutes, anyway," she added.

31

I had another mouthful of hair and her expert hand was exploring the contours of my back when she spoke. "Who are you really working for, David? All this is strictly off the record, of course." Her fingers played a little tune up my spine.

"Later." I took the hair out of my mouth, and her thighs rippled under my hand. Her voice was a whisper. "Tell me now," she suggested. "I won't be listening later."

"I forget."

"No, I'd really love to know."

I sat up, and for a brief second her unmasked eyes were as watchful as a lynx's. Then she rolled them and gazed dreamily at the ceiling through long dark lashes. "I'll tell you," I said. She went on gazing at the ceiling and laid her hand on my chest for encouragement, curling her fingers and walking them up and down me.

"Ready?" I asked. She nodded sleepily. "It's extremely confidential, Romy, so you mustn't tell a soul. Actually, I have been hired secretly by the Tonton Macoute. . . ."

She looked at me sharply, but I turned her head gently so she faced the ceiling again as I went on, talking rapidly.

"The Tonton Macoute is the secret-police organization in Haiti, which is an island in the West Indies. It belongs to a dictator named Dr. Duvalier, who wears a top hat so a lot of the peasants think he's a witch doctor and dare not oppose him. The Tonton Macoute are a very sinister crowd, and the whole island is voodoo-ridden, and in the jungle at night strange sexual rites are performed which . . ."

Romy sat up straight, her expression frigidly alert. Leaning forward over me, she scooped a shoe up off the floor to put it on. She paused, shoe in hand, to express her opinion.

"I don't think you're at all funny. I was worried about you and . . . Oh, what does it matter. I'm going now. I really don't think you're at all funny," she repeated bitterly, still holding the shoe level with her shoulder, her eyes glowing.

"It's not as though you really belong to the ultrarespectable Nord-Deutscher Agency," I went on. "And I can guess who your real employers are."

Her face was frozen stone now, her eyes vigilant and barbed. "What are you talking about?" she demanded quietly.

"The Tonton Macoute . . ."

The shoe missed my left ear. Just.

When I had the room to myself I put through a call to the Frankfurt headquarters of the Nord-Deutscher Agency. They were helpful. Yes, they had a correspondent named Romy Silber and at the moment she was in Switzerland. No, they couldn't say which city she was staying in. With a little prodding they gave a brief description, which could have fitted my Romy, but it could also have fitted many a desirable Fräulein. When they asked me who was calling I began talking and then broke the connection in mid-sentence. As I sat staring at the dead telephone it came to life again. This time it was the police.

6: SAMMET

I said it for the seventh time.

"Inspector Sammet, Sven Heim was a friend of mine. I have come to Zurich to find out what happened to him and to his niece, if I can."

Sammet nodded amiably and shifted his large body in the swivel chair where he sat facing me across his desk at police headquarters. His head was large, too, the silver-gray hair shaggy, his mustache a sweep of iron bristle. He reminded

33

me of a Saint Bernard dog, and his manner was patient and plodding.

"I know, Mr. Martini, but you would be well-advised to leave such matters in the hands of the professionals."

"In this case I didn't feel like sitting at home and reading about it in the newspapers—especially as these outrages have been going on for six months and so far the professionals have got precisely nowhere, if I may say so."

"The trouble is the newspapers are talking about you."

"I know. I asked them to—the London *Telegram,* anyway."

"But, Mr. Martini"—he folded his hands and regarded me with friendship—"the newspapers say you have come over to investigate *all* the explosions."

"I can't help it if they tart things up to make a better story. Does it matter?"

"I'm afraid it does. You see, the fact that you have come because Heim was your friend and the fact that two papers have said you are interested in the previous outrages give the impression that the German explosions are linked to what is happening here."

"Aren't they?"

Sammet took up a pipe and said would I please smoke a cigarette and there would be coffee shortly. He tamped the pipe, and I listened for sounds of activity inside the police headquarters, but the room was sealed off from the outside world, and the only noise was the bubbling in the central heating system which was rapidly converting the room into a tropical paradise. Sammet got his pipe going nicely and explained.

"I can talk to you frankly because after your part in that Hildebrand business over here last year you have a certain status. No—we don't make the mistake of assuming that the Zurich explosions are linked with the others—not at all. So far there is no evidence to suggest that."

34

"The Heim outrage was the fourteenth explosion, and there hasn't been much evidence about any of them."

"You are right, up to a point, that is. But"—the pipe pointed in my direction and moved emphatically—"we do not wish our own tragedies to be positively linked with what has happened outside Switzerland."

There was an expression of mild distaste in his manner, as though cholera might cross the border. I replied quietly.

"Are you saying there are features about the Heim case which suggest it isn't linked with the others?"

"What I am saying, Mr. Martini, is of course completely confidential and must not be relayed to the press."

"I don't know any of the local press."

"You know Romy Silber, who has registered on her hotel form as a correspondent of the Nord-Deutscher News Agency," he pointed out while he examined the bowl of his pipe with grave suspicion. I was beginning to have suspicions about the contents myself.

"You're having me watched?"

"It just happened that one of my men called in at the Schweizerhof and saw you talking to her. The receptionist confirmed her identity."

"He knows her by sight?"

Sammet looked surprised. "No, but she is staying at the Schweizerhof. My man got the impression that she was an energetic young woman." He frowned, but whether he was frowning at Romy's energy or at the state of his pipe I couldn't be sure. "There are odd features about the Heim case," he murmured. "No, I can't reveal them to you, but you should take good care of yourself. It could be dangerous to go poking around on your own."

"Thanks for the warning." I stood up. "I won't wait for the coffee, if you don't mind. You have finished, I take it?"

"For the moment." He leaned back and watched me through a fresh gas cloud of gray smoke. "Did you know that Mr. Heim fought for his country against Russia in what the Finns called the Winter War of 1939?"

"Yes."

"And did you know in what capacity he served?"

"He was a sniper, I think."

"Quite correct, but later, when the Russians were breaking through in the Karelian Isthmus, he was transferred to other duties because of his engineering background. Did you know that?"

"No. What other duties?"

"To delay the Russian advance it became necessary to erect every possible type of booby trap. Sven Heim's job was the planting of time bombs."

7: DEBRIS

It was dark when I reached Sven Heim's house. Seven-o'clock-in-the-morning dark. The explosion had taken place two days before, but the Swiss were still hard at work. Parking my hired car a distance away, I got out. I had no trouble locating the disaster area. Huge overhead arc lights blazed down on the scene, and underneath them orange bulldozers sniffed at the debris. A sizable portion of the villa had been blown into the road, and they were working to clear the obstruction. The wind was blowing off the lake again, so I turned up my coat collar, hid my hands inside my pockets, and walked up.

Heim had lived in a rich-men's suburb on the hill above Zurich. As I walked up the road I passed large two-story villas behind railed walls. The gardens were furnished with small shrubs, and even in the half-glow from the arc lamps they looked neat and tidy. There were lights on in the upper floors of most of the villas.

Close to the salvage operation a small group of people

huddled in the wind. Early-morning ghouls. Cars were parked down both sides of the steep road, and from behind one of them walked a girl. A girl in a Robin Hood hat and a camel's-hair coat. Romy. She crossed the road and trudged up the pavement just ahead of me. I lit a cigarette and caught up with her. "You left this burning when you went last night."

"Thanks." She took the cigarette.

We walked up toward the crowd in silence. In the arc-light glow her face looked bleak, withdrawn, guarded. "I sent off your interview," she remarked coldly.

"Soon I'll be notorious."

"Soon someone will put a bomb under your bed. You really think the publicity will help?"

"It's helped already."

"What does that mean?" She stopped to clean her horn-rims, and I saw that her eyes were alert but there was a hint of sadness in their expression.

"People have started to contact me. Nerve warfare is a two-way tactic."

"You think the time-bomb assassinations are nerve warfare?"

"Terrorist campaigns usually are."

"Be cagey then," she replied offhandedly, and walked up to the edge of the crowd. We stood in the cold morning air and looked at the debris which had buried Sven. It was an appalling sight. There was no relic to show that it had ever been a house, no surviving wall or lone chimney, as there had been so often during the wartime blitz on London. Just a mess of debris in the road and a mountain of rubble in the huge garden. It had been a very big bomb.

"He could never have known what was coming," Romy said quietly.

I didn't reply, but her remark in German caused a small man in front of us to turn around. He was wearing a black overcoat and a dark slouch hat.

37

"You knew him?" he asked Romy.

"I knew him," I said.

He hesitated. "It was exactly eleven o'clock in the morning. I live close by—two roads away. We were drinking coffee when it happened—a terrible sound. I thought for a moment that it was an earthquake. I'm sure the ground trembled, but my wife said I was mistaken. We were stunned, completely stunned. It was only later that we realized a piece of his chimney had landed in our garden."

"Have the police any idea who did it?"

"A madman, they say—a madman from Germany. They have had frightful explosions all the way from Hamburg to Munich. But why should he come here, to Zurich? It has scared us, I can tell you. A friend of mine has advanced his holiday by a week and the whole family is leaving for Morocco today. They say Heim and his niece were blown into a thousand pieces."

He looked as though he wished he hadn't said the last sentence and turned his back on us. Romy moved away, and when I looked over my shoulder I saw her making notes in her book by the light from a car's headlights. A workman swiveled one of the overhead lights, and its beam traveled behind the house ruin and over the lower slopes of a hill that rose immediately behind Sven's back garden. The hill was covered with a dense pine forest. I edged my way around the crowd and walked farther up the road.

The next villa had suffered damage on the side that faced Sven's land, and the wall was covered with tarpaulins. As I climbed the deserted road and left behind the grind and crunch of the bulldozers, the early morning was full of cold silence. I walked past several houses and found a small path that led away to the left between the side walls of two more villas. Using my pocket flashlight, I followed the path beyond the walls to where it began to climb the hill in a zigzag. I climbed some distance up through the dense pinewoods

38

and then left the path and made my way down through the trees. The arc lights provided a landmark, and I reached a position where I could look down on the remains of Sven's home.

His garden ran to the foot of the wooded hill slope, and a gate in the wall was open. From that height the devastation seemed even more pathetic, because the rubble heap looked smaller, less significant. I walked down through the trees to the open gate and stood with my hand on it, gazing down the long garden path, wondering if they had brought the bomb in this way. There was no point in looking for anything in the dark, and I felt sure the Swiss police had already covered the ground thoroughly. It was just that I felt I had to see as much as I could in memory of Sven.

I went back the way I had come and arrived just as a lorry load of debris was being driven away. The road would be open again within a matter of hours. Romy was talking to two men in the crowd, taking notes, so I went back down the hill. Just below the wrecked villa I passed a large gray van. It was parked in an area of shadow, and I almost missed it. The rear doors were half-open and from the interior projected the gunlike lens of a movie camera mounted on a tripod. Behind it a man crouched, operating his weapon. The trappings of disaster's aftermath.

I climbed into my car and lit a cigarette. Behind me the engine of a black Mercedes started up. I reached for the ignition, and the Mercedes slammed into my rear.

8: DORF

"A thousand apologies . . . so early in the morning . . . the reflexes do not respond so quickly . . . I should have first reversed. Of course, of course! I realize that. Now! But

39

now is a little too late! A thousand apologies . . ." He rattled on in German, an animated stream of chatter and word wanderings. "Will you ever forgive me?" he ended.

"No," I said, and got out of the car.

He couldn't keep still. A slim man of about forty, five foot eight or nine, hatless, black hair plastered down over his head, the face white, clever-looking, animated. I walked back to where the two vehicles had connected. They were joined together in loving union, his front bumper locked over my rear guard.

"Let's face it," I told him, "we're married."

"Married! That's very funny . . . to make a joke at a time like this! One thing I appreciate in this dark and bitter world . . . a sense of humor! Only a man of character could crack jokes in the moment of disaster!"

"There's a worse disaster up the road," I said quietly.

"I know, I know! I am here to investigate the matter. You see—I am an insurance investigator, and Mr. Heim was covered by my company. We have a vested interest in the tragedy, so to speak." His keen eyes noted some reaction in my face immediately. "Does that sound too terrible? I see from your expression I have phrased it badly . . . again, a thousand apologies! You must think me a terrible fellow, but first thing in the morning . . . such a struggle!"

I studied him more closely. He wore an expensive black overcoat, and behind his white silk scarf was a glimpse of black tie and evening dress. I now guessed his age as thirty-five, and his pale clean-shaven face was alive with vitality, his whole manner electric, as though he found it difficult to expend his abundance of energy. When he was talking the energy seemed to vibrate, and he spoke with enormous rapidity. His eyes were shrewdly inquiring, his nose long, and his mouth mobile. He put in his mouth a burning cigar he had been holding and produced his case.

"Have one. Please do. I have been up all night, and they

40

are an excellent substitute for breakfast . . . providing you have coffee first, of course!" He smiled, a quick engaging smile. "Strong black coffee, of course. Strong and black —like the colonial's girl friend!"

I shook my head and lit a fresh cigarette. The previous one lay on the floor where I had dropped it when he arrived without warning. "No, thanks. I prefer to eat my breakfast."

"But I have breakfast, too—later! This is by way of being an *apéritif!* My father taught me the trick . . . great, coal-black things he smoked—like the barrel of a torpedo. Home was like a burning forest in those days!"

"And what are we going to do about this?" I pointed to the junction of our vehicles.

"I will pay, of course! Are you going back to Zurich? Good. So am I. We will share a taxi. I will pay. And the matter of insurance will provide no difficulty . . . none at all. I am in insurance myself. I shall take full responsibility. We will breakfast together—I do not refer to cigars! Here, please take my card."

I took the card and bent down in front of his headlights to read it. *Rudi Dorf. Frankfurt. Kaiserstrasse 808.* Just that. Nothing else. No phone number. No company name. I straightened up and put the card inside my pocket.

"We won't get a taxi up here," I told Dorf.

"Oh yes we will! Look, there's a phone box behind that tree. I'll call one and I'll also call a garage. I know. Inside ten minutes we shall be sitting eating croissants. You'll see! Don't forget to lock your car. No one will steal anything in Switzerland, but the police will lecture us like my old schoolmaster. And I have spent all my apologies on you!"

We locked our cars and walked to the phone box. Rudi Dorf walked quickly, brisk little steps which almost danced, humming a tune under his breath, waving the cigar like a toy baton to beat the time. He went inside the box and came out again immediately.

41

"Don't run away! I shouldn't like to lose you—victims are hard to find these days. . . . And my name is Rudi. All my friends call me that. If you don't, I shall feel sure I have offended you! Won't be a minute. I . . . ."

He was chattering away as the door closed. I took up a position from which I could see clearly inside the phone box, which was illuminated, and looked up the road in search of Romy, but she had disappeared. They were loading debris into another truck when Rudi came bouncing out of the box. He hurried across the road.

"The garage has been informed and they are sending someone. The taxi will be here in five minutes. Now, I suggest we pass the time by walking rapidly up and down this road, or we shall get cold. And if you should catch pneumonia, that will be all my fault, too. Don't you agree?"

"I agree with everything you've said for the past ten minutes."

"Everyone always agrees with me!"

I didn't ask Rudi why it had been necessary to make three calls to phone one garage and one taxi.

Breakfast with Rudi told me nothing, and I arranged to meet him in the evening for a drink. We had visited the car-hire people, and Rudi was received as though he had been Nikki Kardehay. I had no difficulty in obtaining a duplicate Citroën, which convinced me I must be meeting all the right people. The rest of the day I spent on the end of the phone in my room at the Schweizerhof calling half the people I knew in Europe. The phone bill would be gigantic, but by the late afternoon I had found out that Kardehay had left Lugano by air early in the morning on his way to Milan. By phoning Berlin, Hamburg, Düsseldorf, and Frankfurt I also found out that Germany was having the seething jitters over the bomb explosions. It had become a first-class political issue which might well affect the coming elections. As to who was responsible for planting the bombs, I heard various outlandish theories but none of them sufficiently sensational or convincing to make me feel I was listening to the rumor Romy Silber had refused to tell me about. The man in Berlin said he had heard a very disturbing rumor and then refused to go any further. He closed the conversation apologetically. "After all, David, we are talking on an open line."

Night had fallen, and I was sitting in the semidark with only the table lamp on as it drew close to the time when I had to go to meet Rudi. I had time for one more call, so I asked the operator to get me a number in Luxembourg. When Anna came on the line she gave me the usual answers about the bomb outrages, and only when I mentioned Kardehay did I hear something new.

"You know, of course, David, that Kardehay is in the process of transferring his headquarters to Paris?"

"No. As far as I knew he was still operating out of Brussels."

"Well, I only learned about it by accident, but he's taken a long lease on a big building in the Avenue de l'Opéra. The whisper is that he's moving there from Brussels."

"Why?"

"No idea, and the same source told me about his weird shadow factories."

"What shadow factories? Why shadow?"

"A little while ago he completed building two huge new factories inside France—one near Clermont-Ferrand, in the Massif Central, and the other just outside Paris. Most mysterious!"

"Why, Anna—why call them shadow factories?"

"Because they've been standing completed now for some time quite empty. Why build brand-new factories and then leave them? The only people at each place are a skeleton staff, and they've been spreading the news quietly that soon there'll be plenty of workers needed."

43

"What sort of workers?"

"Aircraft workers. And the odd thing is that Kardehay isn't an aircraft manufacturer."

9: WUNDERBAR!

"Nice place!" Rudi Dorf gave his bubbling laugh and warmed the brandy glass with cupped hands. "Lots of nice places in Zurich. . . . When I'm forty I shall come here, buy an apartment, and live the life! Lots of nice girls in Zurich, too. You're a bachelor as well? Good. You know what I mean! All the Fräuleins laid out in a row. *Wunderbar!*"

I smiled vaguely and tipped my glass while Rudi's eyes skipped around the place in search of prospects. The Geiger Bar was off the Limmatquai, and at six in the evening money had come in off the streets. The horseshoe-shaped room was closed off at the open end by a huge plate-glass wall which fronted on the street. At the back a chromium bar fitted neatly inside the curve, and the side walls were occupied by booths. The furniture was black leather, the center tables solid hourglass shapes with leather-seated chairs like secretaries', and the girls sitting in them looked like highly paid secretaries. Their boy friends had the air of junior executives ascending a rising curve, and there wasn't a pauper in sight. A portion of floor near the bar was left clear for dancing; a monster Rockola provided dance music in the jazz idiom. No one was dancing yet.

"That funny thing about Sven Heim you were going to tell me about this morning," I prodded.

"Zurich has the most high-class girls west of the Rhine," Rudi said enthusiastically, and ordered a fresh round of brandy. He exchanged glances with a poker-faced redhead at the nearest table and grinned when she looked away.

44

"You did say you'd been sent down from Frankfurt to check on Sven Heim's death?" I persisted.

"A sizable sum is involved, so I thought I'd look over the ground myself. I issued the policy—that was in the days before I was a claims investigator."

"And the policy is valid—even under the circumstances of his death?"

"Most valid—that's the interesting point." Rudi looked artful and then took brandy glasses off her tray before the waitress could serve them. He laid a hand gently on her bare forearm. "One day I'm coming to live in Zurich and on that day I'll serve drinks to you in my apartment. Would you like that? Don't rush into an answer! Give it time—give it two years, because that's when I'll be here. Then, *Wunderbar!*"

Rudi had a way with him, and a way with girls. With a faint smile the waitress told him, Anything you say, sir, the customer is always right! As she walked away Rudi bubble-laughed.

"I *like* Zurich. This is going to be my town! How are *you* getting on with your investigation?"

"Making progress. It's all a bit vague at the moment, but in a few days things may begin to get clearer. Rudi, why was Sven Heim's policy most valid, seeing as he died in a bomb explosion?"

"I have a proposition to put to you, David. Since we are both after the same thing, why not form an alliance and pool our information? Whoops!"

He had eyes in the side of his head, and his long-fingered hand shot out and caught a glass in mid-air. The redheaded girl had just knocked it off the table with her elbow. Rudi saved the glass but the contents spilled on the floor. He waved for the waitress and ordered a fresh drink. Standing up, he talked to both girls at the table, with his back to me. Then the redhead stood up and walked to the empty dance floor with him. I watched them dance. Rudi capering skillfully while the girl held herself erect and tried not to giggle at his antics. Outside in the street someone walked past the huge window. I only caught a glimpse, but he was a big man, and I thought he wore a forage cap.

More couples had wandered onto the floor as the Rockola ground out a Duke Ellington number. And in the center of it all Rudi danced, black hair slicked down the sides of his pale forehead, eyes alive with enjoyment, slim hips oscillating, chatting with the girl nonstop while he performed a series of outrageous steps. When he escorted her back to her table the other girl eyed Rudi furtively.

"Zurich for me, David!" He sat down, his voice loud. "The local talent is creamy." He swallowed brandy. "Does my proposition interest you?"

"Yes, but you'll have to play opening ball—I don't expect to know anything for several days yet."

"But you'll contact me—you know I'm at the Victoria."

"I'll contact you. You said you issued the policy to Heim personally. You knew him?"

"No, not at all. It was five years ago. He came into my Frankfurt office out of the blue—just like that." He made his hand into a jet plane and zoomed across the table. "He wanted special policies, very special policies. So of course I pricked up my ears."

"Why?"

"The ordinary man doesn't like talking about life insurance too much. He prefers to take out a standard policy and then hurries away to forget all about it. But not Sven Heim. Your Finnish friend has his own ideas. He wanted policies to cover death under all circumstances short of act of war."

"What sort of circumstances?"

"Death by accident, including specific deaths such as aircraft crashing and gunshot wounds—things like that." He attended to the brandy-warming ritual. "One of the contingencies covered was particularly appropriate."

46

"What was that?"

"Death by high explosive."

10: EMERGENCY

"Phone message, Mr. Martini. The caller asked you to ring back. He said it was an emergency."

The Schweizerhof receptionist tore a sheet from his counter scratch pad and handed it to me. Romy Silber had been waiting for me when I arrived and now she stood very erect staring critically at the decor. After all, it was only the Schweizerhof, Zurich's number-one hotel. The piece of paper carried a number: 99 49 97. That was all.

"Who was the caller?" I asked.

"He didn't leave a name—just would you phone him at that number immediately you came in. A matter of pressing urgency."

"To him, he meant. It definitely was a him, I take it? It couldn't have been a lady?"

"Definitely a man's voice, sir."

"Shame!" said Romy cynically, looking at nothing in particular, her manner aloof. The receptionist watched her figure without appearing to do so. I asked him to ring for bar service so the lady could have a drink while I made the call in my room.

"A stroke and a slap all in one," she said.

"Pardon?"

"Nothing. You'll find me over there when you come down."

From my room I told the operator I'd prefer to get the number myself, and she gave me a line. I dialed carefully, and at the other end of the wire a man's voice answered at once, as though his hand had been waiting close to the receiver. He spoke urgently in German.

"Who is this, please . . . ? Is there someone there . . . ? Can't you hear me . . . ? Is there anyone there . . . ?"

The voice was guttural, thick, possibly middle-aged, a fat-sounding voice, which spoke emphatically, but underneath I thought I detected a rising note of hysteria. I answered.

"David Martini here. You called me. And you forgot to leave a name."

"Take this down, please. Quickly. I have to go out."

"Go ahead."

"Manfred Klein. Graben 4. Do you know it?"

"You're Klein?"

"Of course. Do you know the address or don't you?"

"Keep your shirt on—and I don't know the Graben."

"You go down the Limmatquai on the left-hand side of the river. The Graben is behind the Hechtplatz, which is near the Quaibrücke. Have you any idea what I am talking about?"

"Not really—although I have located you. Just what is this all about?"

"You must come to see me tonight—at eight o'clock. Not before, not after—at exactly eight o'clock."

"Why should I do that?"

"You are the Mr. Martini whose picture is in the London *Telegram,* the one who has flown over here to investigate certain incidents?"

"You mean the . . ."

"Please! Not over the phone—we are in Switzerland."

"Where privacy is respected."

"The phone is dangerous here—those devices." I felt sure that he had shuddered. "You have come seeking information about this matter—" he paused—"that is true, is it not?"

"It's true. You can come and see me here at the Hotel Schweizerhof."

"That's not possible. They are watching you. When you

48

arrive at the Graben you must wander around as though you are a tourist. At the last moment come into my shop quickly and lock the door behind you. I will leave it open."

The tension filtering down the line disturbed me. Once more I tried to make him change his mind. "Eight o'clock isn't all that convenient—I have another appointment."

His voice rose, and I could imagine him gripping the receiver. He sounded close to breaking point. "If you cannot come at eight, then do not come at all. I shall have left Zurich forever. I shall take with me your last chance of finding out who killed your friend."

"Take it easy—if it's all that urgent, I'll stretch a point and be there by eight. I could make it earlier if . . ."

"No, eight, eight—please, Mr. Martini—*eight!*" There was a pause, and when he spoke again his voice was calmer. "You must excuse me, but I am laboring under some emotion. May I take it that you will be there at eight?"

"You may."

He rang off, and I sat there holding the receiver. When I put it down I reached for the phone book and looked up Manfred Klein. He was on record. *Manfred Klein. Uhrmacher. Graben 4.* But his phone number was given as 92 63 91. I picked up the phone again and asked the operator for 99 49 97. When she phoned back she said there was no reply. Manfred had indeed gone out. I wondered where he had been phoning from. I went back downstairs.

I had come up in the lift, but this time I went down by the staircase. Romy was at the reception desk, and I guessed she had been waiting for the receptionist to finish a call. He put down the phone, and she spoke to him. He handed her his scratch pad. She wrote something on the pad, tore off the top sheet, returned the pad, and then walked over to an armchair. Several businessmen took time off from their newspapers to watch her walk.

Sitting down in the high-backed chair, where she was out

49

of sight of the desk, Romy unfolded the piece of paper, took a pencil from her handbag, and ran it many times across the paper. She was bringing back to life the Klein phone number indented in the surface of the scratch pad. Tilting the paper in the light from a table lamp, she glanced across as the lift doors opened. When I didn't walk out she examined the paper and wrote something on it. That would be Klein's number.

I stood very still behind the staircase wall while she went back to the desk and made a call. As she spoke she leaned her back against the desk so that she could watch the lifts. I turned to the stairs, climbed to the first floor, and then took the lift down. When the doors opened Romy was sitting in her armchair.

"You've been ages," she began at once. "It's lucky I ordered a large gin. I'm an expensive person to keep waiting."

"You'd be an expensive person to keep. Period."

I sat down in the facing armchair while she started her drink. Her glass was full.

"They kept you waiting, Romy?"

"Yes. It doesn't matter. Bar service was pretty busy."

I didn't say anything. The Schweizerhof could accommodate the whole of General Motors and the drinks would still come by return. I went on saying nothing while I looked around the room trying to detect the man Klein had said would be watching me. Everyone looked rich, confident, harmless. Romy was drinking her gin quickly, as though anxious to make it disappear. From beyond the automatic plate-glass doors that led to the street I heard the urgent scream of police sirens. Romy heard them, too, paused with her glass halfway to her lips, and then finished her drink.

"Want another?" I asked.

"No, thanks. I'd like tea now—at Grotti's."

"Tea—after that?"

"Yes. Tea quenches the thirst, gin doesn't. And I'm thirsty. It's almost next door."

I looked at my watch. Seven P.M. She sat with her legs uncrossed, swinging her handbag, waiting to go.

"We'll have to be quick," I said. "I have an appointment soon." More police sirens screamed, and the businessmen sat up in their chairs and peered toward the doors. When I stood up I saw two police cars race past the Hauptbahnhof. People were hurrying along the pavements in the same direction.

"An appointment?" Romy stood up slowly and smiled. "Is she attractive?" she inquired saucily.

"It depends on how you define attraction. I suppose you wouldn't like to tell me why you've come to see me before you gorge yourself on cream cakes?"

"And gorge I will. This is going to cost you a small fortune. I heard some news which might interest you—especially in view of all those police cars breaking their suspensions to reach the Bahnhofstrasse. There's a hot report that for the first time he's been spotted—and got clean away again, too. Someone apparently saw him walking down the Bahnhofstrasse."

"Who?"

"Bruno Fleischmann."

11: TICKTOCK

Entering the Graben was like leaving twentieth-century Zurich to go back two hundred years. The Graben was a small square surrounded by ancient buildings five or six stories high. Stone balconies peered down into the silence, and I was reminded of a monastic courtyard remote from the world.

I stood close to the narrow road that led into the Graben and leaned my back against the stone wall, my eyes scanning each window, floor by floor. Nothing. No sign of a human soul. The feature that bothered me was the second entrance to the Graben—a narrow flight of steps in the corner directly opposite where I stood. The steps went up by the side of a dark building, and at the top was a single lamp. I guessed that the staircase led to a street at a higher level, because farther along I could see the rear end of a black Mercedes perched by a lone stone wall. Anyone standing in that street would have a bird's-eye view of the whole square. There were no lights inside the Mercedes.

My watch said 7:50 P.M., and I was about to walk around the square when a lattice window high up opened. Rose-colored light spilled out into the night, and with it came the soothing rhythm of beat music and a muffled confusion of laughter. No one looked out. I began making my way around the square, keeping close in to the wall, my right hand inside my coat pocket where it gripped the .38 Special Smith & Wesson revolver.

The beat music drifting down brought a comforting feel of life into the deserted square, a breath of the twentieth century into the unknown eighteenth. As I walked, I checked numbers. I had come the wrong way around, of course. Underneath the open lattice three floors above me I heard a girl's merry trill. It broke off in mid-laughter. Have fun, I said, and then I reached Number 4.

The shop occupied a corner site, and across the fascia in gilt, old gilt, was inscribed MANFRED KLEIN, UHRMACHER. The shop looked closed, and only a faint glow of light appeared behind the windows, a glow that came from a long way back. The window had a grille over it, and I faintly made out behind the grille a neat array of clocks, old and new, all of them expensive-looking. I glanced around the empty square and then tried the handle of the closed door, expecting to find it locked. Under my hand it turned, and when I pushed gently the door moved away from me. An automatic buzzer announced my arrival.

I stood quite still in the entrance, listening to the beat music which might be masking more important sounds. Then I went inside, down one step, and closed the door. It had an automatic lock, and the latch was held open by the safety catch. Now I stood listening to other sounds. The shop was large, built on two levels, going a long way in, and it was furnished with an armory of clocks. Slim elegant grandmother clocks, their transparent stomachs exposing the gentle endless sway of their pendulums. Monstrous grandfather clocks, their entrails modestly concealed behind heavy oaken doors. Clocks on tables, touching each other for lack of space. Clocks hanging from the walls. Ticktock, ticktock, ticktock . . . Like the ticking of a thousand time bombs due to explode. At 8:00 P.M. On the dot.

There was no need to consult my wrist watch. In the dim light faces stared back at me, their hands pointing to one angle, as though controlled by a master mechanism: 7:52 P.M. By unanimous verdict. There was no other sound in the shop, no sign of life—human life. The clock life ticked away a thousand seconds. I edged my way around a battery of grandfathers and saw a large booth on the lower level, a booth with wooden panel sides and glass partition tops to increase the wall height without obscuring all the light. It was impossible to see inside the booth, and as I stood and listened I thought about Manfred Klein. The voice on the phone had sounded like that of a man fat, pudgy-faced, short, middle-aged. And then the image blurred.

The pale glow came from inside the booth, and when I stepped down to the lower level I saw for the first time a large gilt mirror on the side wall which showed part of the interior of the booth—a section of bench table running around the interior, a bench table littered with tools and glasses. No Manfred Klein. I thought I heard a slight sound and turned, the revolver in my hand. Impossible to see out into the Graben. The view was broken up and distorted by

53

the rows of displayed clocks, further confused by the grille. The glass in the door was opaque. All the clocks told the same story: 7:55 P.M.

A cuckoo clock high up on the wall exploded, and I nearly jumped to the ceiling. A tiny bird flew out, squeaked, then withdrew. Its face showed 7:00 P.M. Odd man out.

I walked slowly toward the lighted booth, restraining my feet from keeping time with the clocks. Ticktock, ticktock . . . A symphony of metronomes which threatened to send the brain to sleep, but the nerves prevented that. I walked sideways, keeping one eye on the door, wondering how anyone could live with the clocks, and then I saw it.

The revolver muzzle pointed in a reflex action, and then the message reached the brain. The staring face watched me from the mirror. Manfred Klein was fat, was pudgy-faced, was middle-aged, and in his left eye he wore a jeweler's glass which stared back steadily. The right eye was closed in an obscene wink. It stayed closed and the jeweler's glass stayed focused on me. Light from an angled desk lamp just embraced the top of his round head, reflecting off a fuzz of white hair. I remembered a man I had spoken to in a waxworks museum, a man who had stared back at me like this without replying. I crept carefully around the edge of the booth and looked.

They had smashed in the back of his head, a deathblow. And the lower ledge behind which he stored watches had propped his chin, holding it there. In the final clench of muscle his left eye had clamped tight over the most vital tool of his profession, the jeweler's glass, as though reluctant to let it fall, since when it fell it would signal extinction. I checked his pulse, but, unlike the clocks, it had ceased to tick. On the wall behind the booth a giant sunburst clock stared me in the face with its brassy maniac gaze: 7:57 P.M.

I went back carefully through the jungle of clocks. On the way out there seemed more of them, as though they had

54

proliferated behind my back. At the door I tried to peer through the windowful of timepieces, but the Graben came back at me as a maze of zigzags. I opened the door slowly, heard the buzzer, dropped the catch, wiped catch and knob with my handkerchief, and went out into the Graben, closing the door behind me. From the high window the music still played on, a cheerful friendly rhythm. The square still seemed deserted. I walked along the side wall quickly.

At the foot of the staircase I paused, but only for a second. The rear end of the black Mercedes was still in view. Then I ran up the long narrow steps, my mind automatically counting, counting in an odd one-two rhythm which echoed the ticking of the clocks. One hundred and ten steps. At the top I looked back. Yes, the vantage point gave a bird's-eye view of the whole square. The Mercedes was parked in a shadow along to my left, and beyond it lay a dead end. To my right a narrow street sloped up and went around a corner. I climbed the street halfway to the corner and waited. My watch hands pointed to 8:00 P.M.

I watched the shop and, by the light of a street lamp, I watched the sweep of my second hand. Thirty seconds . . . forty-five . . . sixty. The minute hand moved to 8:01 P.M. On the dot the square roared with the detonation's boom. I had heard air-force men talk about taking out a city. The bomb took out Graben 4.

The building shook, quivered, shuddered. Then very deliberately the front wall swayed, leaned, and toppled into the square, smashing itself to pulp, sending up a thick dust storm. Debris shot into the air, high above the ancient roofs, then tumbled back, clattering down the roofs, falling over the brink. A piece of stone struck the wall near my shoulder and ricocheted across to the opposite wall. The explosion must have reverberated clear across Zurich. And then the engine of the Mercedes started up.

I ran up the street, heading for the corner, which must

slow down the vehicle, knowing I wouldn't make it, hearing a scream of brakes, a fierce acceleration just behind me, a horn blowing. I jumped inside a deep doorway, revolver at the ready, but without firing when the car appeared—because I had been warned by the horn. I was close to the corner, and the car slowed as the hood came in view, slid past, followed by the body. As the man at the wheel turned the sharp bend his headlights reflected back from a white wall, reflected back inside the car, so that for a second I saw his face clearly. Rudi Dorf.

12: PHOENIX

The handle of my living-room door turned very slowly from the outside.

I watched it turning from the couch where I sat. Then quietly I reached for the wall switches and pressed them, dousing all the lights except for two near the door. Outside the Schweizerhof more police-car sirens shrieked and then cut off as they went around a corner. The handle was still turning under the pressure from the unseen hand. I sat in the semidark, the revolver resting in my lap, trying to gauge the moment of entry.

The door began to move inward, an inch at a time. I aimed my revolver at the point where the intruder would stand. The opening door paused, as though puzzled by the lighting arrangement. A single siren came and went, and the door opened wide. I blinked once and spoke quietly.

"Come in, Else."

She raised a finger to her lips, walked inside, closed the door, turned the key, and leaned against the panels. We stared at each other. Else was about five feet four, and the long brown sable concealed her slim figure. High leather boots hid her beautiful legs, and a close-fitting fur hood masked her head, so that only her merry little-girl face showed. She tiptoed across the room and stopped in front of me. Her voice trembled.

"Don't shoot, David. I don't want to die twice in two days."

Then she broke down, sinking to her knees and burying her head in my lap while she sobbed her heart out. After a few minutes I got her up off the floor and lying back against a cushion on the couch. Her mood changed at once, and she sat up straight.

"I'll be all right now. That did me good."

I fetched the Bisquit and poured her a meager dose. She peered at it with disgust and then took the glass.

"Is that all I get?"

"For the moment—yes. Sip it."

She took two sips and then drank the lot. Stripping off a glove she placed fingers inside my hand, smiling weakly.

"You see, I'm not a ghost."

Then she started to take off the fur hood, and I waited for the long ash-blonde hair only found in Scandinavia to appear. Instead she revealed a jet-black mane. Only the fact that her hair had been covered had enabled me to recognize her as soon as she entered. She put her hand under the mane and shook it.

"Do you like my hair like this?"

She stroked her fingers through it as though locating the hair for me. I told her she could probably stand another drink and at the same time I poured myself a double.

"Surprised—to see me?" she teased.

"Of course I am, you little fool. What happened?"

"I saw in the evening paper that you were here—at the Schweizerhof, I mean. I'd read you were coming hours ago."

"The receptionist let you come up here on your own?" I asked casually.

"Of course not. He was showing someone into the lift,

and I slipped up the staircase. I had to wait ages for the right moment."

"But you knew the room number," I pointed out.

"Yes, I got that by phoning here earlier. I said there was something to be delivered and we wanted to put the room number on it because it was important and valuable. Don't you think that was clever?"

Her voice trembled again, and she drank more brandy. I studied the face behind the glass. Her cheekbones were high and pronounced, rather like Kardehay's, but her skin was smooth and very white. Mostly, I remembered her long and well-shaped nose, which was tiptilted at the end, and it was this feature that gave her a little-girl look. The impression was strengthened by her large blue eyes, wide-open eyes, which expressed an extraordinary sense of innocence not entirely in keeping with her character. The wide firm mouth smiled.

"You recognized me at once—I'm disappointed."

"Only because your hair was under the hood. What's it all about, Else?"

She took off the sable and laid it carefully over the back of a chair. Underneath she wore a dark-blue woolen dress nipped in around her waist with a leather belt of the same color. It buttoned up modestly to her neck but thrust out generously over her chest. She was smiling impishly in a self-conscious manner when she raised her glass.

"To my return to life."

"Drink it down—your hand is trembling."

Outside in the street a car backfired, and Else jumped, a flush of fear faintly coloring her face. Before she could faint, I asked her again what had happened.

"I left the villa just before the bomb went off. Uncle Sven was suspicious and told me to clear out quick."

"And Sven . . . ?"

Her face crumpled and then stiffened again. "He was in

58

the villa when it happened. I know because I left him there."

"Which way did you clear out?"

"Up through the back garden. At the bottom there's a gate that leads . . ."

"I know—I've seen it. What made Sven suspicious?"

"He thought he heard something in the cellar. You get to it through a flap in the dining-room floor and a ladder leads down. There's an outer door. . . ."

"I remember the layout. What made him suspicious?"

"I was just going to tell you—you don't have to be such a bear," she snapped irritably. The strain was telling on her. Normally, Else was eternally even-tempered. I waited patiently, and she went on. "He lifted the flap, and the outer door was open. That door never blows open—the latch is completely reliable. That made him suspicious. He ordered me out of the house and told me to wait for him in the wood."

"But why should an open cellar door have that effect on him? This isn't making a great deal of sense, Else."

"He'd been like a cat on hot bricks all morning, almost as though he was waiting for something to happen."

"And where have you been ever since?"

"Hiding in the cabin Sven had out in the wilds near Brugg."

She watched me over the rim of her glass, her eyes wide open, the glass concealing her nose. It was a little mannerism I remembered. Else was self-conscious about her nose because she thought it was too long. When she finished drinking I took the glass and filled it again, this time watering it down with plenty of soda.

"You don't have to drown it," she complained.

"Why hide out in the cabin at Brugg? You haven't been to the police, I take it? The papers have reported you dead, you know."

"I was only doing what Sven had told me to do if any-

59

thing happened. He was very emphatic about it and he'd only told me that very morning, when the . . ." She didn't finish.

"You'll have to go to the police," I said firmly. "I only hope they can make more sense out of this than I can."

"Shall I start at the beginning?"

"It sometimes helps."

"Earlier that morning—the morning of the explosion—Sven said that if any emergency arose or if anything happened to him, I should leave Zurich and not let anyone know where I was. I asked him what he was talking about, but he just repeated it. You know what he was like. . . ."

"Else, why were you in the villa that morning? Was it just by chance?"

"No. The day before, just after lunch, Sven had asked me to make a point of staying in with him. I don't know why."

"And that's funny, too. If he'd been expecting trouble, he'd hardly have asked you to be there, would he?"

"I'm only telling you the way it happened," she replied wearily.

"Didn't it disturb you when he talked about something happening to him?"

"Yes, of course, but what worried me stiff was when he handed me the money after he'd said it. Look."

She opened her handbag and took out a wallet. It held a large number of one-hundred-franc Swiss notes and a few of smaller denominations. I reached inside her handbag and extracted her passport.

"Did he tell you to carry this, too?"

"No. I always keep it in my bag. We go to Austria a lot, and I'm scared of forgetting it."

"I see. What did Sven do after he got up on the morning of the explosion?"

"You do dodge about a lot, don't you? After breakfast he went into his study and typed a letter. Then he went out to post it. He was away for about half an hour, and then he came back and got on with some work in his study."

"Who was the letter to?"

"He didn't tell me. He always kept copies of his correspondence, but the files must have been destroyed by the explosion." A shudder crossed her face. "I saw the villa go up from where I stood in the wood. It was horrible."

"What happened to the dog?" I asked suddenly.

"The dog?" Her face went blank.

"Aino—Sven's Alsatian," I said sharply.

"He stayed with Sven."

"When Sven opened that flap and looked down into the cellar did Aino show any signs of alarm?"

"No, I don't think so. . . ." The vague look came into her face again, and she passed a hand over her forehead. "He must have been upstairs, I think. David, it's not so easy remembering all these details after what's happened."

I gave her a cigarette, and she leaned back against the couch to smoke it. The room was very quiet when we stopped speaking, and I wished I couldn't hear the sound of my watch ticking, because the noise took me straight back to the Graben. Else smiled and said it was all right now, I could go on with my questions.

"You shouldn't be carrying such a large amount of money in your handbag," I told her. "Get it converted into traveler's checks."

"David, I mustn't do that. I have to identify myself to change them. The police—everyone—would know."

"I'd like to get the picture very clear in my mind. Just before eleven o'clock—at a time when you thought you'd be staying in all morning—Sven opened the flap, saw something that disturbed him, and told you to run out and wait on the hillside. Is that it? Good. You ran straight out of the house, up the garden, and waited in the wood. Then the bomb went off. Have I got it quite clear?"

61

"Quite clear."

"In that case why were you wearing your sable coat in the house?"

"I wasn't. I'd left it in the cabin at Brugg the last time we were there." She looked at me wryly through her darkened lashes. "Anyone would think I was in the witness box."

"I'm just clearing things up in my mind." I pointed to the handbag. "You'd left that at Brugg, too?"

"Of course not! It was on the sideboard. Sven grabbed it as I was leaving and told me to take it."

I stood up and paced around the room. In the distance a fresh police siren shrieked its urgent message and died. On its way to the Graben? Looking for Fleischmann? I had almost decided what I must do with Else for the moment. She sat quietly on the couch waiting for my next onslaught. I spoke gently.

"You went along the back-garden path and up the hill into the wood. Did you hear anything on the way?"

"No, not a thing."

"While you were waiting on the hill?"

She hesitated. "Not until . . ."

"All right. The bomb went off. What did you do then?"

"I was stunned. It was a terrible explosion. When it was over I ran back down the hill into the garden. Then I stopped—I could see the cellar was buried, just buried. . . . Oh, I don't know—but I knew immediately no one could have survived."

"Go on."

"I was terribly frightened. I remembered the other bomb outrages—but above all I remembered what Sven had said, that in an emergency I must leave Zurich. I suppose in a way I was still stunned. Sven had been so emphatic. I ran. I caught a train to Brugg and then walked the rest of the way to the cabin—I didn't want to risk a taxi. I stayed there most of the time and only went into Brugg for food and to get the papers. That's how I knew you had arrived."

"And you've nothing more to tell me?"

"No. Should there be anything more?"

"It's time to inform the police." I pretended to reach for the phone. Her hand closed over mine and banged down the receiver with surprising strength. I remembered that she was exceptionally strong for her weight and size.

"No," she snapped.

"Why not?"

"Because Sven said so." She lapsed into a state of semi-hysteria. "Damn you! Nearly thirty people have died in these awful outrages. I'm the only one who has survived. Look, I've tried to keep calm, but inside I'm a screaming jelly." She clenched my arm with both hands and spoke from between her teeth. *"They think I'm dead, David.* As long as they think that, I'm safe—with you."

I decided. "Else, I'm taking you out of Zurich tonight. I may have to dump you back at the cabin while I attend to a few things, but there are some odd characters wandering around this town, and you're better out of it."

"Thank God for that. While I remember it, things keep coming back to me, and there's something I should have told you. A message was delivered to the cabin while I was out there. It came through the post with just the address on it—no name. I can't make head or tail of it." She fished inside her handbag. "Here it is."

I recognized Sven's printed letterhead. The note was not addressed to anyone, nor was it signed. It was typed, and the message was brief and to the point: *In case of emergency contact Gustav Glincker, Stiftgasse 85, Innsbruck.*

"You've no idea who sent this?" I asked her.

"Oh yes, I know who sent it. I recognized the broken 'c' character. That was typed on Sven's machine, and I'm pretty sure it was the letter he went out to post on the morning the bomb exploded." She wrinkled her forehead. "Before we leave we must collect my case from the Haupt-

63

bahnhof—I dumped it in the left-luggage place while I came over here."

And then the phone rang. It was the police. Inspector Sammet sent his apologies for not speaking to me when I rang earlier but would like to see me now urgently.

13: BODIES

"You've been here over an hour," Sammet said as he picked up the phone, "so let's hope that this is it." He listened, made one-word replies, and put down the phone. "That was it. Rudi Dorf checked out of the Hotel Victoria just before my men arrived."

"And Romy Silber?"

"She hasn't been back to the Schweizerhof yet." He didn't appear to be greatly interested as he scowled hard at his pipe.

"You do see my point," I said with some exasperation. "I saw Dorf leaving just after the bomb that killed Manfred Klein went off. He was *waiting* when I arrived. The only way he could have known where I was going was by hearing from Romy Silber—who got Klein's number from the scratch pad at the Schweizerhof. It's a pretty plausible line of suspicion I should have thought."

"Unless Klein himself told Dorf."

"What number was Klein phoning from, anyway?"

"His flat."

"And Manfred Klein," I went on persistently. "Where does he fit into the picture?"

"Not really any picture to fit him into, is there?" Sammet remarked blandly.

"Just a watchmaker?"

"That's right. A man who has spent all his life with time

64

mechanisms." Sammet closed his eyes and then opened them again to blow smoke at the ceiling.

"We don't seem to be getting very far."

"Oh, I don't know. The explosion only took place this evening. I warned you not to poke your nose into this business—there have been three explosions in Zurich now. You might even get yourself blown up," he said grimly.

"I nearly was—once on the plane and now this evening."

"So the best thing to do is to go home and leave it to us, don't you think?"

"You'd really like me to do that?"

"Officially, yes. Unofficially"—he tamped the pipe bowl stubbornly with a stained thumb—"I think you make rather a good lightning conductor."

Sammet's attitude puzzled me. Something behind his eyes told me he was worried stiff about the bomb explosions and he was going to some trouble to treat me with elaborate unconcern. I tried once more.

"What about the Heim explosion? I meant to ask you—have you recovered any of the bodies?"

"Bits and pieces, yes. Sufficient for laboratory testing."

"Sven Heim's body, for one," I said cautiously.

"That's right—and quite a few bits of the girl, too."

14: NIGHT EYES

The sense of being followed was present as soon as we drove away from the Schweizerhof. There was a lot of night traffic as we reached the bridge over the Limmat, so for the moment I concentrated on my driving while beside me Else fiddled with a road map taken from her case on the back seat. I crossed the river and headed north through the city.

"Friday night's always busy," Else remarked.

I looked in the rear-view mirror, and a barrage of lights stared back at me. Impossible to identify any particular vehicle. The feeling was quite illogical, based on no tangible evidence. I suddenly realized that I was very tired, but still my brain raced around. Something to do with a color. What color? Else began to give me instructions as to which route to follow, and the lights of Zurich raced past us. I looked in the rear-view mirror again and saw only anonymous headlights. We were on the outskirts of Zurich when Else looked back and stiffened.

"It's still behind us."

"What is?"

"The crimson Cadillac."

Crimson! That was it. The flash of crimson out of the corner of my eye as we pulled away from the hotel. I put my foot down, and we drove fast out of Zurich on the main road which led through Dietikon, Baden, and Brugg to Basel. Beyond the city the moon came out and showed fir-covered slopes on both sides, reminding me of the approach to Vienna. Else went on guiding me, hardly ever referring to the map.

"I know the way so well," she explained. "In summer we used to drive out here every weekend. It's funny how different it looks at night." She glanced back. "There's nothing behind us now. Do you think it's all right?"

"Probably. I'm tired and you're nervous. Zurich must have loads of crimson Cadillacs. In any case, if they'd been following us, they'd have kept farther back. Forget it."

"You don't have to work so hard to reassure me."

"Light me a cigarette and keep your eye on that map— you said it all looked different at night."

"You can't go wrong with me, David," she replied in an overinnocent voice, but when I glanced her way she was busily lighting the cigarette.

We didn't speak again until a while later, after we had

passed through Brugg. The traffic began to thin out, and now it was only occasionally that two great saucer eyes would loom up before us, grow enormous, and then flash past. Behind us the road was empty except for two smaller saucer eyes which kept their distance. I increased speed, and the eyes remained the same size. Pushing my foot down, I took the car up to seventy, seventy-five, eighty. The eyes followed. I began to reduce speed, slowing down more and more. The eyes behind me stayed the same size, as though they were attached to my Citroën by a long string. Else spoke as she leaned forward to peer into the night.

"Keep your speed down. We turn off somewhere along here, and it's a very minor road."

"We shan't be turning off."

"Why not?"

"Because we have company. Look behind us."

She swiveled and talked to the rear seat. "Is that why you've been playing about? I wondered. Wasn't I good not to say anything?" Her teeth chattered over the last word.

Her voice was light and skittish, but I sensed underneath a new feeling of strain and anxiety, the same tone of voice as when she had first entered my room at the Schweizerhof. Her next remark was made as lighthearted banter.

"Big eyes is coming up to have a closer look."

"You're sure?"

She paused, one arm looped over the back of her seat, then she said she was sure. She went on to say that it was *the* Cadillac.

"You mean it's crimson?"

I began to pick up speed rapidly, driving my foot down steadily, praying for the arrival of cars in the opposite direction. We were passing through open countryside, and the highway spread away into the night, completely deserted.

"Crimson," said Else tightly. "And it's got a funny big horn mounted on its hood."

"Bullhorn, probably."

"It's aimed at us just like a gun, David."

"It doesn't talk like a gun," I answered lightheartedly, building up even more speed, so that now the high neon lamp standards rushed toward me and vanished like a succession of blips across a radarscope.

"It's much closer. Why do they call it a bullhorn?"

"It makes a noise like a mating call to cows—they use a thing like that for getting in cattle in certain parts of the world. Else, what's the nearest town ahead of us?"

"Basel. There's a place called Rheinfelden before it, but it's quite small and we're still miles from there."

"How are we doing?"

"Very well—but the Cadillac's much closer."

I could hear it coming now, and when I glanced in the rear-view mirror it was too damned close, much closer than I had anticipated. And I was driving a Citroën.

"He's got a souped-up engine," I muttered.

And then I heard the sound of the bullhorn, a great honking bellow which blasted the deserted Swiss landscape. I had heard that bellow somewhere before. I tried briefly to bring back the association and then gave it up as the Cadillac came alongside.

"Else, he's going to try to ram us over the edge. When I can I'm going to let him slip ahead and then I'll pull up. As soon as I stop, get out of the car. No—don't argue, just get out when I pull up. Get over into those fields and hide. Whatever happens don't come out till that Caddy's gone. If I'm not around, make your own way to the cabin. Stay there until I get . . ."

She reacted instantly, grabbing her handbag and holding the car door handle in readiness. I couldn't see who was inside the Cadillac because its glass was tinted darkly, but I had the impression it was full of men. It blew its obscene horn again, still racing alongside me, still holding a wide

68

gap between us, which puzzled me. I tensed myself to lose speed rapidly, and then the front tinted glass window began to lower. I glanced across, waiting for my first sight of the gun muzzle. Else turned to watch the window as it lowered, and I sensed the rigidity of her body.

A face stared back at me, and I almost swerved. "Christ!" I snorted, and reduced speed. Else's hand gripped the door handle tightly. "Stay in the car," I snapped, "so long as you don't mind bad language. And your name's now Sonia Klinger."

"I rather like that."

"Someone isn't going to like this," I replied grimly.

The Cadillac drove in front of the Citroën, giving me plenty of clearance. When it stopped I pulled in a dozen yards behind it and braked. The doors opened, and men came out from both sides. The man who had climbed out of the front passenger seat walked forward slowly down the track of my headlights, hands held out in a gesture of peace. He stopped in front of the Citroën and waited while I got out with Else. Taking her arm, I moved forward.

"Sonia, meet Larry Biggs, European correspondent of the Washington *Express.*"

Larry Biggs was a short, plump man with a large-domed head. He wore a dark overcoat and, as always, was hatless, exposing streaks of brown hair carefully brushed back from his forehead. His face was also plump, and beneath sad gray eyes a short nose hovered over a postage-stamp-sized mustache. He regarded Else solemnly and said Sonia Who?

"Sonia Klinger. And what the hell do you mean chasing me all the way from Zurich? I don't object to that too much, but when you blow rude noises through that frigging horn— that's the last straw."

"It's my identification signal," he observed mildly.

"It's also the bull's mating call—you've probably just

summoned half the cattle in Switzerland in for midnight milking."

"Can we have a word, David?" He managed to convey the fact that he would like a private word, so I said I'd join him in the Cadillac providing a couple of his men stayed with Sonia. He introduced her to Jeff Tarleton, a husky, soft-spoken man wearing a long camel's-hair coat and a snap-brim hat. Tarleton removed the hat to explain to Sonia that he was from Texas, and he made it sound like an independent state. "I'll be all right with Mr. Tarleton, David," she assured me impishly, so I went forward to the Cadillac with Larry, and we settled ourselves on the back seat. The other men took up selected positions along the roadside as though preparing an ambush. I lowered a window and peered out at them, talking to Larry over my shoulder.

"Are these boys expecting trouble?"

"They've already had some tonight."

"Really? Besides being a newspaper correspondent are you still in intelligence and research for the State Department?"

"You bet!" He produced a hip flask. "Peace offering for scaring the pants off you."

"You should be ashamed of yourself." I gurgled whisky. "This trouble you were talking about?"

"Luckily, I can level with you—that security classification you had from Washington over the Hildebrand business still holds." He leaned back and clasped his hands over his stomach, wearing the expression of a man who expects the worst from the world. "Jeff Tarleton's had a busy time during the past hour. He just rammed a car off the road."

"*What*? You'll get shot—this is Switzerland, remember."

"You're the one who nearly got shot—or did that little episode escape your notice?"

"When was this?"

"Just beyond Zurich. We were using the old tailing technique—keeping a car between us and your Citroën. We dropped back a shade behind the dark Mercedes, and he must have thought we'd turned off. We caught up as he was going around a bend, with you just ahead. He had a gun out of the side window and fired one shot at your tires."

"Never heard a thing."

"You might not—the wind was coming against us pretty hard. Jeff has damn fast reflexes. He drove right alongside the Mercedes before they could put in another shot. By this time you'd put on a burst of speed and were well ahead. So Jeff squeezed him over the edge. He rolled God knows how many times and then burst into flames. That was when we nearly lost you, but luckily you kept on the main road until we caught up."

"Thank God you were following us."

"All a question of timing." He chuckled. "We don't know who the gunman was. We have his car number, but ten gets you one it was a hired job."

"Let's just hope the Swiss police don't catch up with you. It's a serious offense to push cars off the roads over here."

"It's an even more serious offense to commit bomb outrages," said Larry quietly.

"You're working on them personally?"

"Night and day. I haven't had a decent night's sleep in four months. This is the biggest thing I've ever been on—it could alter the whole balance of power in the West, and even hand Europe to the Russians on a plate. There's a rumor growing and growing as to the organization that's behind them. Once that rumor breaks in the press the repercussions could be world-wide."

"And that rumor is?"

"That the organization behind the bomb outrages is the CIA."

2 AUSTRIA: RENDEZVOUS

15: ESCAPE ROUTE

It was the middle of the night, and we were close to the Swiss-German border. Ahead of us Jeff Tarleton drove the Cadillac with Else in the back. I sat behind the steering wheel of the Citroën with Larry alongside me. As we drove along the lonely second-grade road I repeated my question.

"You're quite sure you can get Sonia over the border tonight?"

Larry looked at his watch. "It's tomorrow already."

"I mean before dawn?"

"The answer is still yes—just. Stop fretting. Jeff will take her out and look after her well. He's an ex-paratrooper, so if the wrong people turn up they'll find they're dealing with no pushover."

"And no Passport Control post is involved?"

"None at all. She'll have to do a little walking over rough ground, mind you."

"Sonia will walk."

"You wouldn't like to tell me what this is all about?"

"Part of our deal, Larry—remember? You asked me to help you with the bomb outrages and I said yes, on one condition: that you take Sonia Klinger out of Switzerland and make sure no one gets at her. What's this outfit you have at Friedrichshafen, anyway?"

"As you know, it's the nearest German town to Switzerland in the area. We have a small communications unit in the middle of the town. She can have her own small apartment and just sit tight while you clear this thing up with me." He paused. "You wouldn't involve me in anything, would you?"

"She's committed no crime so far as I'm aware."

"Forget it, forget it." He laid a hand on my arm. "I shouldn't have asked that, but this business I'm on is driving us all crazy. Look, the Caddy's pulling in. I'll bring her back here for a word with you, and then Jeff will take her across to Germany."

When I was alone in the Citroën with Else I went over the whole business with her, explaining that she would be safe with these people but that I still wanted her to keep up the fiction of her new identity. She seemed quite happy about the idea of having Jeff as a protector. "He's very well mannered," she told me impishly. "He even calls me ma'am!" She giggled. "I suppose if I want to get in touch with you I phone the Schweizerhof?"

"For the moment, yes. If I move on, I'll arrange for messages to follow me. But when you contact me don't forget you're Sonia."

"By the way, David, I know he's going to sneak me into Germany, but whereabouts shall I be staying?"

"At Friedrichshafen. Is that all right?"

"As a matter of fact," she said, "that will do rather well."

16: FILM SHOW

The screen showed a scene of fresh devastation, another mountain of rubble that had once been a family's home. I eased myself back in the chair inside the small theater under the Bahnhofstrasse and accepted a cigarette from Larry, who sat in the chair beside me. The little theater was in darkness, the only sound the steady whir of the camera inside the projection booth. We had one row of seats to ourselves, but there were other people behind us. As the film scene switched to a crowd watching the wrecked house from behind a roped barrier I leaned forward.

"Braunschweig," said Larry. "Willi Beckmann died in that—the Christian Democratic politician. He'd made several anti-American speeches," he added.

The faces in the crowd were just faces in a crowd, all gazing bleakly at the camera. I concentrated hard and so far I had seen no one I recognized.

"Whose idea was it to take these pictures?" I asked.

"Mine. There's nothing on the first three outrages, of course. It was only afterward that I had a sniff of this CIA rumor building up, so I jumped in with both feet. We're co-operating with Interpol, the German and Swiss police. The Dutch and the Danes have been helpful, too. I suggested that if there were new outrages a film unit should be rushed to the spot to photograph the sight-seeing crowds. At the time I was just being thorough—it seemed a long shot that anyone connected would come back afterward. Now, it's the only shot we've got." He spoke emphatically. "If only we could spot just one person we know—or one person we don't know at the scene *of more than one of the outrages. . . .*"

"You had a film unit outside Sven Heim's house?"

"That's right. I haven't seen it yet—it comes on as a tail-piece at the end of this lot. No one at all you recognize?" he asked hopefully.

"Not so far, Larry. Was Beckmann's body recovered?"

"Yes, quite intact. The explosion blew him clear. He was stone-cold dead, of course. Sometimes the victims are blown to pieces, sometimes just badly disfigured. Once or twice they've survived whole—like Beckmann. We have every possible variation of corpse in this grisly business. This is Regensburg. Arthur Riedel, Germany's leading air-frame specialist went up in that mess. There wasn't much of him left, I can tell you."

A low wooded hillside. Large modern houses standing in clearings. In one clearing a cone of debris. The camera switched and eyed the usual crowd hypnotized by the after-math of explosion. The crowd eyed us back. I leaned for-ward, and the figure on the screen moved back, out of the camera's probing gaze. Larry sat up.

"Something?"

"Wait till I've seen the whole show."

Augsburg . . . Hanover . . . Kassel. Larry's voice in-toned the roll call of the death cities and their victims. In the gaps between his commentary he told me about the rumors.

"We're particularly vulnerable to this CIA rumor, if it ever hits the world's headlines, because of two factors. One, there's growing resentment back home in Congress about anti-American sentiment in Europe, and this is known. Some of our less-tactful senators have seen to it that it should be known. Added to that is Washington's growing strategic anxiety that Europe is going to opt out from the world scene. That's the first point. Second, most of the lead-ing figures who have died in the outrages have been re-ported as expressing anti-American sentiments."

"So the rumor theory is that the CIA has gone wild and is

eliminating important anti-American personalities from the European scene—in Germany, that is?"

"Something like that. There's been a lot of talk in the press this past year of agencies like the CIA and the KGB living a life of their own—and that doesn't help. The thing we just can't figure out is what this campaign of outrages is intended to achieve—apart from terrorizing the whole of West Germany—and that's what will happen if we don't stop them soon."

A familiar voice spoke in my ear from the seat behind mine, but the voice lacked the normal bubbling laugh.

"The outrages, Mr. Martini, are intended to influence decisively the coming West German election. Of that I have no doubt at all."

Larry introduced me. "Meet Rudi Dorf, a senior official of the German police force."

"We've met," I said briefly. "Sold any good insurance policies lately, Rudi?"

"No one ever suspects an insurance man, David." Rudi chuckled and offered me a cigar, which I refused.

"How can they influence the election?" I asked him.

"The New People's Party, which doubtless you have heard of . . ."

"A bunch of Nazis," grumbled Larry.

". . . an extreme right-wing party," Rudi corrected. "They are violently anti-American and have made the withdrawal of all foreign troops—which are mainly American —from German soil the leading plank in their platform. If this rumor is headlined in the world's press at the right moment, they could have a landslide victory in the election, even though at the moment they are a minority party."

"Münster," intoned Larry. "Theodor Bathe, aerodynamics specialist. Blown to pieces."

"Also anti-American?" I asked.

"He was reported to have said American business was

colonizing Europe, and the statement received splash treatment. Later, he denied saying anything of the sort and claimed he was on holiday in Egypt at the time."

"Denials are always too late," said Rudi.

"This looks familiar," I remarked, and leaned forward.

"Heim's place. This is the bit I haven't seen. Well, well, if it isn't our old friend Mr. David Martini!"

The glow from the arc lights had been just sufficient to record my brief glance at the camera inside the gray van. Then the film spluttered.

"That shows a time lag," Larry explained. "They don't operate the camera nonstop, of course. Personally," he complained bitterly, "I haven't got one damned thing out of this. So, after six months we are still exactly where we were when I started. Several major European police forces, Interpol, us—all that effort . . . What's the matter, David?"

I was leaning forward in my seat, staring hard at the screen. The crowd parted to let a car move up the road past Heim's villa, and I had a clear view of him, a very clear view. I pointed.

"Him!"

And then the film died. The shot had been taken on the last few feet of film. I sat back, and they put the lights on. Rudi leaned over the back of my chair, and Larry sat tensely. "Well, David?" he prodded.

"That man was at Regensburg. Run through the film later and you'll spot him—only a brief shot, but he was there. And he was outside Heim's villa the morning after the bomb went up—no, the second morning after. Now we can start moving."

"For Pete's sake, who is he?" demanded Larry.

"Josip Riz, so-called chauffeur to billionaire Nikki Kardehay."

17: SCRAMBLE

". . . everything on Kardehay, everything you can dig up, it doesn't matter how trivial it may seem. When I say everything, I mean everything. . . ."

Larry was talking on the phone to Washington, and I found it interesting. I had never before witnessed him putting the pressure on his superiors. He moved into action like a well-controlled bulldozer, his voice flat, grinding down the opposition. From the third-floor window above the Bahnhofstrasse I watched Zurich start to light up in the dusk. It was Saturday evening, my third day in the city, the night of October 28.

Else would now have spent twelve hours in Friedrichshafen, and during that twelve hours neither Larry nor I had had a wink of sleep. We had driven straight back to Zurich from the border and taken up residence in this large room which was Larry's temporary headquarters. It looked as though he had worked from here for years. Six Americans in their early thirties, all looking rather alike in shirt sleeves, sat at a long table recording phone reports as they came in, while two more collated the reports. I looked at some of these, and they told me nothing.

I had spent some time on the phone myself, calling more people in Europe I knew, and what they said told me nothing I didn't already know, which amounted to almost nothing in itself. Tremendous activity, no progress. I could see Larry's point. Six months of this would drive even a hardened warrior into the ground. The door opened, and Rudi Dorf came in, smiling as though everything was hunkydory, but I thought the smile was a little forced. He waved and listened to Larry's closing barrage.

". . . so now you know what I need, what I must have. And I need it transmitted over here in six hours. You're six hours behind us on time scale so by rights I should have it now!" He chuckled. "Just so long as you've got the message. Bye."

He rammed the phone down and glared at me. "So there you have it—a scramble, may the good Lord and Washington forgive me, because personally I don't believe it."

"Believe what?"

"That Kardehay is mixed up in this thing."

"But Josip Riz . . ."

"Riz, yes—but he's probably playing his own game. And I may tell you, Washington doesn't go much for it either."

"Why not?"

The central heating was turned on full blast. Larry stood up, rolled his sleeves back above the elbows, and came over to me, hands pushed deep in his trouser pockets.

"Because, David, we know Kardehay. Sure, he's an ex-Hungarian, came out at the time of the '56 uprising—I know all that, but he made his fortune in the States, in the West." He lit my cigarette, his own, and then Rudi's cigar. "When Kardehay arrived in New York he was nothing but a brilliant mathematician; he'd been a lecturer at the university in Budapest. He studied the stock market, borrowed capital, used his mathematical expertise to calculate the odds, and plunged in on the American Exchange, where the real risk stocks are. In ten years he was worth a billion dollars and started buying up whole industries—small, key firms at first and then bigger ones. He went for the sophisticated stuff—electronics, things like that. Two years ago—and I must admit I don't understand why—he transferred his operations to Europe, with Brussels as his headquarters. So—" he paused to emphasize—"we really can't see a man like that being mixed up in a terrorist campaign with political undertones."

"You're thinking about the Russians?"

"I must admit the thought had crossed my mind."

"Cross it off your mind—this thing has nothing to do with Russians or Chinese or any of the old bogies."

"What makes you say that?" asked Larry thoughtfully.

"Call it a hunch, but I know Kardehay personally—don't forget I've negotiated with him, and during the pressures of negotiation you learn about a man. I think I know how he sees things."

"Just how does he see them?"

"From his own standpoint night and day. He doesn't give a damn for America or Russia or any of them any more. The only person who counts in Nikki Kardehay's world is Nikki himself. And now, can we have another look at those lists of victims? I've made some notes."

"Bully for you! We've made a million of them, and that list of victims shows no pattern—no pattern at all, unless you count their anti-American viewpoint."

We sat down at the table, and Larry waited skeptically. I showed him the lists I had drawn up, and we argued about my argument. After fifteen minutes he was listening without comment and asked me to run through it briefly again for Washington. When he had the tape recorder ready I started.

"First of all, forget the anti-American statements these people have made, or are supposed to have made. Forget all about that. Now—I'm including Sven Heim in this—up to date fourteen outrages have killed thirty people, including people who happened to be in the houses at the time the bombs went off. Of the fourteen leading personalities who died, six were prominent West German politicians, and the other eight were directly connected with the *aircraft* industry, again including Sven Heim—the only victim killed outside Germany, but still within the aircraft category. No, I'm not including Manfred Klein, because I think he comes into a category all his own."

"And the anti-American bias straddles the two categories," Larry interjected. "All the politicians were critical of the States and two of the aircraft men are on record with the same kind of view."

"*Forget* that aspect, Larry, for the moment. The other factor is the size of the bombs used."

"Size of the bombs?" Larry blinked.

"It's all down here. The explosions varied in ferocity. Sometimes huge bombs were used—of the type, probably, that killed Sven—and on other occasions the bombs were smaller. The one that killed Willi Beckmann, the politician, was the smaller type." I leaned over the table. "But in the case of the aircraft men always a big bomb was used."

"You think that makes up a category?"

"I think it makes it worth our while to draw up another list fast—a list of top German aircraft people still surviving who can be warned on the quiet that they may be potential victims. Put them on their guard and tell them that if anything suspicious happens they must contact the police at once."

"That's a helluva long shot," Larry protested.

Rudi had been examining my lists and now he watched us both debate the point.

"Have you any other shot to fire at the moment, however long?" I inquired.

"It will just cause more alarm," said Larry flatly.

"I don't know," intervened Rudi. "We have nothing else to go on, and there is something curious about David's list. I'd be prepared to co-operate on those lines."

"We'd better give it some thought," replied Larry. "Quite some thought."

A phone rang, and one of the men at the table said it was for Larry. He took the phone and listened, then he swore and rattled the receiver cradle, listened again, and rammed the phone down.

"Broken connection," he said grimly, staring at me. "David, I have some bad news, and you're not going to like it one little bit."

"What's happened?"

"Sonia Klinger has disappeared."

18: DEAD LETTER

It was waiting for me when I got back to the Schweizerhof. I took it upstairs and read it by the light of the table lamp.

Dear David,

Will you forgive me—after all the work you have put into this transaction? But I have to tell you that I have irrevocably changed my mind about selling the jet engine to Mr. Kardehay.

This means there is now no need for you to fly to Zurich with the agreement. I shall not be signing it. Instead, I would like you to send me your bill for the agreed fee—the whole of it. I would have sent a check with this letter but I am unable to compute your expenses, which you will of course include.

When we meet I will explain why I changed my mind. I have informed Mr. Kardehay of my decision. Else sends her love.

Sven

The letter was dated October 22, four days before I had been due to leave for Switzerland, and was typed on a printed letterhead which carried Sven's home address. I read the accompanying letter from my secretary, Judy, which explained that the fool of a new postman had again delivered mail to that bitch of a woman next door, who hung on to it for days before bringing it around. Judy also said that she had tried to phone me but I had always been out, so she was sending it on. Her last sentence was almost comic. She hoped that under the circumstances I wasn't finding Zurich too quiet.

When the phone rang I was just thinking of going to bed.

A Mr. Dorf was downstairs and wished to see me very urgently.

19: DEADLINE

"Bad news," announced Rudi with a cheerful smile, "very bad news." I felt that he savored the drama of being the bearer of ill tidings.

"What is it now?" I asked wearily. "And help yourself to that brandy."

"Larry asked me to come because it isn't something to talk about on the open phone and he's pretty busy. He's already hearing from Washington. I think he'll be up all night."

"While I remember it. Romy Silber . . ."

"Is my assistant. A most competent girl, especially when it comes to obtaining information."

"She tries, she tries very hard," I assured him.

He grinned devilishly. "She told me you were a hard nut to crack."

"The bad news, Rudi—I can't wait to hear the very bad news."

"We're up against a deadline now. Larry is nearly going around the bend."

"What deadline?"

"I told you about the New People's Party in Germany. Their chairman and leader is Kurt Langer, you know."

"Yes, Rudi, I do know."

"But, of course, he is only the front man—the man with the golden tongue who makes all the speeches. The really dangerous one is the party secretary, Walther Loeb. He stays in the background but is the strong man."

"Pass that bottle," I said. "This sounds like a long session."

"Oh, it needn't be. I forgot—you also have not had much sleep. None at all, really. As for myself, I slept the sleep of the just at the Victoria."

"At the Victoria?" I blinked. "I thought you'd left there."

He bubble-laughed. "The good Inspector Sammet had to tell you something. I saw him earlier today. I don't think he fully appreciated your offering as a prime suspect a senior German police official!"

"A scream," I agreed, and drank brandy.

"I have just heard from a very reliable source inside Germany that Langer is shortly going to make a major speech in Munich on the bomb outrages. He is going to point the finger of accusation at the American Central Intelligence Agency."

"He can't do that without evidence," I said sourly.

"Oh yes he can. He will simply avoid mentioning the name, but it will be perfectly clear who and what he is talking about."

"When does he make this speech?"

"A hall is booked for the night of Friday, November 3."

"Are you quite sure? That's only six days away."

"Quite sure. So now we have only six days left to do what we have failed to do for over six months."

"You're just trying to make me lose a night's sleep."

"I think you're going to lose that, anyway. Larry wants you to come straight back to the Bahnhofstrasse with me. The reports on Kardehay will be coming in all night long."

20: TELEGRAM

I spent the whole night and all Sunday morning reading the reports on Kardehay. I thought I had known something about him before I began negotiations on behalf of Sven Heim, but as Washington spewed out more and more reports I realized I had known very little about him. I hadn't known, for instance, that he had another headquarters, called the Torre, which was situated high up in the Alps near the Brenner Pass, close to the Austro-Italian border.

In between reports coming in on Sunday morning I read a newspaper. The Zurich bomb explosions were the headline story, and there was a reference to Bruno Fleischmann having been seen in the city. When Larry finished another phone call and brought me coffee he looked even more baggy-eyed than usual.

"I still haven't heard from Tarleton since the connection broke," he explained apologetically. "He's out looking for her. The trouble was he expected someone to try to get into the apartment. He didn't count on her walking out under her own steam."

"Can't be helped."

"Anything in the paper? I'll have to write a piece myself for the *Express* someday."

"Nothing except the bomb business—and the Egyptian President has again boasted that they are close to air mastery over the whole Middle East."

"He's talking through his fez. They've hardly got an air force at the moment. Excuse me—must be another report."

I ate lunch in the room with Larry and Rudi, and it was midafternoon before I went back to the Schweizerhof. As I walked in, the receptionist handed me a telegram which had just arrived. I read it twice and I thought I understood it.

Gone to see Gustav. Please come urgently. Sonia.

21: GUSTAV

Night had fallen again when I got off the Vienna Express at Innsbruck, the ancient Austrian city which guards the northern entrance to the Brenner Pass.

I took a taxi from the Hauptbahnhof to the Hotel Maria-Theresia, checked in, washed, borrowed a street guide and an umbrella from the receptionist, and walked out into the main street, the Maria-Theresienstrasse. It was still Sunday, the night of October 29.

Innsbruck is over seven hundred years old and shows her age. Untouched by air raids, mellow color-washed walls still line the main street, and antique balconies suggest a hint of her imperial past. Just beyond the city the massive Alpine range looms over the roofs, but on that night the mountains had vanished in a fury of rain squalls. It was bitterly cold, and the foehn moaned along the deserted street. I put up the telescopic umbrella, checked my map, and walked down to the bottom. A signpost pointed back the way I had come. BRENNER.

The Stiftgasse was a narrow twisting alley of gloom leading off an arcaded street near the foot of the Maria-Theresienstrasse. At eight o'clock in the evening the rain thrashed down like a movie storm, bouncing off the cobbles and then surrendering itself to the wind, which threw it against my trouser legs. No one was about, and the buildings on either side were so high it was like walking into a canyon. A dozen yards from its entrance the alley curved and lost the street lights completely, so now only single wall lamps, suspended high up, vaguely lit the darkness. I huddled my coat collar closer around my neck and tried to hold the umbrella steady in the wind.

Number 85 was a dark alcove of shadow midway between distant lamps. With my pocket light I checked the name above the bell push and realized that something was wrong. It read E. EGGER, LEICHENBESTATTER. Undertaker. Flashing my light above the door again I reread the number. The Gothic numerals had confused me. This was Number 83. I walked a few steps farther, shone my light into the next alcove, and saw a large single door of heavy ancient wood. The door was split in the center, and hinges showed along

89

the split where it could be folded back. In the right-hand section was a smaller door. I read the card and pressed the bell above it. GUSTAV GLINCKER. DRUCKER. So Gustav was a printer. High up out of sight a gutter overflowed. I moved close in to the door to escape the cascade. I was pressing the bell a second time when the small door opened inward as though of its own volition. Above the inside frame an oil lamp glowed smokily.

I looked for the person who was opening the door. I peered behind the door. No one there. A thick cord was attached to the handle. The cord ran over a pulley wheel, turned the wall corner behind an iron staple, and then disappeared into the shadows. I stood there, aware that I presented a perfect target to anyone standing in the darkness, wondering about the coffins. Lying on the cobbled floor of the chamber were several large wooden coffins, their metal handles reflecting tongues of oil-lamp flame. Beside them were several stacks of cut panel sides, waiting to be made up into complete coffins. Three or four loose handles were scattered on the floor. I decided that Mr. Glincker rented storage space to his undertaker neighbor, Mr. Egger.

Something moved in the shadows, and I felt sure someone was standing watching me. I heard a creak of old, old wood, and a large square of light appeared in the left-hand wall, exposing flickering oil lamps in the room beyond. I had a glimpse of stone walls and wooden benches, and then, next to the wooden flap he had pulled open, I saw a man standing.

He was very small, stockily built, and his crumpled suit hung loosely on his squat body. He wore his thick gray hair brushed back from his forehead, and he watched me through enormous horn-rim spectacles. The gun in his right hand was aimed at my stomach.

"I'm David Martini," I said in German. "I've come to see Mr. Glincker."

Still holding the pointed gun in his right hand, he made a

waving motion with his left hand which I took to mean he would like the door closed. When I pushed it the cord followed the door movement freely. I turned around, and the squat man used sign language with his left hand for me to come forward.

When I reached him he had opened the door completely. The window flap he had previously drawn back was the upper half of a stable-door partition. On the wall I saw a handle, which he had used to open the front door by remote control. He motioned me to go forward in front of him, and I went up two steps into a stone-flagged room. The oil lamps hanging from the walls flickered eerily and juggled sinister shadows across the stonework. I looked around quickly, but we seemed to have the place to ourselves. On the benches around the room lay several sticks of type and above them were dozens of pigeonholes which contained more lead type.

At one time each pigeonhole had carried a printed letter on white paper to identify the contents, but now most of the paper was worn and faded, so presumably Mr. Glincker knew just where everything was. A small flat-bed printing press occupied part of the right-hand wall, and in the corner a wooden staircase led up to the next floor. I stood looking at another door in the facing wall, which I assumed led into a side alley.

Wood creaked behind me. When I turned he had closed both door flaps and dropped a wooden bar. He stood with his back to the closed door, still holding the gun, which I now saw was a 9-millimeter Luger. Even without the weapon Gustav would be an incredibly evil-looking man. His forehead was low and compressed, his nose short and flat, and behind thick lips a single tooth showed where the upper lip twisted. His spectacles highlighted the whole impression. They were very thick pebble lenses, and behind the glass mad pinpoint eyes stared at me without moving.

91

"I'd just as soon you put the Luger away," I suggested.

He waved a finger across his lips several times in a negative motion, and for the first time I knew that he was dumb. As I said it again slowly his pinpoint eyes followed my lip movements.

"I am David Martini. I have come to see Mr. Glincker."

He nodded, lifted a finger in a wait-a-minute gesture, and then heavily climbed the open staircase behind the flat-bed press. The staircase was clumsily made of huge beams and planks and led up to a minstrel's gallery which was partly enclosed. While I waited I looked at the old Gothic type faces that littered a wooden table in the middle of the room. At one moment I heard a click which I thought I recognized but I continued to gaze at the type. When I looked up at the gallery it was deserted.

Quickly, I walked over to the back door, which was set inside an arched alcove. Lifting the latch I inserted a small piece of type under it so that now the door could be opened from the outside. Then I went back to the end of the room near the staircase. The wall was masked by a six-foot-high free-standing cupboard, which was open at the front. Its many shelves were divided into more pigeonholes full of lead type. The cupboard stood well away from the wall, and when I went behind it I saw that a portion of the wall was covered by a large piece of canvas held there by nails driven into the mortisework. There was no sound from the gallery as I lifted the canvas. Behind it was the only new piece of equipment in the place—a giant meat safe set into the wall. The door was slightly ajar, the mechanism switched off. When I opened the door it was almost big enough for me to step inside. It was also empty. I closed the door, wondering why the safe seemed not only bizarre but also unpleasant. When Glincker came down I was studying his pigeonholes.

Instead of the Luger he now held a newspaper in his right hand. He spread it out carefully on the table over the type, and I saw it was the airmail issue of the London *Telegram* that carried the report about my journey. It also carried my picture, and he pointed to it with satisfaction. I faced Glincker and spoke carefully.

"I . . . have . . . come . . . to . . . see . . . Else . . . Heim."

He frowned and looked annoyed, shaking his head in a way that conveyed to me that there was no need to talk at that snail's pace. From then on I spoke normally.

"Miss Heim is a friend of mine, and she told me she was coming to see you."

I waited, and he nodded impatiently.

"Where is Miss Heim staying? It's very important that I find her quickly. She may be in some danger."

He stared at me a moment longer and then picked up the *Telegram* and neatly refolded it along the creases. The paper had covered a line of type, which he pointed to. Picking up a triangular piece of cracked mirror, he held it over the type, handed me the mirror, and indicated that I should repeat his action. When I did so I saw it staring back at me in half-decipherable Gothic letters reversed in the mirror, so that I read it the right way around. HOTEL REGINA.

Gustav escorted me back through the chamber of coffins. This time I noticed a connecting door in the side wall that would give direct access to Mr. Egger's establishment. When he opened the small front door a spray of rain blew in my face. I stepped out and turned to thank him, but the door had already shut. As I reopened the umbrella a cyclonic gust whooshed down the Stiftgasse and blew it inside out. Throwing the remnant into the gutter, I turned up my coat collar and walked deeper into the Stiftgasse. The side turning off the alley was so narrow that the stone walls brushed my shoulders. Pushing open Gustav's back door silently I went inside.

Gustav had his back to me, and although the door had opened noiselessly the sound and feel of the wind warned him. He swung around, his open mouth expressing fear and amazement that I had entered through a locked door. In his left hand he held a Polaroid camera, and the fingers of his right hand were in the act of withdrawing the developed print of the picture he had taken of me from the minstrel's gallery. I shook my finger at him and removed the print.

"You mustn't go into business on your own, Gustav."

22: RENDEZVOUS

I checked out of the Hotel Maria-Theresia and carried my case up the street to claim the room I had just booked at the Hotel Regina. The receptionist took me up to the fifth floor inside a glass cage, and as we walked down a long corridor a girl walked out of a bathroom and came toward us. It was Else, her hair now its normal ash-blonde color, wearing a blue dressing gown splashed with yellow dragons. Behind the receptionist's back I winked and when I looked back she stood pointing and stabbing her finger at her room.

Inside my own room I pulled back the curtains and looked down into the rain-swept street. Opposite my window the shallow roofs had wire fences just above the gutters to bank up the winter's snow. I waited five minutes and went along to Else's room.

"What the hell do you think you're playing at?" was my greeting.

"I feel so much better now I'm properly dressed," she replied, and raised her hair on both sides with her hands.

She wasn't properly dressed. Now, her dressing gown gaped open, and underneath she wore a transparent see-through nightie. Semicircles of white rounded breasts stared back at me through the opening. She sat on the end of the bed and dangled her legs, eyes mischievous, manner animated in the way I remembered.

"Why run out on Tarleton?" I demanded.

"Because Sven had said I should contact Gustav."

"How did you do it—get away from Friedrichshafen?"

"There were two of them guarding me—Jeff and another man. I had a flat at the top of a building, and they took turns eating at a snack bar that faced the entrance to the block of flats. My food was brought in. Part of the time one guard stayed in another flat farther along the corridor. You have to go out the front entrance—and I had a bag. How would you manage that one, David?"

"Stop boasting about it," I told her irritably.

"I waited until Jeff was in the snack bar and called in the other guard for a cup of coffee. I had my dressing gown on and a towel around my head—he thought I'd just had a bath. That put him off guard, and when he went back to his room I put the towel and dressing gown in a holdall and walked out. I was dressed underneath in an outfit they hadn't seen, and earlier I had got the porter to take my bag to the station. . . ."

"And Jeff, watching in the snack bar across the street, saw a blonde leaving a large block of flats without any luggage?"

"That's right—I'd washed the dye out of my hair earlier and kept it covered up under the towel."

"Don't look so darned pleased with yourself. They were watching for someone trying to get in at you. You played them a dirty trick."

"Are you annoyed with me, David?" she teased, and crossed her legs. The gown fell sideways and showed long slim legs to high above the knees. I pointed at them.

"Stop trying to play mothers and fathers—you're not old enough. You risked your passport crossing the border into Austria, then?"

"My hair was back to the right color, my passport's made

out in the name Hildegarde Else Heim, and when the reports of the explosion appeared in the papers I was only briefly mentioned as Else Heim—a common enough name, and no picture. I didn't think I'd have any trouble. I came here by train and ate in the dining car."

"And saw Gustav to tell him you were staying here. Now where does Gustav fit into the picture?"

"He was a very old friend of Sven's. We lived here once, for six months. I'm sorry about Jeff Tarleton, David, but I feel much safer here in Innsbruck. It's so away from the world."

"So when you heard you were going to Friedrichshafen you were tickled pink—you knew you daren't try and cross a Swiss border on your passport?"

"That's right. Don't look so bearish, David. Isn't it a cozy room?" Modestly, she pulled the dressing gown back over her legs without attending to the panorama higher up.

I stood up and went over to the window to think. When I pulled back the curtains it was still a dirty night. Rain pattered on the glass, the drops running down in snake patterns. The window was double-glazed with a half-inch gap between the two sheets, but I could hear the moan and whine of the foehn coming down from the distant Brenner. Behind me I heard the bounce of springs.

"The bed's terribly comfortable, David."

The headlights of a car came up the main street; it slowed and stopped opposite the entrance to the hotel. It stayed parked there for over five minutes, a slant of rain passing through the beams. My vision was blurring from staring down when a man got out of the car. He walked across the street and disappeared inside the arcade which led to the lobby of the Hotel Regina. Two minutes later he came out again, climbed into the car, and drove off. I dropped the curtain.

Else was perched on the end of the bed again, her gown

open all the way down, her white face flushed from the warmth of the central heating. She watched me through her lashes as I came close to her. I picked her up, one arm under the legs, the other around the small of her back. As she waved her legs and squirmed vigorously I took her around to the side of the bed, lifted her high in the air, and then dropped her heavily.

"Stop acting like a randy schoolgirl—and get a good night's rest."

I was walking out of the room when she shouted in Finnish, something that didn't sound too complimentary. I went back to tell her to keep the door locked and bolted and got a pillow in the face for my trouble.

The phone call came through as soon as I reached my own room—a hoarse, muffled voice, which spoke in German.

"Mr. Martini? Listen. Take the 3:15 tram from the Berg Isel stop tomorrow afternoon. Get off at the second stop—at Schloss Ambras—and wait there. Bring Miss Heim with you. I can tell you what happened in Zurich."

23: TRAM RIDE

The mountain peered in at me through the window when I woke up next morning. A snow-tipped peak of the Nordkette Range. During the night the rain squalls had vanished, and now the sky was ice-blue, a perfect backdrop for the Alpine silhouette. When I opened the window the air was cold, but sunshine bathed Innsbruck.

I went along to Else, and she said we could have breakfast together in her room, so I went back to my own room and ordered coffee and croissants for one. While waiting for the breakfast to arrive I shaved and fretted over the time I had to waste until the afternoon rendezvous, but I had a feeling this meeting could be important. Shortly after my own breakfast arrived, Else herself arrived, carrying her breakfast tray and wearing thick woolen pajamas under her dressing gown.

"I had to put these on," she explained cheerily. "I had nothing to keep me warm in bed last night!"

"Don't start that again."

I dabbed fresh soap on, and she grabbed me from behind, wrapping her arms around my bare waist. "David, you look marvelous just in your pajama trousers." The hands crawled up over my chest. "Ticklish?" I dabbed a brushful of soap over my shoulder and planted it on her head. She let go and yelped. "I washed it only yesterday!"

"You can spend the morning washing it again—I have phone calls to make. After lunch we're going for a tram ride."

"Goody!" She clapped her hands together. "Where to?" came as an afterthought.

"Igls—at least you are. I get off at Schloss Ambras, and you go on up and wait for me."

"What happens at Schloss Ambras?"

"I'm meeting someone—and kindly remove your hands from my stomach. I'm trying to shave."

Ash-blonde hair came up under my right arm, and I dabbed soap on a tiptilted nose, but this time she refused to retreat, and her hands fiddled purposefully with my pajama cord. When I lost my trousers I lost my temper, locked the door, and the first thing I did was to spank her. The second thing I did was under provocation, and I consoled myself with the thought that we had a free morning.

The tram climbed out of the Berg Isel station pit, headed across a bridge over a river, and then left the road altogether as it began to ascend the mountain on its solitary

98

track. On the right we passed unfinished spans of a new *Autobahn* to the Brenner, and through the trees the sunlit city began to fall away and level out.

The line snaked up through a dense pine forest, and we were the only passengers aboard the single tram car. Else said it was like a tram out of a fairy tale and she wished we could travel on it forever and ever. As the gradient grew steeper the ancient buildings of Innsbruck receded and there was no sign of life anywhere. I checked my watch. The second stop the man on the phone had said. Several minutes later we pulled up in the middle of nowhere, and an Austrian in walking boots climbed aboard and went to the front. We continued the ascent, swinging above a lower stretch of track now, so the view was on the right—the white-tipped Olympus of the Nordkette Range in the distance, while below, Innsbruck had flattened out into a faraway city.

"You stay on board," I reminded Else.

"I'll behave."

"It's more than you've done so far."

The tram pursued its way along the track through the forest, and the rest of the journey was spent in silence. Then it rounded a curve and stopped. Else touched my arm. "Take care."

The Schloss Ambras halt was a large cabin-like waiting room by the side of the track. No one was waiting for me, and I watched the rear end of the tram disappear around a curve and then I was alone with the forest. Inside the open cabin there was a long wooden seat. On the far side of the track the ground rose abruptly to a small bluff, and it was the crest of this bluff I watched, since it was the approach point I would have chosen myself if I wanted to surprise someone waiting at the halt.

The sound of the tram climbing up toward Igls had faded, and now the oppressive silence grew. I strained my ears for the tiniest sound, a crunch of foot on pine needles, a scrape

99

of boot on rock. Nothing. Not even the cry of a single bird. Peering behind the cabin I found a bed of moss. I went back to the front and something watched me from the crest of the bluff. A dog. Sharp-pointed ears, wide-open jaws. An Alsatian. It stared down at me and I stared back for a moment, until I remembered the tactic of ambush: show the dog in front and come up behind. I went inside the cabin and sat on the bench, the revolver in my lap, just in case.

I didn't hear him come, but then I hadn't expected to. The dog gave no sign of his approach, although he must have seen him coming. A face peered around into the cabin.

"About time, Sven," I said.

24: HUNTSMAN

He was dressed in the clothes of an Austrian huntsman, his green corduroy trousers pushed down inside leather knee boots, a cartridge belt slung over his jacket shoulder, a soft green hat with a feather in the band pulled down over his large head. In his hands he held a rifle.

"You guessed, David?" he inquired.

"Let's say I had a shrewd suspicion. Else did very well in the beginning at playing bereaved niece, but you know Else." I grinned. "She couldn't keep it up, and her sense of fun kept breaking through. Then the fact that you'd planned for an emergency suggested to me that it was unlikely you'd come a cropper when it happened. Oh, and when you called at the Regina last night to make sure I'd turned up to look after Else I recognized your walk."

"You must think I'm crazy."

"You don't look it, Sven. What happened in Zurich?"

"I was suspicious. The day before the explosion a man I'd never heard of rang up and made an appointment to see me at the house at eleven o'clock the following morning. He said his name was Mendel and said it was about a large sum of money which had been left to Else by a distant cousin who'd emigrated to the States and then died there without any other relatives—so Else was the natural heir. But there were complications—they concerned Else's age. He wanted to meet me privately, and it was important that Else should also be there."

"Didn't all this sound too fishy for words?"

"Yes and no. Else did have a cousin who went to America, and we'd no idea whether he was dead or alive. Someone must have a good research department."

"What had all this to do with Mendel?"

"He said he was acting on behalf of the American lawyers and he was a partner in a Frankfurt law firm."

"So you left it at that?"

"Of course not. He said if anything urgent cropped up that meant I couldn't keep the appointment I was to phone him at the Schweizerhof. I let ten minutes pass after he'd called and phoned the hotel. They did have a Mr. Mendel staying there, but he'd gone out for the day."

"So you took precautions?"

"Yes. I gave Else a large sum of money and made her keep her passport in her bag. I told her to clear out of Zurich in an emergency."

"And the following morning?"

"It was close to eleven, and I was very much on the alert. I heard something in the cellar, and when I opened the flap the back door was open. I chased Else out through the French windows and went down to investigate. I didn't find anyone, but I found the suitcase. It was almost too heavy for me to lift. During the Winter War, I was a bomb-demolition expert—near the end of it, anyway. I'd read enough about the outrages, God knows. David, when I lifted that case I smelled it was a bomb."

101

"So you ran out to join Else on the hillside?"

"That's right. We saw the van leave. . . ."

"What van?"

"The laundry van—only it was the wrong day for it to call. We saw it drive away from the house, and a few minutes later the bomb went off—exactly at eleven it was."

"Then you skipped over the border at some remote spot and came here, leaving Else behind to let you know what was happening?"

"Yes. When she heard you were coming she phoned me, and we fixed up a way to get you here without any risk of anyone knowing we were still alive."

"You should have gone to the police," I told him.

"I like to fight my own wars," Sven said, and shut his mouth.

He was still standing up, tall, heavily built, watching me gravely. In his late fifties, his face was weather-beaten and brown, the type of brown the sun produces at high altitudes even in winter. His nose was hawklike, his mouth thin-lipped and firm. I glanced up to where the dog waited on the crest.

"You brought Aino with you?"

"Yes, we came out over the hills."

"I'd wondered how they managed to make sure the victim was always at home in time for the explosion. So now we know—they ring up with some cock-and-bull story and make an appointment. But why make sure that Else would be there also?"

"I don't know—unless it made the story more convincing and they don't care if other people get blown up with the main target." He gripped his rifle firmly. "I will shoot someone for this. And that is something you can depend on, David."

"You need a target yourself first." I looked at him carefully. "Or have you already found one?"

102

"You sent Else on up to Igls, I suppose? I rather thought you'd do something like that—just in case there was trouble waiting for you here."

"You're not answering my question, Sven. Was it purely the call from Mendel that made you suspicious?"

"I've told you."

"All you've told me is the method they use. Did you really expect me to swallow this?"

"I've told you," he repeated stubbornly.

"You were warned, weren't you—beforehand?"

"No."

"Why is Gustav Glincker such a good friend?" I asked casually.

"I happened to save his life years ago. During the second war against Russia—when we fought with the Germans in 1942 and '43—Gustav was with the German Army. A Russian mortar shell fell close to him, and I pulled him out of the barrage. It was the shock of the mortar burst that struck him dumb. That is all."

"So," I pressed, "if Gustav heard that you were in danger, even if he was on the other side, he might well warn you, mightn't he?"

"Leave Gustav alone," Sven said fiercely.

"Why run away?" I prodded. "Why not go to the police?"

"A great deal of protection they are," he blazed. "Six months these outrages have been going on and the police still know nothing. I prefer to deal with things myself."

"Why choose this part of the world to hide in?"

He hesitated. "Because we once lived here."

"I see." I gave him a cigarette and asked the question as he bent over the flame. "Why take out insurance against death by high explosive?"

The cigarette didn't jump. He simply looked surprised.

"How do you know about that? Oh, I suppose the police found them at my bank. That's simple—I wanted to make sure there would be something for Else at a time when I had very little money. I'm cautious, as you know, and one works on one's own experience and what one hears. I shoot a lot, and a friend of mine who also shot a lot filled his rifle with a defective cartridge. When he fired, it killed him, and for some reason his policies were invalid."

"I see." I paused and watched the dog watching us, its head on one side. "Sven, what made you call off the Kardehay deal?"

The rifle barrel tilted, flashed reflected sunlight. Sven turned his head, squinted up at the crest where the dog was sitting patiently, and slapped his rifle stock. Aino disappeared, and a moment later came bounding around the foot of the bluff. He stood between us, wagging his tail.

"Have to be going soon now," commented Sven. "You have a right to know—I received another offer for the engine."

"I see."

"No, you don't see at all." He bent down and ruffled the dog's ears. "When the deal is concluded you'll be there."

"Where did the offer come from?"

"Cairo."

"You're selling to the Egyptians?"

"No. I went to Egypt, you know—there and back all inside twenty-four hours—just to see. I saw," he added grimly.

"It's more than I do."

"Let's just say that I want my engine used for peaceful purposes and that"—he squinted along the barrel—"is why I canceled the deal with Kardehay at the last moment. I really must go now."

"Where to?"

"I have a cabin up on the mountain. For the moment I don't want Else around. She knows you were coming to meet me, of course. We've met since she arrived in Innsbruck. Just make sure the wrong people don't get near her, David."

"She can have full protection from the Americans if only she'll behave herself. I'm working on this with a pal of mine from Washington."

"You'll need help. No, I'm not saying any more. You know us Finns—bloody-minded and independent as the devil."

"The devil's in this thing somewhere."

"I'd say you were right. I've dragged you a long way to explain but—" he paused and looked straight at me—"it's not necessarily out of your way."

"One dark night men will creep up on that cabin of yours and that will be that. You'd do better to come with me."

"I don't think so, David. I'm a marksman. Remember?"

"In the dark?"

"With my sniper-scope—yes. There's a new infrared sight that works pretty well. The Americans are coming to Innsbruck?"

"They'll be on the way as soon as I reach a phone."

But the Americans were on the way already. I collected Else from the Igls tram terminus, took the next tram down to Innsbruck, and called Zurich, only to learn from Rudi that Larry was on his way east. And yes, they had put into operation my long shot. A register of possible targets among German aircraft specialists had been drawn up, and the Zurich nerve center was on the line sending out warning signals nonstop. "*I* think it's a good idea," Rudi told me, "although Larry has reservations, but Germany is *my* territory." He ended up on a joking note which I didn't think very funny. "Don't forget the deadline," he said.

It was early evening when I parked Else firmly in the lounge of the Hotel Regina and went out to see Gustav. The weather had turned sour again, and just before night blotted out the mountains a heavy cloud sea smothered their slopes and sailed in over the city. As it turned out, Gustav was not at home. I tried the front door and then went around into the side alley. The back door was also locked, so I decided to come back later with Larry. But his arrival was delayed because the express was late, so after dinner with Else I went back alone.

25: CRACKED MIRROR

It was raining again, a heavy substantial rain which beat on the cone of my umbrella and then spilled over the circumference so that I walked inside a curtain of rain. No wind swept down the Stiftgasse this time, but from the entrance I saw that the lamp on the distant curve had gone out. The corner was a cavern of darkness. I paused at the entrance and looked at my watch: 10:00 P.M.

The Stiftgasse looked derelict, and I walked inside slowly, listening carefully, but all I heard was the beat of rain and the slosh of my sodden shoes. When I reached the corner I glanced back and saw the lights at the end of the alley. They glowed eerily in the rain-swept night. My flashlight beam located Number 85, and my thumb was almost touching the bellpush when I noticed the small door. It wasn't quite closed.

I switched off my flashlight and thought about it. Gustav was a man who would always lock up at night carefully. When I had left previously, I had heard him close the latch and ram home the bolt. At a superficial glance the door was shut, as though someone unfamiliar with that door had entered and pushed it behind him, thinking that it had closed. I left the umbrella in the alcove and pushed the door gently.

The large chamber was pitch-black and damply cold.

106

I shivered and watched a line of light escaping from the stable door where the two panels met. The noise of the rain interfered with my attempt to listen, so I risked closing the outer door. Faintly, in the far corner, the winding handle rattled, and I aimed the Smith & Wesson in the direction of the sound. Then total silence except for the sharp patter of rain. I wondered what Gustav was doing and whether he had gone up into the bedroom which I felt sure led off the minstrel's gallery. In that case, why leave the downstairs light on? I beamed my light quickly over the coffins, and then switched it off, using the line of light from the door to lead me toward it.

Reaching the door, I listened again, my ear pressed against the upper panel. A splinter penetrated my skin but the panel held firm against my tentative pressure. Gustav must have gone upstairs. He had dropped the bar that locked the door. Behind me something scurried in the darkness. I aimed the light and switched it on. Two tiny eyes gazed into the beam and then vanished in a flurry. A rat. Reaching down with my left hand I pressed gently against the lower panel, and it moved under my touch. For another long minute I listened carefully. No sound at all. Holding the revolver in my hand I got down on my knees and pushed the lower panel open slowly.

The panel was half-open, and now I could see the reflected glow of the oil lamps, the shadows quite still because of the absence of wind. The panel opened wider, and I watched for Gustav's legs standing by one of the benches, thinking that he might be staying up late to set type. I had an idea that he was a man who would work irregular hours. Then the benches came into view, and there was no sign of life. Quietly, I crawled forward under the panel, instinctively looking up at the minstrel's gallery. Empty.

I stood up. The bar had been carelessly dropped, so that it held the upper panel fast but had not been engaged in the lower slot which locked the bottom panel. I couldn't see Gustav making a mistake like that.

I began to walk around the room toward the free-standing cupboard which masked an area in front of the wall, the most likely point of ambush. When I peered around the end the space between cupboard and wall was deserted, but the canvas sheet over the meat safe had been caught up inside the closed door. Also I could hear a faint hum. The refrigerating mechanism was working.

Creeping back around the cupboard I looked up at the gallery again. There was no one there. I returned to the safe, pulled aside the canvas, and opened it. I had found Gustav. He was coiled up in a foetal position and faced me. A thin layer of ice had formed over the lenses of his pebble glasses. As I lifted his chin the body flopped flexibly. I couldn't detect a pulse beat, and I didn't check for heartbeats—his shirt front was ripped and smeared with blood. He had been stabbed several times, and from the location of the wounds any one of the stabs would have killed him. When there is plenty of time professionals like to be sure. From the smears along the edges of Gustav's jacket I guessed that the assassin had wiped his knife clean on his victim's clothes.

After closing the meat-safe door, I wiped the handle and replaced the canvas. Then I went over and checked the latch of the back door. It was bolted firmly. Still watching the staircase I worked it out. The murderer hadn't left by the back door, which should have been the natural exit. But he could have left by the front door after dropping the bar so that it closed the upper panel and left open the lower door for him to leave by. He might have done that to delay discovery of the body in case someone called. But why switch on the refrigerator plant? There was one other possibility—that the murderer was still upstairs. I glanced at the center table, sensed movement, stepped back. The hurtling knife scraped my right knuckles, and I let the revolver fall. It spun

108

across the stone floor and disappeared in a space below the benches. I could be fairly sure of finding it, given a few quiet minutes to search.

The man on the gallery was tall and thin, dressed in a dark overcoat, dark slouch hat, his face long, thin, pinched, jaw deep, pointed. He moved to the top of the staircase, another knife in his right hand. I watched the knife hand intently, waiting for the flickering movement that would give me a half-second warning of his next throw, but instead he came down the stairs at me. His shoes were rubber-soled, another professional sign, and the steps creaked as he came down fast, mouth tight, hand extended in front of him, knife pointing slightly upward. As he reached the bottom step I lifted a form of type off the table and threw it straight at his head. The chase bars broke into separate components and loose type rained in his face. Stumbling backward, he half sat on the stairs, the knife point aimed upward for my forward move. I stepped backward and put the table between us. Getting up from the steps, he catfooted slowly around the table and suddenly lunged the knife across it, but I jumped sideways, still close to the table, slashing my stiffened hand across his stooped body. The blow was aimed for his neck, but instead it struck the side of his face. I nearly took the head off his shoulders, and the vibration up my arm shook like a dental drill. Groggily, he waggled his head, hand still gripping the knife, and then he came around the table fast. Throwing a heavy composing stick in his face I stunned him for a second and kicked him in the kneecap. He bent forward, but still held on to the knife, held it in front of his body, crouched, and his eyes stared upward, waiting for a one-second chance to deliver the thrust. Running around the table I darted up the staircase, and as I reached the top he began stumbling up behind me, hauling up his body by the banister rail, the knife still gripped in his other hand. I ran along the gallery as though desperate to find cover and then suddenly ran back again. He was several steps from the top when I kicked, and the kick landed in his chest. He lost balance and began to fall over backward, his left hand clawing frantically at the rail. Running down two steps I aimed another savage kick, which struck him hard in the stomach. Now I kept up the momentum of my kick, pushing, thrusting, and then the banister rail gave way. He went over sideways, taking the rail with him. There was a rending groan of breaking wood. As he landed between the free-standing cupboard and the wall he rolled to take the smash of the fall, and his back hit the cupboard. The top swayed gently and then resumed its normal upright position. I ran down the staircase, slipped on the composing stick lying on the floor, and grabbed the table for support. I straightened up, started to dash toward the cupboard, and saw the shadow —the shadow of a man standing half-erect, hand extended, waiting.

The cupboard was tall and narrow, its pigeonholes crammed with old type. There was probably half a ton of lead inside those pigeonholes, half a ton perched upright and which had swayed when his body hit the base. Holding my hands apart, palms open away from me, I ran forward and hit the cupboard amidships. It swayed under my onslaught, and for a moment I thought it would stay erect, so I continued the pressure. Then it fell away from me, crashing downward, its top just missing the meat safe. It fell like a bomb, and I heard him scream. Once. Then the cupboard lay on its back and from one side a hand extended. The fingers parted, and the knife lay lifeless on the stone.

Two minutes of feeling and fumbling under the bench found the Smith & Wesson, and when I withdrew my hand it was filthy with the dirt of ages. Running up the staircase again, I went along the gallery and opened a heavy wooden door. It opened noiselessly on its well-oiled hinges, and I looked into Gustav's bedroom, which was small, oblong, and had a tiny window overlooking the side alley. I looked out of the window and saw nothing, hearing the rain flailing down on the cobbles. The single bed was a wreck of clothes thrown on the floor, and the mattress had been ripped open. The edges of one torn fissure were smeared red. All the drawers from a small chest had been taken out and turned upside down, the contents thrown in a shambles across the floor. I wondered whether the thin man had found what he had searched for, knowing that if he had put it in his pocket I would never be able to lift that cupboard off him. My watch registered 10:15 P.M. and I wanted to leave the place quickly. The row could have disturbed people next door, although from the thickness of the stone walls I didn't think that was likely.

Standing in the gallery again I looked down on the carnage, remembering I hadn't checked Gustav's pockets. In any case, the thin man would already have attended to that. Then as I gazed around the room below I thought of something. I went down the staircase.

The cracked triangle of mirror was still in the drawer I had seen Gustav put it back into. Tilting it at an angle I held it over the isolated line of Gothic type that occupied a place all by itself in the center of the table. The heavy Gothic word stared back at me, staggered in the middle by the crack in the mirror. BRENNERO.

26: WILDERNESS

It was winter. The passage of months seemed telescoped into hours as the Trans-Alpine Express approached the high Brenner.

As the express began to lose speed I gazed out at the snowbound wilderness. Thick snowflakes drifted beyond the

111

window, floating down through the Alpine air and changing direction chaotically before they reached the ground to add fresh layers to the white carpet already hiding the earth. Across deserted mountain slopes black fir trees stood silent and still like nature's sentries. I rubbed a large hole in the misted glass, and Larry peered through it.

"Not very encouraging," he remarked.

Else clapped her hands. "I think it's gorgeous—ever since I was a little girl I've loved the snow."

"You're still a little girl," I growled.

"I've apologized to Larry about leaving Jeff Tarleton," she protested, "and he's accepted my apology."

"Jeff," said Larry drily, "will be coming up here himself soon. I'm sure he'll be pleased to see you."

Else beamed. "And *I* shall be pleased to see him. He's tremendous fun."

Larry frowned. "It beats me, Else, how you could get clean away from him, cross a border on your own passport, and come all the way to Innsbruck to contact your uncle."

"It's the little-girl look," I told him. "She just looks far too young and innocent to get up to some of the things she plays at. Larry, why were you on your way to Innsbruck when I phoned?"

"As we dug deeper and deeper on Kardehay some funny things started turning up. This place he calls the Torre—did you know that it's situated slap-bang on the Austro-Italian border? From the map the frontier seemed to run right down the middle of that damned place. Up there you can breakfast in Italy and lunch in Austria just by switching rooms. And Torre—that's an odd name."

"It means 'tower.' "

"That makes good sense. I checked on its history. It used to be a great prison for long-term criminals, and then the state abandoned it as being too cruel a place. I gather it's built like a fortress—but one thing that interested me was

112

that he protects it like a fortress. The reports weren't too clear, but apparently he has his own private army to keep out intruders. As if there'd be any—Brennero is the nearest main-line stop, but the Torre is miles away high up in the big Alps."

"Anything more?"

"There's this character Josip Riz. During the war he was a guerrilla. Came the so-called peace and he's in Italy, up to his neck in the black market, for which he duly serves a prison term. Years later he pops up again—inside the States as a strong-arm man for the Cosa Nostra. We think he jumped the Mexican border to get in. Then there's a blank, and just before Kardehay leaves New York to come to Europe, a Joseph Rich appears on the payroll of Kardehay Enterprises. It's only when he's gone that we find Mr. Rich is really Josip Riz. So why should a respectable millionaire like Kardehay have such a man in his employ?"

"Perhaps his experience recommended him."

Beyond the window a snow-covered bank loomed close to the line. I rubbed a fresh hole in the glass and saw a deep narrow gulch. No water ran down, but from its mouth protruded a tongue of ice. Else said she was going to have a wash and left us alone. When she had gone Larry leaned across the compartment.

"This business of Sven—I don't understand it. Why go off in the wilds like that?"

"He's a Finn. They fight private wars and jealously guard their privacy."

"And he wouldn't tell you any more about that trip to Egypt?"

"No. He's obstinate. The Finns are like that. They fought Russia all on their own in 1939, remember."

"We compiled your lunatic register, David. Now that we know the method of approach it may not be so lunatic. I spoke to Rudi before we left Innsbruck, and he's warning all

113

the potential victims of how it's done—that business about someone phoning for an appointment to be kept at the man's house, I mean."

"We can only hope—there's not much time left, Larry."

"Don't keep reminding me. You think we'll get Else through Italian Passport Control? I didn't really like bringing her up here."

"No alternative really. Either you or I must keep an eye on her, and your boys hadn't reached Innsbruck when we left."

"They're coming straight on to Brennero, anyway. You really think Gustav Glincker was connected with the bomb outrages?" he asked with a curious expression on his face.

"It makes sense. Someone warned Sven of what was coming, and the only person who could do that was someone linked with the organization behind all this. Gustav fills the bill because he owed Sven his life—and Gustav was murdered last night."

"It's a good thing we eventually decided not to contact the Austrian police. You had a point that they might hold you as a witness for God knows how long but"—he smiled faintly—"that isn't the main point."

"What is?"

The outskirts of Brennero were moving past outside now, old buildings huddled in a narrow valley between the Alpine giants, roofs thick with snow. Larry handed me a copy of the *Neue Innsbrucker* he had been reading, pointing with his thumb.

"You won't find a word in there about Gustav Glincker, but you may still find it interesting."

I read the report quickly as Else came back into the compartment and put on her sable.

The murdered body of Erich Egger, undertaker, who lived at Stiftgasse 83, was found late yesterday evening by his assistant, Paul Herzog. A macabre aspect of the murder is that Egger was lying in one of his own coffins. . . .

27: TORRE

"We'll reconnoiter this Torre place by car—it's the only way we can get there," said Larry. "And by the way, I think we were followed here."

We sat alone in the lounge bar of the hotel at Brennero. Larry was crouched forward over a crackling log fire as though he couldn't get close enough to it, while Else was upstairs changing.

"Followed?" I queried.

"Chap in a long mildew-green coat. He was in a car near the Hotel Regina when we left. I next spotted him on the platform at the Hauptbahnhof. Now he's just been through the lobby."

The room we sat in had old beams in the ceiling, dark paneled walls, heavy wooden tables, their surfaces highly polished, armchairs upholstered in dark-brown leather, brass-studded. In the fire, flames crawled over a huge centerpiece log, and outside the snow fell like a blizzard. There was a distinct feeling of Christmas just around the corner. Through the glass-windowed doors leading to the lobby I saw Else come out of the lift. She was wearing a dark-blue skirt and a Tyrolean sweater of many colors. Then my heart skipped a beat.

"What's wrong?" asked Larry.

A tall man in an astrakhan coat and a Russian-style fur hat had just come in from the street. He took off the hat and shook snow away, looking every inch a Hungarian. Behind him stood another man, a man dressed in a windbreaker and fur-banded forage cap. They took no notice of Else as she came through the swing doors.

"It looks as though we came to the right place after all," I said grimly. "Standing in the lobby is our friend Nikki Kar-

115

dehay. He's got Josip Riz with him. I hope to God they don't know Else."

"Does Kardehay know you?" I asked Else urgently.

"No, luckily. I saw him out there—he's like his pictures."

"We'll have to keep you out of the way. If he comes in here, you're Sonia Klinger. If he starts talking to you, for Pete's sake watch it—he's as sharp as a knife."

"I can be sharp, too."

Larry scowled and fingered his mustache. "Ten gets you one he's with us inside ten minutes. I'm getting a feeling about our Hungarian-American friend."

"I don't bet on certainties," I said.

Five minutes later Kardehay came into the lounge alone. He walked up to the bar and ordered a drink without appearing to notice me. As always, he was faultlessly dressed. He wore a midnight-blue two-piece suit. His cream shirt intensified the richness of the blue, and an inch of cream cuff projected beyond the sleeves. He was sporting a sun-gold tie, and as he waited he lit a long cigar. For no reason I could imagine he bought himself two drinks. The barman bowed over the tip, and then Nikki came over to us, holding a drink in each hand.

"Welcome to Brennero, David! If I'd known you were coming, we'd have ordered sunshine!" His brown eyes flickered mischievously over Else. "But perhaps you've brought your own! Your usual double whisky will be acceptable, I trust." He laid the glass carefully in front of me and sat down, addressing Larry. "You must excuse the informality of my approach, but here we are on the Brenner and the arrival of fresh society is a rare occasion. Now, what can I get you? We will drink to the occasion!"

The barman waiting at his shoulder took the orders and I made the introductions. Sonia Klinger. Larry Biggs, correspondent of the Washington *Express*.

"Ah, Mr. Biggs," said Nikki sardonically, "so that's

116

where we met. I have a photographic memory for faces and I remember you well. It was three years ago in the ballroom of the Hotel Plaza, New York. Prince Rupescu was giving one of his absurd parties—he's an old rascal, of course, but he does know how to give a party."

"I'm afraid I don't remember," said Larry quietly.

"But I remember you distinctly. Washington *Express,* you said? That's funny—have you always been with them?"

"For years and years and years—don't remind me."

"Now it's all coming back to me." Nikki pressed slim fingers over his high forehead, then he snapped them. "Jo Jo Johnson told me you had something to do with the State Department. Excuse me, I'm neglecting the charming Miss Klinger." He took the brandy glass from the waiter's tray himself and served it to Else, his thick eyebrows shooting up apologetically. "Accept this as a peace token. Now, a toast. To a wonderful day at the Torre—for all of us!"

He drank while I stopped the glass at my lips. His eyebrows asked me why.

"What are you talking about, Nikki?" I inquired.

"You are staying at the hotel." He spread his hands wide. "I asked the receptionist. So you are all invited there for lunch, and afterward I shall take you on a personally conducted tour of the Torre. I refuse to take no for an answer. That's settled? Good. It will be a unique experience. You are Austrian, Miss Klinger? Viennese, perhaps?"

I held my breath. Else spoke good German, but the accent of the Viennese is peculiar and unique. I thought Nikki would know about things like that. Else gushed.

"Yes, but I'm from Feldkirch—that's in the Vorarlberg. My father was Austrian but my mother was Swiss-German. I'm a Teutonic cocktail!"

That's muddled it nicely, I thought. Heaven knew what sort of a German accent such a union would produce. I didn't think Nikki knew either. He said he liked Feldkirch, and I stopped breathing again until I realized from her conversation that Else had brightly chosen a town she knew well.

A little later Nikki explained to Larry that now he remembered Jo Jo Johnson had said that he was the State Department's nonfavorite journalist because of the articles he wrote on their foreign policy. Larry carefully didn't look relieved, and we endured another half hour of this trip-wire talk before Nikki looked at his watch, said it was time to go, and perhaps we would like to get ready while he made a phone call.

Upstairs I arranged with Else that she should have a diplomatic stomach upset which prevented her coming. At the last moment Jeff Tarleton arrived and said the other men who had come with him had scattered to different hotels. I handed him over to Else, feeling sure that this time she'd be lucky to get into the bathroom without Tarleton at her side.

Downstairs Nikki waited for us in the lobby. Accepting my reason for Else's absence with expressions of concern, he led the way out of the hotel. It was snowing heavily. The only person in sight was a porter who leaned out of an upper window to push snow off the telephone wires with a brush. It fell with soft plops, and the foehn began to blow strongly as we entered the waiting Mercedes. Nikki took the wheel, and I sat beside him; Larry occupied the back seat. There was no sign of Josip, and I wondered whether he ever acted as chauffeur.

The Mercedes traveled up the mountain road in chains, but other vehicles had followed the same route recently, and Nikki drove the car wheels inside well-defined ruts. I watched the snow fall beyond the fan-shaped area kept clear by the windshield wipers. It was building up to a blizzard, and Nikki leaned forward to peer beyond his own fan-shaped window.

"I'm following the ruts so we shan't go over the precipice," he explained genially.

"Happy landings," muttered Larry from the back.

"Can't see more than a few yards," went on Nikki. "I hear you can only die once. Not having had the experience, I can't vouch for it."

We were moving higher all the time through a landscape of the utmost desolation. At times the snow slackened, and a long way off I could see down into what I took to be the Brenner Pass area. Ahead of us was a dreamlike suggestion of mountain, an immense white slope which went up forever. Nikki pointed.

"The Torre is behind there."

"Why choose such a place to live?" asked Larry.

"Oh, I'm only here part of the time. I come here to think and plan—away from the distractions of the world."

"I heard it was some sort of a headquarters," Larry remarked.

"I use it partly as that, too. It's a good strategic position—midway between northern and southern Europe. Dear, dear"—he leaned well forward—"it is getting bad, and this is rather a dangerous road. Not nervous, David?"

"Just hungry."

"Soon be there! You were asking me about the Torre, Mr. Biggs. I use it as a testing station as well. Plenty of open space for that sort of thing. At the moment we're working on a new type of lifeline for ships in distress at sea. It's a rocket-powered lifeline, and we waste too much money firing the things across the slopes. Haven't hit anybody yet. Not so far as I know," he added. "If we did, I doubt if they'd survive to report our little misdemeanor. Ah, this is more promising."

The guide ruts made by other vehicles had turned off to the right, and ahead of us the road was marked by a wire fence. It was only snowing lightly now, and I was surprised

119

to see that the road surface had been recently cleared. Huge piles of snow banked up one side of the road. I asked Nikki about the clearance.

"A snowplow from the Torre has cleared the way for us. I phoned to let them know we were coming."

"That road off to the right," said Larry, "where does it lead to?"

"It's the supply road up to the Torre for heavy vehicles. In fact, it is the only road that actually goes up to the place."

"Where are we going then?" I asked.

"This also leads to the Torre, but there is a tremendous abyss between where this road ends and the Torre itself. I have surmounted that obstacle with an interesting feat of engineering. You'll see! The abyss itself is so deep that the locals say it is the home of the devil. I don't think they're referring to me."

28: WATCHER

The monorail car appeared through the curtain of snow and came toward us at incredible speed. Standing by the parked Mercedes we watched it come, a flash of red in the white world, seeming to defy all the laws of gravity as it flew forward suspended *below* the overhead railway supported on trestle towers.

"It seemed the best way over the abyss," Nikki remarked, "and the other road's such a long way around."

We climbed the steps inside the concrete terminus tower and stepped out onto a platform where the monorail car waited for us. The interior of the car was rather like a funicular coach, and the separate compartments were linked by a corridor. Nikki took us along to the front compartment, where we joined the driver, who sat on a long leather seat behind his desk-top control panel. A huge bay window occupied the nose of the vehicle, and large wipers were keeping the glass free of snow. At a nod from Nikki he closed the automatic doors and we moved forward into space.

It was a sensation rather like flying, but always at the same level. I stood up to see better, holding a handrail, and below us the ground whizzed away. Snowflakes splashed on the nose window and were immediately brushed off by the wipers. I strained my eyes to catch my first sight of the Torre, and then we were over the abyss. The driver pressed a switch. We slowed and then stopped, hovering over the chasm. Nikki said he always found the view fascinating. The gorge was about fifty feet wide and bottomless. Under the car snow fell into the drop, was caught in a powerful air stream, and boiled and churned just beneath the brink. Ahead of us rose the Torre.

The ancient prison was built of gray stone and climbed the almost vertical mountain slope in a series of three giant steps, each step a massive rampart with square guard towers at intervals. It looked completely uninhabited and reminded me of an abandoned Greek monastery. Windows had been cut out of the bleak stone walls, and at the lowest level they were covered with grilles. I couldn't imagine the reason for the precaution, since below these windows the ground fell sheer into the abyss. And above the highest rampart the mountain went on up toward an unseen summit lost in the snow.

"Alcatraz was a rest home compared to this place," said Larry.

"I thought you'd like it."

Nikki spoke to the driver, and the car moved forward, spun around a wide curve at the base of the lowest rampart, reduced speed, and passed through an archway in the stone wall.

* * *

"Imagine the monstrous crimes which haunt these old walls, Mr. Biggs. Blackmailers, murderers, and rapists have trodden the steps you are now walking down."

We had finished lunch and now were descending an iron staircase into the second level of the Torre. Above our heads an open catwalk ran along the full length of the vast hall, and behind the catwalk were rows of ancient cells. More cells lined the floor below on all sides. Nikki led the way, and I followed behind Larry. As we went down, there was no sound except for the steady tread of our feet on the metal steps, which echoed weirdly, one ghost step behind our own. All the cell doors behind the catwalk stood open, as though waiting for occupants.

The atmosphere was chilly and damp, the hall starkly lit by green neon strips hung high up from the ceiling, so that in the floor area we approached the illumination had faded to a greenish glow. Under my palm the iron handrail was worn smooth, the work of a thousand unknown lost hands which had helped their owners up and down the grisly stairway.

"The locals won't come within miles of this place," Nikki went on cheerfully. "They think the ghosts of long-dead criminals prowl the mountain slopes at night."

"You can keep it—all of it," said Larry tersely.

"You get used to it. You even get used to working down here."

We reached the ground floor, and I saw that the cells were larger. During their active life they had probably housed three or four men each. As we walked along the hall Nikki pointed out that several of the cells had been converted into offices. Instead of iron grilles there were varnished wood doors with porthole windows. He took us inside one office, and a blast of warmth met us. Two men dressed in white coats and wearing green eyeshades worked at drawing boards. They stood up as we came in, but Nikki told them to continue, and they sat down again after a

122

glance in our direction. No introductions were made, and the men seemed completely absorbed in their problems. The walls were lined with painted board to conceal the stone, and in one corner a radiator chugged quietly, as though struggling with an air lock.

"What are they working on?" I asked.

"This lifeline business. We're having trouble firing it far enough. I'm determined it shall be a revolutionary advance. We'd better get along now —there's a great deal to see, and you'll want to be back before dark."

We walked past a dozen converted offices, and when I glanced through the porthole windows I saw more men at work as though they sat in the middle of a modern city. At the end of the hall Nikki opened a heavy iron door, and we went into another new cell block. Here the building seemed more derelict, and the lights were fewer. During the next half hour we were shown a small generating station, a water-purifying plant, and the test range where the lifeline system was put through its paces. All the time Nikki rattled off a commentary.

"Make some of our own power . . . also feed in off the main grid . . . cost me a fortune to get a power line up here. Yes, we supply our own water—far too far away from the public authorities. . . . This should interest you. They're actually firing at the moment."

From inside a glass booth in the northern wall of the Torre we looked down over the mountain slope. It had stopped snowing now, and below us hooded men in winter clothing were pushing a small platform trolley along a short railway which ended in the middle of nowhere.

"We keep the track free of snow by underground heaters," Nikki explained, and lit a cigar after offering his case.

Mounted on the trolley was a small mechanism that vaguely resembled a cannon. The trolley stopped, and the hooded figures fussed around it.

123

"They're dropping the telescopic legs now—you need ground support before you fire the thing."

In the next room a movie camera projected through the window, and the operator stood waiting, his gaze fixed on the men in the snow. In the distance I could see a squat building like a blockhouse and I asked Nikki what purpose it served.

"Control point. They have another camera inside, and we plot the trajectory. Ah, here we go. Any moment now."

The figures moved away from the platform, leaving one man behind the cannon-like instrument. We waited for a moment and then heard a coughing thump. A projectile streaked from the mouth of the cannon, trailing the lifeline behind it, soared through the air, reached its apex, and then curved downward, landing with a flurry of snow.

"We'll get it," said Nikki briskly. "God knows when, but we'll get it."

"How big a staff have you up here?" I inquired.

"Thirty, including domestic staff."

"It's a wonder they don't all go crazy," commented Larry. "I'd say there was a certain shortage of recreation in these parts."

"You think so? Not at all. The only thing we lack is television—the mountains get in the way of that. We've just got time. I'll show you."

I pressed my face close against the window and looked sideways. Just beyond the end wall of the Torre the mountain curved away from the abyss and alongside it a vast new building stretched away out of sight. Windowless, it was constructed of concrete, its walls high, the roof shallow.

"What's inside there?" I asked.

"Living quarters for the staff, including their own cinema. They don't mind working inside the Torre but they prefer to live outside its walls."

We walked back a different way, through endless stone-flagged corridors lit at intervals by vertical neon strips. When Nikki opened a modern door with a porthole window we walked into a different world.

"Recreation!" said Nikki ironically.

The indoor swimming pool was green-tiled, surrounded by a terrace of black marble. Overhead floodlights shone down on the greenish water, and at the far end there stood a high diving board. A girl reached the topmost platform, waved briefly, held out her arms, paused, dived. Arrow-like, she pierced the water and vanished. The tiny splash settled, and the pool resumed its normal glasslike sheen. Under its surface I saw her swimming toward us. Nikki chuckled.

"She's new here, and I'm sure she'll be expensive—but the boss needs recreation, too. You might be able to do me a small favor."

"Name it," said Larry. "That lunch we had entitles you to a big favor."

"She only came here yesterday and all she has is an overnight bag." He grinned sardonically. "I imagine she wanted to look over the ground first. Her things are still at a hotel in Brennero, and she wants to go and collect them. Do you mind if she travels back in the same car?"

The blurred form was close now, hands aimed upward as she prepared to break surface.

"Be a pleasure," said Larry.

The girl emerged.

"A pleasure," I repeated.

She reached the side and slowly climbed a metal ladder a few feet from where I stood. Pausing at the top, she held on with one hand and removed her bathing cap, shaking jet-black hair over her shoulders. She wore a gold-colored bikini which appeared to be several sizes too small. From above the brassière strip the upper halves of full rounded breasts gleamed wetly and nakedly, held in close juxtaposition. A drop of water ran down her long neck, traveled over her chest and disappeared. As the water tickled she shook the upper half of her body and then, taking her time, reached fingers under the bottom of her pants to adjust them. I heard the elasticized material return to her body.

Nikki introduced Romy Silber, and she nodded to us without any sign of recognition, took a towel off the ladder, dried her hand, and laid it on Nikki's sleeve.

"The pool's marvelous—can I come here any time I like?"

"Of course."

"You'll keep the heating turned on? I never, never bathe in less than seventy degrees."

"You see what I said!" Nikki cocked his head at me. "Expensive!"

"And you will remember to get that new Italian film sent up from Milan?"

"I've ordered it already!"

"Then all I've got to do is to go back to Brennero to collect my things."

She spoke as though she were alone with Nikki, and his eyes watched her with amusement. Now she stood with her back to me, and I deliberately studied the line of her pants where they crossed the lower portion of her rear. As though she sensed my gaze, her hands came around her sides and she hitched up the pants. Nikki studied me cynically over her left shoulder. She turned around.

"I'm sorry, Mr. Martini. It's rude to stand with my back to you."

"Worse things have happened to me."

She looked at me arrogantly and said she'd better go and get dressed, but Nikki laid a hand on her arm.

"These gentlemen have very kindly agreed that you can share the car taking them back to Brennero."

"I see. I will be able to get back here tonight?" she inquired anxiously.

126

"If the snow holds off, yes. Otherwise the car will bring you up in the morning. It wouldn't be nice if you went over the precipice just after we'd met, would it?"

"Don't say things like that—I'm superstitious. Are they leaving soon?" She indicated us with a flick of hair.

"Within the hour. The sooner the better."

"I'll go and get dressed."

She walked off along the black marble, towel slung over her shoulder, feet padding softly, knowing we were watching her, her body somehow saying to hell with Nikki's damn friends. Larry watched her leg movement and fingered his mustache. I lit a quick cigarette and spoke quietly.

"I could recreate with her myself."

"I told you," beamed Nikki, "we have everything on the Brenner!"

We went back to his quarters on the highest level of the Torre, and this time there was no iron staircase to climb. Instead, we ascended inside a small lift.

"Cost a fortune to install this," Nikki remarked. "It goes up between two walls and we were just able to squeeze it in."

His main living room was a large chamber that faced the abyss. It was luxuriously furnished; the blue carpet was wall to wall, the armchairs modern Scandinavian, upholstered in black leather, and one corner was occupied by a chromium bar. While we waited he served drinks. The most alarming feature of the room was a huge plate-glass window which took up most of the front wall, and, since the glass reached to floor level, standing close to it gave the feeling that it would be quite easy to fall over the brink.

"So now you've seen my mountain retreat," said Nikki, and handed us the drinks.

"Most impressive," remarked Larry. "There was something I wanted to ask you. . . ."

While they chatted I wandered over to a smaller side window in the southern wall. Here the view was awe-inspiring

—the snowbound slopes rolled away in a series of drops toward unseen Brennero. Late-afternoon mist floated over the distant valley like steam from a cauldron. I picked up a pair of field glasses and focused them on a distant ridge where I felt sure I had seen movement. The blurred lenses resolved, and the ridge jumped at me. At the summit a man stood quite still, and I had the impression he was watching the Torre. He was too far away for me to distinguish his features, but a matchstick shape bisected his silhouette. I felt sure the shape was a rifle.

29: IRON DEVIL

We held a council of war in my hotel bedroom, and I fired my opening shot at Romy.

"We couldn't talk in the car with that driver there, but now I want to know—what the hell's going on and what were you doing up at the Torre?"

"Do you think Nikki will be disappointed?" she fenced. "I'm sure I dodged the driver. I came out the back way from that other hotel, but someone will have to collect my bag. Don't worry, I paid the bill—but what am I going to sleep in?"

"You'll be up all night answering questions, don't you worry." I ignored Larry's attempt to intervene. "All right, how did you get there?"

Larry intervened. "It was Rudi's idea. I didn't like it, but she belongs to his outfit, so . . . After you'd seen Josip Riz in that film on Saturday morning Rudi went into action. He knows that Kardehay likes the girls—he's been married twice and they both left him; all that money, too. Well, Rudi put Romy on a plane for Milan and told her to get next to Kardehay. She checked in at his hotel and . . ."

Romy interrupted drily. "I was an instantaneous hit with

our friend. Don't think it's gone to my head—he was out *looking* for a girl, a new girl. I sensed that the moment he ordered me a drink. In no time at all he was inviting me up to what he called his weekend place. Christ!" She closed her eyes and shuddered. "Heaven preserve me. I was only there one night, but I thought I was going to have fun keeping the bed to myself. But he only tried it once. I was holding him at the door when one of his minions came and told him there was a long-distance call, so I preserved my reputation."

"Do you know where the call was from?" I asked.

"Cairo."

"See anything funny while you were there?"

"If there is anything funny, it's happening in that huge building on the northern side. The concrete one with no windows. They work through the night in there."

"How do you know?"

"Kardehay has his sleeping quarters on that side, and I had a room farther along the corridor. It overlooks the very end of the building, and light escapes from the ventilator things on top. I nearly froze to death leaning out that window to see more of the roof. I think they work three shifts. I heard noises at midnight, and when I looked out, the door into the building was open. One lot was filing out while another lot went in."

"How many—any idea?"

"Yes, I concentrated on the new arrivals. I counted about eighty men going in."

"And he said he had a staff of thirty," I said.

"That doesn't include the lot coming off duty," Romy pointed out. "Or the guards. I had the feeling there's a small army of them. I can't be sure of that," she said carefully. "They're armed, too."

"In what way?"

"The ones inside have automatics in small leather holsters. The mountain patrol carries rifles."

"Mountain patrol?"

"Yes. I took a chance there. Kardehay seemed pretty busy with phone calls most of the evening, so I went down the staircase to the next floor. I had to dodge into a lavatory when I heard someone coming. After they'd gone I stood on the seat, and from the little window I could see down into a yard. It was full of men wearing hoods and snow goggles. They were putting on skis, and I saw them go through a gate and ski out over the mountain."

"Anything else?"

"Give me time. Give me a cigarette," she added. She took off her jacket. Underneath she wore a tight-fitting, polo-necked sweater. As she leaned close to reach the match flame, the tip of her breast pressed into my arm. Larry was over by the window, peering through the curtain into the street. She nuzzled me, sucked in a deep breath of smoke, and looked up as Larry came back. "God, it's a relief to be down here with you two. I was never so happy in my life as when I saw you from the top of that high board."

"How were you going to get out?" asked Larry.

"When we got to Brennero I'd insisted that I leave my bag at the other hotel. He was rather amused, but it gave me an excuse for coming back down here. At least, I hoped it did."

"Any sign of what they're making up there?" I asked. "That is, apart from lifelines."

Romy looked puzzled, and I explained to her the demonstration Nikki had given us of the lifeline apparatus. Since her bedroom window had been at that end of the Torre perhaps she'd seen them firing their cannon?

"No, I didn't. I didn't even see that little railway they push the trolley out on."

"I thought so," I said. "He just showed us that to give us the impression he's running an experimental establishment up there."

Larry snorted. "Just as he invited us up to show that

130

there's nothing funny going on. But those guards are there to protect something. I'm rapidly coming to the conclusion, David, that you've hit a bull. I only hope it's our bull."

"Talking about bulls," remarked Romy, "I'd better keep indoors here or Kardehay will know I'm still around."

"You're going out of the danger zone," Larry rapped. "I'll get one of my boys to take you down to Milan on the night train. In the morning he'll take you on to Zurich by plane."

"And," I added, "he can take Else with him as well."

"Else?" queried Romy.

"We'll tell you about her later. Larry, can you get some-one to pick up Romy's bag from the other place?"

"We'll fix that just before the train arrives."

Romy kicked off her shoes, slipped her feet underneath her, plumped up pillows, and leaned back.

"Send this other girl out by all means," she urged, "but I'm staying." She looked at me with mock arrogance. "I have been some help already, I take it?"

"You've been a load of help—in fact, you've done your stint, so we're packing you off to a rear area."

"*My* rear area is quite comfortable where it is, thank you very much. You never know—" she waited while Larry went over to look out the window again "I may come in useful one way or the other." She stared directly at me, and the tip of her cigarette glowed redly.

"It's no good," I told her. "We're putting you on the night train. With an escort."

"You'll have to phone Rudi first," she replied coolly.

So we phoned Rudi. And Romy stayed.

"I call it the iron devil," said the old man. "It goes straight up into the sky, hovers a bit, and then flies off. It makes the devil of a row."

I sat with Larry in the crowded lounge bar in front of the

131

log fire. It was eight o'clock at night. Upstairs in her room, Romy was reading a magazine. Else and her escort were aboard the train on their way to Milan. The old man was named Pietro. He sat in the next armchair and had already cadged half a liter of beer off me.

"This bird," I said, "if it makes so much noise, why don't they hear it down here in Brennero?"

"The mountain gets in the way—the mountain where the Torre is. And then the wind blows the noise north into Austria."

He made wind-blowing motions with his hand and then took the fresh tankard I had ordered off the waiter's tray. Raising it in solemn salute he drained half the contents while I paid. Larry kept his voice low, but he deliberately spoke in Italian so Pietro could hear.

"He tells stories so you'll buy him free beer."

"I like stories . . ." I began, but Pietro shook his head.

"I saw it happen many times."

"During the day?"

"No, always at night. Up on the mountain near the Torre."

Larry snorted with disgust, and I wondered whether he had a point. Under shaggy brows Pietro's eyes were bleary, and as he put the tankard down he nearly missed the edge of the table. His long green overcoat was folded over the back of his chair, and behind him Italians gossiped and joked. The room was a babble of voices. Under the light of a copper lantern the barman sweated in his fever to keep up with the orders.

"The Torre is miles away," I reminded Pietro. "Do you live near it?"

"No one lives up there except the Hungarian. My cabin is on the far side of the valley. I can see the Torre through my telescope. I don't sleep, so often I sit up and watch the stars."

He drained his tankard and put it down where I could see that it was empty. I pretended not to notice it, but I did notice that a small fat man with blond hair who sat behind Pietro had leaned toward us. I wondered whether he was listening to our conversation.

"Why iron?" I asked.

Pietro took out a pipe and concentrated on filling the bowl, his eyes wandering briefly over the tankard. Calling the waiter, I ordered another half-liter. Larry whispered in my ear.

"Let's go upstairs before the old soak ruins you."

Pietro stopped his pipe-filling operation and asked me what I had said.

"Why did you call it an *iron* devil?"

"The moonlight shines off it—it looks like iron."

"Does it make the noise when it's coming up or when it hovers?"

"All the time."

The waiter came back with another half-liter, and I held out my hand quickly. I kept a firm grasp on the beer as I asked my next question.

"How long does it stay hovering?"

"Half a minute." He thought about it. "No longer." He frowned, his eyes watching the full tankard, so I pushed it across the table. The blond-haired fat man stood up and made his way through the crowd toward the exit.

"What happens when it first appears—tell me again."

"It comes up out of the ground, then it stops in mid-air, and after a while it flies away behind the peak. It makes the devil of a noise." He drank deeply and then tittered. "The mountain is haunted, you know."

"Really?"

"There are lights on it—lights that move across it in the dark. I once counted fifteen lights. They are the spirits of criminals who died inside the Torre."

133

"I see."

I finished my whisky, and Larry chuckled. Old Pietro had acute hearing in spite of the din. He glared at Larry. Then another man came across to Pietro and said something I didn't catch. Pietro smiled and said he was just ready for another. He drained his tankard to prove his assertion, and the other man went toward the bar. Larry stood up.

"Time to go." He spoke in English. "You've had your bedtime story, David."

30: CASUALTY

Romy was sitting up reading her own bedtime story in a magazine when I arrived. After leaving the lounge I had waited downstairs with Larry while he took a call from Zurich. I was surprised to see her wearing a dressing gown, which she pulled closer over an openwork-lace nightdress.

"Jeff Tarleton brought my bag," she explained, "so now I've unpacked." Stretching her legs under the bedclothes she leaned back on the pillow. "I think I'm going to get out of bed—I'm as stiff as a board. It must be from leaning out of that damn window at the Torre. The wind was blowing like a banshee."

"I've just met a man who believes in banshees. Larry will be along in a minute."

"I'll wait till he's gone."

The only light on was her bedside table lamp. I went over to the window and parted the curtains cautiously. The snowbound street was deserted and extended into the distance between the old buildings. It was a fine night, and the light from the street lamps reflected back from the ground brilliantly, making the scene unreal and dramatic. Farther up the street a very old-fashioned-model car was parked by a bank of snow without any lights. As I watched, several people came out of the hotel and walked around a corner. The street was empty again. Behind me Romy stifled a yawn.

"Take no notice of that," she said. "I'm glad you came up—I was bored just sitting here reading. You might have brought me a drink," she added. "Mr. Tarleton went down and got me one. He has such nice manners."

"I know—he called you ma'am."

"Yes, he did. Anyone out there?"

"Not a soul—yes, there is now."

The old man in the long green overcoat started walking down the silent street toward the parked car. Pietro walked unsteadily, hands thrust deep inside his pockets, head down. His trail of footprints in the snow formed an elongated zig-zag pattern. I thought perhaps I'd better go down, and then he stopped. He stood quite still for several minutes, head up now, as though sniffing the night air.

"What is it?" asked Romy. I heard a swish of bedclothes, a patter of feet, and then she stood beside me.

"The man who believes in banshees. I thought he was drunk, but now I'm not so sure."

Pietro was on the move again, walking now with quite a steady stride, head down again. The footprint pattern stretched behind him in a straight line. He reached the parked car and, to my relief, walked on past it.

"They're amazing, these hardened old drinkers," I said. "They put away liter after liter and still manage to walk home."

"Look, David, a snowplow."

Pietro was slowing down again, but still walking in a straight line. The orange-colored snowplow emerged from a side road and turned down the street behind Pietro. The driver sat inside an enclosed cab and maneuvered his vehicle so that it began to shovel snow into the gutter. I heard the door open. It was Larry. He joined us at the window.

"Pietro's going home," I told him. "Larry, have you got a car with chains available?"

"We've got two now—some more of the boys have arrived from Milan. Why?"

"I'm thinking of driving back to the Torre. I'd like to take a look at that new building."

"Tonight? Up that road?"

"It's not snowing—and I don't think the road's as bad as Nikki made out. He spent half his time trying to scare us."

"You can't use the monorail. You're thinking of the supply road, I suppose?"

"No. There's a lower road which comes out beyond the Torre—I've checked it on the map. The abyss is much narrower up there, and there seems to be a covered bridge over it. . . ."

Romy's fingers closed over my arm. "Look."

The snowplow was very close to Pietro, who was still walking up the street, a tiny distant figure. The odd thing was that the orange machine was no longer shoveling snow. Now it traveled straight down the cleared stretch, and it had considerably increased speed. Opening the window, we heard the faint vibrations of its motor, a fast humming sound. And as we watched it came up behind Pietro, who still walked steadily on, quite accustomed to the presence of such a machine. It was almost alongside him when it swerved violently, and the entire machine drove over him. It was reversing into the street as Larry and I ran from the room.

The cold air hit us as we left the hotel and ran through the snow. The long street was once more deserted. No sign of the orange machine, no sound of its engine. I hoped that Romy had managed to get straight through to the police, and then we reached him. Pietro lay in the snowbank, a tangled heap. Larry made a face, bent down briefly, and straightened up.

"He's dead, of course. Where the hell is that machine?"

We found it by following the trail of red smears in the white snow. They led up the nearest side street, and the snowplow was abandoned against a wall, the driving cab empty. I looked at Larry, who was puffing.

"I'm going up to the Torre tonight. Where do I find the car?"

31: SNIPER

The Alpine world was white, palely lit by moonlight, the grim northern wall of the Torre a rugged silhouette. A glow of lamps located the windows, one of them the bedroom where Romy Silber had spent the night, leaning out to watch the strange building in the distance. I feared and welcomed the moon; it exposed me to view across the snowbound slope but also showed me the guard fence which protected the building. I moved toward the fence quickly.

It was bitterly cold in the still night, but I wore a fur-lined jacket Jeff Tarleton had lent me, and my feet moved smoothly inside ski boots borrowed from the hotel proprietor. The snow was crisp and hard. My feet made little sound. Somewhere in the night a dog howled, and I paused, looking back the way I had come. Beyond the northern end of the Torre the abyss curved away from the mountain, and the covered bridge I had crossed was a long way down. I moved up close to the fence and wondered why it looked so easy to pass.

The fence was formed of several horizontal wires between concrete posts. The top wire was chest-high, just too high for a man to step over. But it would be quite easy to lift a wire and climb through the gap. The posts were much higher, too high to peer over to examine their fourth side. Standing midway between the two posts, I looked at them carefully. Then I began to shovel snow away from under the lowest wire. It took me fifteen minutes to clear a gap, and I was lucky. Under the wire the ground shelved slightly, and I thought I would just have enough clearance to wriggle my body under the wire without touching it. I took my time, chin dug into the ground, body pressed into the earth, moving forward inch by inch, refusing to relax when my back had passed under the obstacle, remembering to splay my boots to avoid their heels catching the wire. When I climbed to my feet my chin was frozen. Automatically, I rubbed the circulation back into it as I checked the inside of a post. Small alcoves had been cut deep into its surface, and inside each alcove rested a black plastic box. Alarm bells. Any vigorous movement of the wires would have put the alarm system into operation. I hoped that this was their major contribution to the defense of the hangar-like building.

I was halfway between the fence and the outer walls, shuffling rapidly across the hard snow crunch, when I saw the iron posts. They were arranged in a circle around the building, about twelve feet apart from each other, as though a new fence was in the process of erection. Each post stuck about four feet above the ground, but it was the distance between them that bothered me. Cautiously, I walked closer. Then I saw the trail of footprints leading from the end of the small railway that carried the lifeline trolley. The footprints came toward me, passed within inches of one iron post, and then stopped. Other footprints returned to the railway. I walked up to this post, saw that it was just a post, and followed the prints to the railway, guessing that I had probably discovered the secret of the second obstacle line. Midway between each post they had buried land mines, and the iron poles indicated where it was safe to walk.

The outer wall of the building was at least forty feet high, and the huge doors in the end wall were firmly closed. I listened and thought I heard the hum of machinery. Stand-

138

ing well away from the building I tried to see light coming from the ventilator cowls, but Romy had looked down on them. I began walking along the base of the wall, away from the Torre. There were no windows—only an endless surface of concrete. I glanced up at the sky and saw clouds coming over the distant peaks. If they didn't go away, I was going to have difficulty getting back. I needed the moonlight to pass over the two obstacle lines.

I was close to the end of the wall when I found the ladder, an iron contraption which ran up the side of the concrete vertically. The rungs were covered with snow, and when I gripped them I felt ice under the surface. I listened carefully and then began to climb.

Wearing ski boots made it difficult. I wondered whether I was attempting a suicidal operation, but I had to see inside this building. I went on up. The protruding tips of the boots forced me to climb on the balls of my feet, which increased the danger of a slip, so I climbed slowly. As I climbed snow broke off under my changing grip, and my gloved hands closed over ice-skinned iron. Inside the gloves my fingers began to lose their feeling. I compelled myself not to hurry, not to try to get it over with quickly.

The thick jacket hampered my movements, and to encourage myself I looked up. I was surprised to see that the roof still seemed a mile away. When I glanced down I saw the ground far away below. Even from this height a fall could prove fatal. My teeth clattered with cold. I clenched them and continued the ascent. Much higher up I found a round ventilator close to the ladder, but the grille was closed. I pressed my ear against it and heard again the faint hum of machines working. Before resuming the climb I looked sideways along the wall. Its surface sheered away and had a dizzying effect. In the distance a light in the Torre went out. If anyone watched there, as Romy had watched, they were bound to see me, pasted against the concrete like

139

a fly. Hell and damnation, I told myself, get on with it! Then it happened.

I lifted my right foot to feel for the next rung, and my left foot slipped on the ice and lost its hold. My bent arms dropped to their full extent, my hands took the full force of my falling body, and I hung in space. I heard a cracking sound and thought the rung was going. A piece of broken ice streaked my face. The strain on my fingers was telling as my feet fumbled desperately for a hold, slithering back off the icy rungs, the boots getting in the way, pain screaming down my upper arms, all feeling going from the crooked fingers. I got a toe hold, a foot hold, rammed the other foot in alongside, going up two steps to relieve the pressure on my tortured wrists. Then I just hung there, sucking in great sobbing breaths of bitter air, curiously without interest in the proceedings, feeling I'd sooner stay there forever rather than move again.

The final lap I risked at a faster pace, in spite of the ice, and when my head emerged above the wall I saw that the ladder continued on up the roof surface to the summit. A low-railed catwalk followed the ridge line from one end of the building to the other. It had been put there for maintenance purposes, I supposed. Dotted at regular intervals along the roof surface were ventilator cowls, and now I saw a glow of light filtering from all of them. Romy had been right. They worked regular night shifts.

Still perched against the side of the wall, I made a mistake. I paused to look down from my vantage point, and near the corner I had walked toward I saw a high bank of snow. As I watched I heard the sound of an approaching engine. An orange snowplow came into view, headlights focused on the moving heap of snow it pushed forward in its scoop. Then it began to clear a large area, piling more and more snow against the bank. I froze against the ladder, not daring to move. The driver inside the cab had only to look up once to see me. I waited fifteen long minutes before he drove away. Then I scaled the ladder up over the roof.

The iron catwalk running along the roof summit was barely a foot wide, its surface very slippery, and I had to stoop slightly to hold on to the handrail. On both sides the snow-covered roof sloped and slithered away. I kept my eyes on the walk. The ventilator cowls were staggered at different levels, the nearest still several feet below the catwalk, but first I went to the end and peered over the edge.

The entire area in front of the building had been cleared of snow, and the plow was stationary, its lights switched off. Just beyond it the ground sloped, and down the slope ran a broad concrete ramp leading to another huge building. It was similar in appearance to the one I stood on, and massive doors occupied the end wall I faced. So far as I could see there was no one about. I wondered about the ski patrols and then turned my attention to the nearest cowl. It was going to be difficult—I could see that—but it was the only way I could hope to find out what was going on underneath me.

The cowl was square, about a foot in width, and it projected perhaps two feet above the roof surface. I hoped it was strong enough to take my weight as I climbed under the guard rail, sat down on the roof slope, hung on with my hands over my shoulders, splayed my legs, and let go. The cowl rushed up to meet me. I grabbed my arms around the metal to take the impact and then sat with it between my legs, the top just below eye level. Warm air streamed in my face, reviving me wonderfully. I sat there for a moment, warming my gloved hands, the heat penetrating my legs below the jacket.

Inside the grille louvers the fan was whirring, but I had a clear view down between the blades. The factory floor was far below, but the building was lit by strong neon lighting, so I could observe my fragment without difficulty. To the

141

right the unfinished tip of a fuselage projected into my range of vision. Pygmy-sized men in dark clothes fussed over the fuselage tip, while beyond them a white-coated man worked inside a glass booth. That was the extent of my view as I crouched down to peer inside the cowl, blissfully warm. I watched for several minutes without seeing anything else, and then the man inside the booth stood up. I could see him through the booth's transparent roof, and I wondered what he was doing as he stood quite still. A minute later a man appeared, walked up to the booth, paused outside, and then the white-coated man emerged. As he walked out of sight the other man followed him. I couldn't be quite sure, but I was fairly confident that the second man carried an automatic weapon.

It was going to be tricky getting back up to the catwalk— I had slightly misjudged the distance. Turning on to my stomach would have made the second stage easier, but in the process I would have propelled myself over the edge, so I stayed on my back where I could see the cowl. Very carefully, I eased my body up the roof away from the cowl, maneuvering to place the soles of the ski boots flat against the upper side of the cowl, and then slowly extending my legs full length. Now I was lying stretched flat on my back over the icy roof slope, held there only by the pressure of my boots on the metal surface, feeling the snow dissolving away the recent warmth. Reaching one hand up over my head, my right hand, I fumbled for the upright that supported the handrail. The other upright was too far away for my left hand to grasp it; I would have to haul myself up backward relying on the strength of one hand. The tips of my fingers brushed the upright bar, and that was when I knew I had misjudged the distance.

I lay there for a moment watching the stars, faint specks in the glow of moonlight. Tentatively, I dragged my heels up the roof, using the tips of the boots to give leverage against the cowl. If I slipped now . . . The upper joints of my fingers curled around the bar. Not enough. I eased my heels higher, boot tips lower. The second finger joints wrapped around the bar. Another inch would do it. My right arm was stretched to the limit, the muscles protesting with a growing ache. Under the tension my knees began to tremble. Damn them! I eased up a shade farther, and my hand locked on the bar. Done it! I gritted my teeth for the final haul. My feet were now clear of the cowl, and this gave my body a tendency to slip toward the right. I took a deep breath and pulled. I had covered half the distance, and my arm was crooked at the elbow. Suddenly the cramp started, kneading, twisting, ripping at my upper-arm muscle. The agonizing pain grew, screamed in my brain. Without realizing it, I let go. . . .

The roof slithered away under me, my body tobogganing forward, hands futilely digging down for a hold. In the effort to save myself my head banged hard against the snow, and light flashed in my eyes. Then I went over the brink. The ground soared up. I was going to miss the snowbank—the trajectory of my fall carrying me . . .

I lay half-stunned, amazed I was still alive, up to my chest in snow, spitting snow, seeing rolling black waves, feeling my consciousness slipping away. No! I snapped my teeth closed, bit my tongue, and the pain steadied me. It was a reflex action that padded my hands into the bank on either side, giving me the balance to haul up my legs. Then I fell on my hands and knees into the snow. I seemed to stay in that position for an eternity. When I straightened up I stumbled down the side of the bank and just saved myself from falling again. The clouds were close to the moon. I had to get past those obstacles before the clouds masked the moonlight. "Must get past them . . . tell Larry." I was talking to myself now. I stumbled away from the bank and headed out across the snow.

My ski boot scraped the iron post—I passed so close to it.

Now for the fence. Not far. The light was fading. Was I losing consciousness? Pull yourself together. The clouds over the moon—that was it. I looked up and saw the moon disappear. It was pitch dark. My feet slid backward and forward automatically. What was the next move? Flashlight. I checked, and it was in my pocket. Don't shine it too soon in case the snowplow driver comes back. I checked my revolver, and that was safe in my other pocket. I felt dazed and worried that I might black out. Don't think about it—just keep . . .

I fell against the wire, and the alarm bells started ringing. Feeling around in the dark I grabbed a wire, lifted, and clambered under it. Moving forward in the dark away from the wire, I tripped. When I picked myself up I put on the light—I had to see my way. Behind me, over to the left in the direction of the Torre, a horn began to wail mournfully. That was nice. General alarm. Just like a breakout from prison in the old days.

I had gone some distance when I saw them—three lights which moved over the mountain slope. I thought I was seeing things, but when I rubbed my eyes and looked again they were still there, equidistant, moving toward me in a row. Pietro's haunted spirits. More lights appeared, but they were much farther away—pinpoints of light which moved more slowly. I kept going, forcing my boots through the snow, hoping I was heading for the covered bridge. When I remembered that I was also heading for the abyss, I put the thought out of my mind.

The three moving lights were much closer when a glow spread over the mountain and suddenly the moon turned full on. The three men on skis were less than half a mile away, and the lamps attached to their heads changed direction, coming straight for me. Across their backs I saw the outline of their rifles. The covered bridge was still a long way below me, a cabin-shape of shadow in the moonlight. I

144

knew it was quite impossible for me to outrace the skiers, so I turned to face them and took out the revolver. At that moment I saw the man on the ridge.

The ridge was farther north, midway between where I waited and the advance of the mountain patrol. With the full strength of the moon behind him I could just detect his movements—the lifting of the rifle, the pause. It was a long-distance shot, and now I could hear the skim and swish of the approaching men. The shot rang out sharply, echoed. The skier on the left suddenly lost his balance and went down in a flurry of snow. Then a second shot. Another man flung up his poles, swerved violently, and crashed. The third man was close now, and he had been warned. He changed course and moved in a series of zigzags, body crouched low. My mind calculated his course, and I knew he was still coming for me. As he reached the limit of one turn, and turned again, the third shot echoed in the night. I saw him jerk convulsively, then appear to recover his balance, brace to jump a sharp drop, leap forward, crumbling in mid-air. He fell crazily at the foot of the drop and lay still. When I looked back at the ridge the man had gone.

I was fairly close to the covered bridge when I fell down. Wearily, I climbed to my feet as the pain shot through my head again. I continued trudging toward the bridge, which now seemed to be vibrating slightly. The vibrating continued in tune with the buzzing inside my head. Then it got worse, and I was falling. Just before I blacked out I remembered the man on the ridge. He had shot like a marksman, and I thought he must have been using a sniper-scope.

3 GERMANY: TARGET

32: REST CURE

I opened my eyes, saw the mountain peering in at the window, so I knew it was Innsbruck, saw Larry, closed my eyes, and pressed my head deeper into the pillow.

"What day is it?" I asked.

"Wednesday, November 1—don't worry, you've only been out a few hours. How are you feeling?"

"As though I could lie here forever—with a little encouragement. Is Romy about?"

"Doesn't sound as though there's much wrong with you that a few days' rest wouldn't cure. And that's what the doctor's recommended. You've been examined and you're sound in wind and limb, except for a bruise on the side of your head."

"A roof came up and hit me. How did I get here?" I tried opening my eyes again, and this time the light didn't hurt so much. The sky was brilliant, cloudless, and the snow-tipped peak perched comfortably on the opposite roof. Snow. The memory of all that snow made me close my eyes again. "What time is it, Larry?"

"Eight o'clock in the morning. We brought you down here out of the danger zone in an ambulance—borrowed from the Italian government. Everyone is being very co-operative. Jeff found you—inside that covered bridge."

"Inside it? I blacked out half a mile from it."

"Well, you must have got up again, done a zombie walk to the bridge, and blacked out again."

"I just don't remember. What was Jeff doing up there?"

"I sent him up—I sent a carload up. After you'd gone I worried about it. They were coming up the lower road and heard shots. The mountain slope was in the way, so they couldn't see what was going on. By the time they could, nothing was going on. And the horn had stopped wailing. Jeff thought it came from the Torre and said it sounded like a banshee."

"There are banshees on the mountain. Pietro was right. I'll tell you about that in a minute."

"Well, Jeff found you inside the bridge sitting on the floor with your back against it. You had Mr. Smith & Wesson in your hands as though you were expecting company. You were also out cold."

"You can say that again—I was cold. What about old Pietro?"

The swimminess came back again, so I opened my eyes, and it went away. I sat up against the pillows.

"Nothing on Pietro." Larry made a face. "The snowplow belonged to the town and had been left in a carport place just off the main street. Someone grabbed it on the spur of the moment to mow the old boy down. The police wanted me to stay there a few days, but I called the police chief in Milan and he vouched for me." He looked dubious. "You're supposed to be resting instead of talking your fool head off."

"I'm going to talk my fool head off now, so listen carefully. That new building on the north side of the Torre . . ."

At the end of fifteen minutes I felt a lot better, and Larry knew as much about it as I did. He asked a few questions and told me that they had found my car where I had left it parked by the roadside, so someone had driven it back to Brennero. He was going out of the room to phone Zurich when Romy arrived carrying a tray. Behind her back he looked her up and down in mock amazement and then went out, closing the door firmly behind him.

"Sitting up already, I see. Just as I thought—a complete fraud," said Romy coolly.

She put the tray down on the bedside table, and I looked at a coffeepot, cream jug, sugar, two cups, and a bowl with a lid hiding its contents.

"I'd like a drink," I said firmly.

"Coffee," she replied equally firmly. "You've been in a state of mild shock. The doctor said you were suffering from exposure. Alcohol is bad for you. And stop looking at me like that."

I went on looking. Romy was dressed in a black cashmere sweater which hugged her affectionately. Her ski pants were skin-tight, and the only decorative touch was a string of pearls. She watched me grimly for a moment and then turned sideways to pour coffee. When she had the pot in her hand I leaned over and traced a line with my finger down the ski pants. She swore.

"Damn you, I'll spill this."

"You don't have to—just keep still."

"Lie back and relax," she commanded. "You'll have a relapse. I know, I'm a trained nurse. How do you like your coffee?"

"Hot and strong. You may add a little cream. And, since you're nurse, I think the bed needs remaking. I can sit in that chair while you attend to it."

"You're staying in that bed for several days. I was here when the doctor said it. Here."

She thrust the cup at me and stood with the flat of her hands over her hips, watching me drink. This morning her black hair was tied behind her head with a green ribbon. Folding her arms under her chest she cuddled herself and spoke crisply.

"I've been delegated to stay here and see you do stay in bed—what do you think about that?"

"I don't remember putting these pajamas on," I said. "Who do they belong to?"

"Me. I have several spare pairs with me."

"We must be just about the same size. Except," I went on, "that you're slimmer around the waist and narrower across the shoulders." She glared. "Cheer up," I told her. "You're also much fuller in the chest. I can tell all these things—from the pajamas."

"I'll leave you to drink your soup on your own."

I looked down at the jacket. "And powder blue doesn't really suit my complexion."

"I'd say they should have left you up on the mountain. Now—drink your soup. I'll take that cup."

"Don't like soup."

She took the cup, put it down on the table. "What the hell do I have to do to get you well?"

She bent down to pick up the soup, and I grabbed her around the waist. She resisted temporarily, and then her mouth came down over mine savagely. My hand went behind her neck, and she lost her ribbon. Black hair spilled down over my hand and tickled it. She wrenched herself free, her eyes large.

"Now will you drink your soup?"

"I'll try a spoonful. You'd better fix your hair in the bathroom—Larry comes back and finds you like that he'll think we've been wrestling."

152

"I thought we had."

She strolled off into the corridor leading to the bathroom, and I shouted after her. "Just a preliminary skirmish." I thought I heard a click, and this reminded me of the time Gustav had taken his surreptitious photograph. So long ago. All of three days ago. By the time Romy came back I had polished off the soup. I pointed to the empty vessel with satisfaction.

"I've decided to behave myself."

"Really?" Her eyes were still large. "Feeling better?"

"I'm ready for anything. Mind you, the patient isn't all that warm inside here. You forgot the hot-water bottle."

"There's one in the bathroom—I'll fill it."

"There's one here." I grabbed her wrist and shifted over to make room. The mountain seemed to be peering in even more closely. She giggled when I pointed the fact out to her and adjusted the sheet. I warmed my cold hand under her sweater.

"Now you're suffering from exposure—and you *are* fuller in the chest."

Her hair was all over the place. She sat up and pulled it back on each side of her head, looking at me gravely.

"If Larry comes in it won't matter—I'm still decent. I've got my sweater on."

"You'd better push those ski pants under the bed, I suggest."

"Where are they?"

I reached down and lifted them off the floor. Bouncing out of bed on the other side she took the pants and went toward the bathroom, but I called her back.

"You can have your pajamas, too—they're at the end of the bed. I'm getting up now."

"Are you sure . . ." She came back into the room,

153

naked from the hem of her sweater down, fiddling with her pearls. I got out of bed and padded across the carpet.

"Am I sure of what?" I asked.

"That you're fit enough to be—walking—around. . . ."

Her voice trailed off, and she stopped fiddling with her pearls. Five minutes later she sat up on the carpet, picked up her sweater, and looped it over her arm.

"Next time the pearls come off, too," I promised her.

"You're fit enough."

When Larry came into the room I was washed, shaved, dressed. I could tell from his carefully controlled manner that he was excited about something. He looked me over carefully.

"Romy told me you were up. She said you'd made a lightning recovery."

"I've had my rest cure. The soup did it," I added.

"You remember that crazy idea you had about drawing up a register of potential bomb victims? I told you that I phoned Rudi from here and described that phony appointment ruse Sven Heim told you about?"

"You did."

"Well, Rudi warned the whole bunch of them about how the approach might be made. He hoped it would act as a warning signal. Well, it's paid off."

"How?"

"A leading jet-engine technologist, Fritz Bauer, has just made a similar appointment with an unknown man for this afternoon. He warned Rudi. We'll have to hurry. A plane is coming to pick us up from the airport here."

"Where are we going?"

"Germany—Mannheim."

33: MANNHEIM

"That's Bauer's house," said Rudi as he drove the Mercedes along the suburban road, "the one we're coming up to with a big fir tree in front."

I sat beside Rudi; Larry shared the back with a German police inspector. It was a wealthy area, the empty road wide and tree-lined. Each two-story house sat behind a large front garden with plenty of breathing space at the sides. The postwar architecture was beginning to mellow, and several houses had closed the jalousies against the watery afternoon sun. It gave them an appearance of being unoccupied, and I guessed that behind the closed jalousies lived housewives who talked about the sun fading the carpet. Behind iron-grille gates wide driveways led to two-car garages.

The house behind the big fir had the jalousies open, but there was no sign of life. Farther along, a road sweeper collected a pile of autumn leaves.

"One of our men," said Rudi. "We daren't put them in too close or they might be spotted. We wanted to put men inside the house, but Bauer won't have it. He's become almost fanatical about this business—Arthur Riedel, who died at Regensburg, was a close friend of his. Bauer acts as though everything depends on him."

"In a way it does," I said. "What time is the appointment?"

"One o'clock. Not long now—we just have time to get back to the observation post. Really, I'm almost beginning to wonder. It looks too peaceful for a bomb outrage."

We were almost past the house now, driving at the same slow pace Rudi had maintained since entering the suburb. A six-foot laurel hedge concealed the lower floor.

"Peaceful?" I grunted. "I'll bet Bremen, Regensburg, Kassel—all of them—looked peaceful enough before the bombs went up. And the details of the appointment are damned close to Sven Heim's experience."

"I suppose they are. This man who phoned—Schenck—is supposed to be from Holland. He told Bauer on the phone it was a confidential matter concerning Lotte and he'd like her to be present at the interview. Lotte is Bauer's fiancée—there's quite an age gap between them. Apparently a legacy has been left to the girl, but there are complications."

"All this made sense to Bauer?"

"It would have but for my earlier warning. You see, Lotte had a German father and a Dutch mother. Her parents separated, and she was brought up in Holland. They're both dead now."

"The research department this organization runs must be pretty good."

"If we're right about this," Rudi pointed out. "We don't know that yet."

"We shall by the afternoon. What's behind Bauer's house?"

"I'll show you."

"Rudi, this man Schenck—is he just a voice on the phone or did he give an address?"

"He told Bauer that in an emergency he could be reached at the Palashotel. We've checked. They have a Mr. Schenck staying there, but he's out somewhere. The Dutch police are checking the passport number, but we haven't had their report yet. Here we are."

We turned down a side road, and when the hedge of the last house ended I saw an open field. Rudi gestured across the field.

"Bauer's house is seven along from here."

"Any gate in that wire fence?"

"Not from Bauer's garden. We'd better turn back now—we're almost at the *Autobahn.*"

I leaned forward with interest. "The *Autobahn* to Bavaria?"

"That's right."

"Rudi—for God's sake put a man inside that house."

"Bauer won't permit it. He says the house may already be watched, and this time we've got to track them down—the whole lot. He's got political pull, too. I can't push him too far. He insists that he'll keep the appointment as arranged."

"God help him." I looked over my shoulder to where Larry was sitting glumly on the back seat. "And what's the matter with you?" I inquired.

"I was thinking about the Heim explosion. We know both Sven and Else are alive, and yet relics of the bodies of a man and a woman were found in the wreckage. Who on earth were they?"

Noon. We stood in a large room on the top floor of a big office block on the outskirts of Mannheim. A pair of Leitz Trinovid binoculars stood mounted on a tripod in a fixed position, and when I looked through them I could see the front of Bauer's house near and clear. The house was half a mile away.

"We should be closer," I said.

"Bauer insists . . ." Rudi spread his hands.

"You're willing to take the risk to wrap up this thing?"

"These bomb outrages are the biggest political issue in Germany today. And, as Bauer insists . . ."

Rudi lit a fresh cigar and started pacing restlessly around the room with a lithe, easy walk. Larry sat in a chair, hands crossed, a forgotten cigarette in his mouth. At a table a German policeman sat wearing earphones, testing a two-way transmitter. A second policeman guarded the door.

No one spoke, and the tension was rising like the ticking

of a bomb. A third policeman came in, carrying a high stool. Adjusting this, he settled himself in front of the tripod, peered through the binoculars, adjusted their angle a fraction, and waited.

"Bauer is due any moment," said Rudi.

"Due back home, you mean?" I asked.

"No, he's calling in here on his way home. It's a natural thing for him to do; a firm on the fourth floor makes his blueprints. He'll see them and then slip up here."

"What for?"

"I want him to see this setup. It may make him feel more comfortable."

"He's cracking up?"

"You'll see whether he's cracking up."

Rudi put the cigar back in his mouth and resumed pacing. His natural talkativeness had deserted him. Five minutes later there was a tap on the door, which the guard opened to admit a short, stocky German of about forty. He wore his sandy hair in a crew cut, and his wide jaw expressed determination. We all stood up automatically as Rudi greeted him and made the introductions. Bauer nodded and asked if he could look through the binoculars. We waited while he peered through them. He spoke briskly.

"I would hardly recognize my own place—it looks so different from up here."

"We think you shouldn't go ahead with this—going back to the house," said Rudi.

"I have made up my mind. You will adhere to what we arranged, won't you?"

"We haven't spotted anyone watching the house yet," Rudi persisted. "One of my men could take . . ."

"You wouldn't spot them watching if they're organized like this—spying from another building. I have decided. You will keep strictly to the arrangement?"

"Yes," said Rudi unhappily.

Bauer nodded. "Good. One more thing, Mr. Dorf. I brought Lotte with me and left her in the next room as you suggested. I'll collect your police girl and go back to the house with her." He almost smiled. "She does look rather like Lotte. And, Mr. Dorf, I don't want Lotte watching the house from this room. Look after her. I must go."

We watched him go, and when the door had closed no one said anything. Larry broke the silence as he fumbled for a cigarette.

"Plucky little so-and-so. I hope this Schenck bastard really is from Holland."

34: GOOD-BY

"Schenck wasn't from Holland."

Rudi put the phone down and stared across the room at us bleakly. We had both automatically stood up again. Rudi went on talking.

"That call was from the Dutch police. They had trouble locating Schenck—apparently he's on holiday in Madrid. The real Schenck, that is."

My watch said 1:00 P.M., the time of the appointment. I walked toward the door. "We'd better get over there."

"Wait a minute," said Rudi.

"We've waited too many minutes. Did you put a man inside the house?"

"Bauer wouldn't . . . You saw him yourself."

"Get a patrol car—I'm going over. On my own if necessary."

"Hell," protested Larry, "tell him what it's all about."

"What what's all about?" I demanded.

The policeman behind the binoculars peered closer to the eyepieces, and we all watched him.

"Well?" rapped out Rudi.

"A gray van approaching the house, sir. It's just stopping outside. A man has got out; he's opening the gates. They're backing the van in—I think it's a laundry van. Can't see them now."

"Let me look!" Rudi glued his eyes to the glasses while Larry and I ran over to the window. The road was deserted. Up in the sky three small planes performed acrobatics, mock-chasing each other. I swung around on Rudi.

"Can't you phone Bauer? Where's your nearest man on the spot?"

"Wait," said Rudi, still peering through the glasses.

"Yes, wait," Larry repeated.

The room was full of silence, and the body heat of tension seeped through the silence. I opened a window. The noise of traffic from the *Autobahn* drifted in with the fresh air. Rudi left the tripod and went over to the phone. When I looked through the binoculars the house jumped at me. As I watched, Rudi issued a stream of instructions. Silence. The receiver banged down. Then he was talking in a different tone. I guessed he was using the two-way transmitter.

Over the top of the side hedge along Bauer's drive I could just see a gray line—the roof of the van—parked close to the garage. It appeared to be a large vehicle. There was no sign of life from the house. Then I detected movement at the windows and began reporting.

"They've just closed the jalousies . . . upper windows . . . can't see downstairs. The van's on the move . . . farther in. Garage doors must have been opened . . . it's stopped . . . half in, half out."

Behind me I heard the phone ring. The guard's voice answered. It was a brief conversation. The receiver banged down again, and he spoke to Rudi.

"The other observation point, sir. They report two men got out of the van, carrying something. Looked like a suitcase, very heavy—they carried it between them."

"Anything more yet, David?" Rudi asked.

"Not yet. Except those jalousies. What are you doing?" I kept my eyes screwed to the glasses.

"We have far more men on this thing than you realize. That road looks deserted, doesn't it?"

"Too damned deserted for my liking."

"Good. I find that encouraging."

"I don't see your road-sweeper man."

"He can't sweep the road all day," Rudi snapped.

"Take it easy, you two," suggested Larry.

We waited. I lost track of time watching through those binoculars, although by now I realized that the policeman was standing close to me, his notebook ready for recording anything I said. When I started speaking he took it all down.

"The van's on the move, I think . . . yes. Now it's stopped again . . . halfway down the drive. Still stuck . . . engine must have stalled. On the move again . . . coming out . . . turning, away from us . . . big vehicle. Driving off the way we went . . . just a minute . . . turning off that same side road. Gone."

I straightened up and took the crick out of my back. I should have used the chair. They stood inside the room like stone figures, Rudi with his head cocked to one side, ear aimed toward the window I had opened.

So I bent down again, feeling that I must see that house. I waited. And waited. The bruise at the side of my head began throbbing. Behind me no one moved or spoke. My back began to ache. I stayed crouched. Larry coughed and suppressed the cough as though not wishing to disturb the silence. I heard feet tap up and down on the floor. Rudi. Not wanting to start pacing, unable to keep still. Christ!

Something flashed. The lens image filled with gray dust. Through the open window came a distant boom, and the image was full of nothing. I stood up and looked direct. A cloud was growing over the house, a cloud of gray-black smoke, billowing, climbing higher, ascending as a vertical column into the sunlit sky. Rudi stood perfectly still, his out-stretched hand holding a smoking cigar. Larry gazed through the window, his face expressionless. The policeman stared, open notebook still held ready. Bending down, I looked through the binoculars and waited. Rudi was chattering over the transmitter now, his voice harsh and urgent. Gradually the dust thinned out, settled. And then it hit me. The dust had cleared, the view was excellent, the pile of rubble very high.

"Good-by, Mr. Bauer," I muttered.

35: EYE IN THE SKY

We climbed aboard the plane, the door closed, the motors started, an ear-vibrating hum. The passenger cabin was small but the seats were comfortable, six along each side of a central passageway. I sat behind Rudi and in front of Larry. Rudi twisted around to speak.

"It's soundproofed—we'll be able to talk."

"That laundry van must be miles away now," I said.

"We have a vehicle behind it—equipped with a radio transmitter. Our radio operator up front with the pilot is in constant touch."

"Where is the van now?"

"On the *Autobahn* heading south."

"Toward Stuttgart?"

"That's right. Let's hope it sticks to the *Autobahn*—much easier to follow."

"Your pursuit car may be spotted."

"I don't think so. We have a series of cars in touch with each other—twenty minutes is the maximum time one vehicle shadows the van, then another takes over." A hint of his normal exuberance crept back into his manner. "I told you we were organized!"

162

"And we follow in the air?"

"Exactly. That gives us two eyes watching the same objective."

"If they're going any distance this plane will be spotted."

"I don't think so. Camouflage has been arranged. You'll see!"

The machine began to move forward for take-off, and Rudi went along to the pilot's cabin. We were fastening our safety belts when Rudi opened the pilot's door, saw that we were secure, and disappeared again. The cabin had large windows, but to see out properly involved standing up. When the machine was air-borne we unfastened our belts and stood up. We looked down out of the same window.

The plane gained height rapidly, and in a few minutes I saw the green-dark plateau of the Black Forest flowing steadily toward us. Rudi came back and took us to the other side, where he pointed out the *Autobahn,* a concrete ribbon coiling away into the distance. He spent several minutes scanning the ground with his binoculars and then he held them steady.

"Got it. See where the road curves near that big factory?"

"The one with the chimney?"

"No, it has a water tower to one side. . . ."

"Got it. Go on."

"Coming up to the curve—four vehicles, well spaced out . . . Do you see?"

"Yes, the front vehicle is just starting to go around the curve."

"That's the van. They've just reported back on the radio. Our man is the third vehicle back." He chuckled. "It's a Rolls-Royce. Who would suspect a Rolls? It has British plates, too. We *are* well organized."

"Don't overdo it, Rudi. We can lose them yet."

Behind me something was happening, and I heard Larry swearing. When I turned around I saw two yellow trainer planes wheeling and diving. One came too close for comfort and soared up over our heads. A third plane came up fast on the starboard side, headed straight for us, and dived underneath. Rudi grinned.

"How do you like the camouflage?"

"Aerial circuses," grumbled Larry. "What the hell is going on?"

"Camouflage. David said that we could be spotted by the van, and he was right if they have a long journey ahead of them. One plane is ultimately suspect. But four planes performing maneuvers are a quite different proposition. We're supposed to be the target plane, by the way."

The door to the pilot's cabin opened, and the radio operator spoke to Rudi. "We're moving away from the *Autobahn* for fifteen minutes. Providing they stay on it, we'll pick them up again at Pforzheim."

Rudi unfolded a large-scale map of southern Germany and spread it across a seat, his voice low, almost talking to himself.

"I wonder where they're headed for? Wherever it is, let's hope they arrive before nightfall." He glanced at the sun and then at me. "What would you put your money on?"

"I'd keep it in my pocket. It could be anywhere—south to the Swiss border or east toward Bavaria. They could even go west and cross the border into France."

Rudi nodded and started tapping his fingers. Being confined inside a plane wasn't exactly his forte. Larry was staying by the window as though hoping to catch sight of the van. Outside, two of the trainer planes engaged in a mock dogfight and then broke off to fly around and around us. I wondered how old the pilots were. Rudi looked up from his map.

"I think they're heading for the Black Forest."

"You're guessing."

"Not entirely. I have a feeling."

"You were prepared for something like this happening," I said. I made the remark as a statement.

164

"We were prepared for every eventuality and we organized for it," replied Rudi smoothly. "When this particular contingency occurred, we reacted. That's all."

I stood up and looked down on Germany. The Black Forest lay immediately below, a sea of dense green fir forest. Here and there the sea flowed around large islands of open countryside and then rolled down again into gorges. The whole vast area was interlaced with a network of tracks. But I stood watching for some time without seeing a soul.

The plane was losing height when we passed over Pforzheim. The yellow trainer planes were flying sedately in formation a long way to port now, one plane stepped above another. We were well out of sight of the van, so there was no need for demonstrations. Larry came and stood beside me.

"It's a relief not to have those apprentices using us as live bait."

Rudi looked up sharply. "Those pilots are highly experienced—they couldn't have put on the show they did otherwise."

"I've nothing against your boys that keeping a healthy distance from us won't cure."

We circled Pforzheim several times, and the trainers circled with us. Then the radio operator appeared, speaking quickly. "The van's still on the *Autobahn;* it's just coming into Pforzheim. Car Zero Five reported."

Rudi consulted a notebook. "That will be the Citroën— bright crimson." He stood up and hoisted his glasses. "A crimson Citroën—should be easy to spot."

I strained my eyes along the cement ribbon on the starboard side. The traffic was fairly heavy but spaced out in several convoys. Our plane began to lose a lot of height, and one of the trainers buzzed us. Larry sighed and concentrated on the view below as I pointed.

"Back from that large clump of trees—six vehicles in

convoy. The Citroën's third from the front, and I'd say the van is leading."

Rudi swiveled his glasses. "That's it." He went forward to issue instructions. The three trainers had vanished. When I pressed my nose against the glass I saw them high up, coming down in dive-bomber formation. They screamed past thirty yards away, pulled out of their nose dives, and took up formation alongside as though acting as escort. Rudi came back, flapping his map.

"I think it's Stuttgart. Looks very much like Stuttgart."

"That thing you didn't tell me about," I said. "I'd like to hear it now."

"I don't quite follow you, David."

"Back in the building at Mannheim, it came up in conversation and then got lost."

"Tell him," urged Larry. "We wouldn't be here now if he hadn't suggested that register."

Rudi lit a fresh cigar and examined the glowing tip. He put it back again in his mouth, puffed quietly, removed it, and began speaking.

"You know they pulled bits of bodies out of Sven Heim's bombed villa. There was something peculiar about them."

"You're telling me there was—Sven and Else are both alive."

"No, I'm talking about the state of the relics, which were sent to the Swiss police laboratory. They have good pathologists, and during the examination they discovered traces of ice crystals."

"I see." I thought about what Rudi had said. "What conclusions, if any, did they draw?"

"That they came from bodies which had been preserved in a freezer—possibly in a refrigerator."

166

36: DEVIL

Well beyond Pforzheim, not too far away from Stuttgart, it all went wrong.

Without warning the van left the *Autobahn* and turned deep into the Black Forest on a side road, heading for an area that was almost totally uninhabited. Half an hour later it turned onto a track that led nowhere.

Rudi radioed the pursuit cars to stop following and to take up positions on the fringe, to wait for the van to emerge into civilization again. With our escort of trainer planes we followed at a discreet distance, flying backward and forward over the same flight path. Rudi was showing signs of anxiety now and couldn't keep still. Alternately, he studied his map and stood up to gaze through the glasses.

"It leads nowhere, nowhere at all," he said.

"Just where does it lead?" I asked.

He spread out the map and showed me. The track the van was following went a long way and eventually ended in the middle of a small hollow surrounded by forest. We estimated the remaining distance they had to cover and the approximate speed of the van, which was not very fast in that type of country.

"They'll have spotted us now for sure," I said.

"For sure," agreed Rudi. I didn't think that he was really listening to me.

"They could escape us in the dark," I warned him.

Crushing out his cigar, he left us without a word and went into the pilot's cabin. When he came back he had recovered some of his normal bounce.

"I've decided—it's all arranged. We're flying direct to Stuttgart Airport. There'll be a fast car waiting for us, and it will drive us as far into the forest as possible. From there we'll have to walk to that forest bowl."

"Let's just hope the van is waiting for us," I said.

We seemed to have been walking for hours and it was pitch-dark. We all carried flashlights, and a policeman who knew the area led the column. The immensity of the Black Forest enveloped us, and the only sound as we went up the narrow path was the noise of our feet breaking dead twigs. It was also cold, the cold air of high hills that are not quite low mountains, but it was not the cold of the high Brenner.

Behind the police guide walked Rudi, and I followed him in front of Larry, who cursed quietly and systematically at intervals. Larry had never been a man for country walks. Behind him walked a second policeman, who carried a walkie-talkie set on his back, and when my feet ached I reminded myself of his burden. Two more policemen brought up the rear.

"How much farther?" whispered Larry. "I'd just like to know, that's all."

We paused because Rudi had heard the question and he consulted the guide. Apparently we were approaching the last ridge now—the ridge that overlooked the bowl. The man with the walkie-talkie had words with his machine and then told Rudi that the car patrols had just reported no sign of the van coming back onto the *Autobahn*.

We stood listening, forming a semicircle around the footpath. The sky was full of dense cloud, which for a moment parted to let a shaft of cold moonlight shine down. The tall trees watched us, and it was impossible to detect a sound. Larry shuffled his feet.

"Let's get moving—the grass is always greener on the other side of the hill."

Ten minutes later we had nearly reached the top of the winding footpath and the trees were so close we could reach out and touch them. The guide had sprained his ankle,

168

which slowed us down, and now I was in the lead as I fumbled my way through the darkness. The moon shone fitfully, but all lights had been switched off because we were close to the crest of the ridge. As it happened, I was the only one who saw it. When I reached the crest a freak shaft of moonlight peeped through the cloud curtain and vanished.

In the brief second of illumination I saw the bowl, perhaps seventy feet down a gradual slope, its floor smaller than I had expected, possibly thirty feet in diameter. And on the far side of the bowl at the bottom stood the gray van. Two men sat beside it on the ground and then, as though the moon shaft had been a signal, they stood up. The clouds smothered the moonlight, and they were gone. I told Rudi what I had seen in a whisper.

"We've got them cold," he said.

"When we've collared them," warned Larry.

We had our heads close together, and Rudi sounded excited. "There's no way out for that van except the way they've come, and the patrol cars are waiting for them. We've got them all sewed up. I think they're waiting for someone to arrive, and that someone may be coming up the path behind us."

The policeman with the sprained ankle hobbled into the group and kept his voice so low I could hardly hear him. "I know this place. There's a path around the outside of the bowl through those trees. It brings us out opposite here, where the rim of the bowl is lower."

"Good, good!" replied Rudi. "We'll wait over there. It's just a matter of patience now."

"There is another way in and out," I objected. "From the sky."

"No plane can land down there—no long-distance machine. And if they send a helicopter, there will be plenty of time for Joachim and Karl to disable the pilot—with their rifles, if necessary."

"I see your point, Rudi, but do me a favor—get that chap

of yours to radio back alerting NATO Air Command. All radar stations to go on full watch immediately."

"As you wish." Rudi gave instructions, and we waited while the policeman went farther away from the bowl to transmit the message.

We were deep inside the forest, walking slowly as we followed the hobbling guide, when I stopped and listened. Rudi bumped into me. "What's the matter?"

"I can hear something coming—a jet, I think."

"A jet can't land in that bowl."

"Listen."

We were now some distance below the outer rim of the bowl, and the guide had just assured a somewhat irritable Rudi that the path turned upward in a minute. The sound, which had started as a mutter, was now increasing at a terrifying pace, a long endless screaming hiss which suggested enormous power. We couldn't see a damned thing, and I was wishing we'd stayed in our earlier position. The scream was developing into a prolonged roar with a hissing undertone like the descent of a bomb. It was on top of us now.

"The bowl," I yelled. "Get up the bowl!"

I began running upward through the dense forest, feeling with my hands for tree obstacles. Then I switched on my light, ran up faster, tripped over a tree root, sprawled, dropped my flashlight, and the light promptly went out. I got to my feet and felt my way up, passing myself from tree trunk to tree trunk. The hellish din of hiss and roar was quietening down. I knew why. It had landed.

We had come down the path much farther than I had thought. The pine needles underfoot made the ground slippery and difficult to hurry up. Behind me I could hear the others coming. Flashlights bobbed crazily between the trees, and then one came up beside me. Rudi.

"You were right," he panted. "At least we've alerted the radar stations."

"Save your breath. My God! Look!"

We reached the top together and stared down into the bowl. There was no sign of the two men now, and the plane was beginning to rise, fire spurting in the night from its twin jets poised vertically, aimed at the floor of the bowl, churning up a vast cloud of soil dust as they turned the bowl into an inferno. Foot by foot it climbed, vertical as an arrow. Then it rose level with the rim where we stood and went on. Up, up, up.

"Down," I shouted, and we dropped flat.

The machine climbed—fifty, one hundred feet—and hovered, quite stationary, as though held by some unseen force. As we gazed up, the jets began to rotate, mobile fire cones in the night. Then the plane was on the move again, heading upward in a tremendous power climb. The swiveling jets turned the fire thrusts away, and abruptly the flames vanished. The hissing grew fainter and fainter and was gone as Larry arrived with a policeman. I still lay sprawled on the ground alongside Rudi.

"If the jets had turned our way earlier, we'd have had it," I said.

"What was it?" Larry asked quietly.

"Veetol—vertical take-off plane. Pietro's iron devil."

37: BUNKER

It was warmer inside the headquarters of the military sub-control unit for the Stuttgart Area. It was warmer because the unit was housed in a giant concrete bunker hollowed out of a hillside under the Black Forest. I looked at my watch. Midnight.

On a wall map of Western Europe a uniformed orderly was inserting redheaded pins. They plotted the aerial course followed by the Veetol earlier in the night. At a nearby table

Rudi sat listening to fresh reports coming in. The reports were being relayed to Colonel Greif over the phone. Greif sat at the head of the table and wore civilian dress. Facing Rudi across the table, Larry sat drinking cognac. I went over to refill my glass as Greif put down the phone.

"What's the picture now?" I asked.

Greif stood up, went over to the map, picked up a two-foot pointer, and gestured toward the map like a schoolmaster. Like his manner, his voice was precise.

"We have no reports from ground observers—none at all. The absence of moonlight made personal observation impossible."

"Surely it would be going too fast, anyway?" I queried.

"Not necessarily. Over flat terrain we get some surprising results. But this time we had to rely entirely on radar. The system was alerted just in time. We picked up the Veetol here first." His pointer zeroed in on a position close to Esslingen, just east of Stuttgart. "Then it flew out to here, ten miles east of Ulm. From there it proceeded to Memmingen, and the next point of contact was over Saint Gallen. . . ."

"It turned," I interjected. "It headed back southwest."

"I thought that curious, too. From Saint Gallen it moved in a direct line along here and passed over Sargans. . . ."

"Just a minute—that's Swiss territory."

Rudi intervened. "I asked them to alert every tracking station within five hundred miles of Stuttgart—every tracking station that would co-operate, that is. And the Swiss are very co-operative."

"What happened after Sargans?"

"They lost it," Rudi replied.

"When they lost it," I persisted, "what was the final point of contact and where did it appear to be heading?"

Colonel Greif waved his pointer. "Beyond Sargans all contact was lost. Direction of flight was then east—east across the Austrian Arlberg. That put us into a dead end—

the Austrians haven't the equipment capable of tracking a Veetol."

"What course would you guess it was taking?" I asked.

"Straight along the Inn Valley, past Innsbruck, and on to the east. It must have flown low, too. It was never picked up by the NATO radar chain on each side of the Alps in Germany and Italy."

"Could it have done that—flown so low? On a pitch-dark night, flying below peak level down that long narrow valley at jet speed—it would be suicide."

"Theoretically, yes. But in actual practice it might be done." He gestured toward the phone. "I've been talking to one of the NATO air commanders. If the pilot reduced speed to the bare minimum necessary to keep the machine in flight, *if* he knew the area extremely well, and *if* he had a navigator who used his own radar equipment with exceptional skill—then it might be done. And now, if you'll excuse me for half an hour, I have to attend to something. I'll be back as soon as I've dealt with it."

Greif took the orderly with him, and the three of us were left alone. I refilled my glass with cognac, while there was still some left, and spoke to Larry.

"Well, we can make a pretty good guess where that Veetol did go. It reached Innsbruck, all right. From where we're sitting it then turned south and went straight over the Brenner to land on the mountain near the Torre."

"That," said Larry, "is a guess we're going to have to follow up. It's a good thing I left my people in Brennero. I'll just check to make sure Mr. Kardehay will be in residence."

He spent some time on the phone, and from what he said I gathered that Nikki Kardehay was no longer on the Brenner. Putting the receiver down he made a wry face, waiting for me to ask the question, so I asked it.

"All right, where do we go to see Kardehay?"

"Venice."

173

4 ITALY: DEVIL

38: WAR COUNCIL

"The deadline is right on top of us," said Romy. "I've just flown back from Munich after an interview with Loeb, the secretary of the New People's Party."

The living room of Larry's hotel suite in Venice was on the second floor. Beyond the open window a *vaporetto* chuffed down the Grand Canal, passing a black gondola. Its wake rolled the gondola from side to side while the gondolier's body moved to counterbalance the sway. The window was open wide to let in the warm balmy air of late afternoon, and in spite of Romy's urgent statement there was a more relaxed feeling around the table. Larry sat at the head, presiding over the conference, while I faced Romy, and farther down the table were four of Larry's men. One of them was Jeff Tarleton.

"Rudi sent you to Munich?" I asked Romy.

"Yes. He wanted me to try to check the deadline. When you flew to Mannheim I took the express from Innsbruck up to Munich. I went to see the party chairman, Kurt Langer, but Loeb saw me instead. I interviewed him in my capacity as a reporter for the Nord-Deutscher Agency."

"That must be wearing a bit thin now."

"Not at all—I really do work for them, but they have an arrangement with Rudi."

"Which capacity comes first?"

She couldn't resist it. "I'm a woman first," she replied, not looking at me, "a trained police girl second, and a reporter third. The Agency doesn't mind. They get scoops from Rudi —and that"—she looked along the table—"is strictly confidential."

"What did Loeb say?"

"He admitted under pressure—which was his way of making me feel how important it was—that Langer is going to make the bomb outrages the main theme of his big Munich speech."

"Today's Thursday, November 2, so that means tomorrow night, doesn't it?"

"That's right—at eight o'clock. He's addressing a huge public meeting, and half the world's press will be there. Loeb has let drop a hint."

"What hint?"

"The same thing he implied to me—that the organization behind the bomb outrages is American. He means the CIA, of course."

Larry's voice was grim. "It's 4:00 P.M. now, so that gives us little more than twenty-four hours to show who really is behind them. You'd better outline that idea you said you had, David."

I leaned forward so they could all hear me. The window was behind Romy, and I could see the peaceful afternoon sky of Italy's late summer, a clear pale blue full of sunlight. Somewhere, a long way off, a steamer hooted.

"We've got to get inside the Torre again," I started. "That

178

last trip at Kardehay's invitation was laid on to show us how harmless the place is."

Larry shook his head. "We've been over that once already. Since we arrived this morning from Stuttgart I've spent half my time on the phone with Captain Ferrano in Milan. He'd like to help, but Kardehay draws a lot of water in this part of the world. The Italians are hoping he'll build factories in the south, and he has political pull. Ferrano can't give the go-ahead for any kind of investigation of the Torre unless we provide a solid link between Kardehay and the bombings."

"There's the flight of the Veetol. . . ."

"Which was not picked up by the radar on this side of the Alps. I tried that, and Ferrano won't play."

I banged my fist on the table. "We've got to put the pressure on Kardehay and we've got to provide Ferrano with a reason." I looked down the table. "Jeff, you're sure that Josip Riz is with Kardehay in Venice?"

"Quite sure. Kardehay has a place on the Grand Canal farther up beyond the Rialto Bridge. I watched it myself, and Josip Riz is definitely in residence. I also found out that Riz lives there when he's not off with Kardehay on a trip."

I turned to Larry. "Those films showing Riz are on the way, aren't they?"

"Be here this evening, maybe earlier."

"Then we'll try to use Riz to put on the pressure, and make him the reason for Ferrano, too. We'll spring it on Kardehay when he least expects it, plus the fact that Else Heim survived the bomb explosion, plus the flight of the Veetol." I paused. "I've already prepared the ground. I've been to see Kardehay this morning."

"You have?" Larry frowned. "Doesn't that rather give him warning?"

"The main thing is it starts making him feel uneasy. I

179

want to rattle his confidence in the hope that he'll make a slip."

"He'd be surprised to see you," suggested Larry.

"I think he was, but he didn't show it much. Just asked how I was getting on with my investigation into Heim's murder. I told him that was why I was in Venice—that the trail led here."

"It might not do any harm at that."

"I also told him that you were here with me. I think that did upset him."

"Incidentally," Jeff broke in, "this place has been under observation since noon. From a building opposite, across the canal—man with field glasses. Another character is at the front watching the entrance. Maybe we'd better draw some curtains over that window."

"No, leave them." Larry's manner became more animated. "It shows we've rattled Kardehay already. I'm beginning to think David's idea has something in it. Let's hear the rest of it."

"Kardehay is holding a big private party at his place tonight, and I think we should go. It's fancy dress. The climax is to be a gondola trip down the Grand Canal later this evening—from his place to St. Mark's Square. The party will break up after that, and I want to show him that film somewhere soon afterward."

"My place," suggested Jeff. "It's close to St. Mark's and the room's as big as a barn. I'll be waiting for you to arrive with everything set up. Let's hope Riz comes, too."

Romy put both hands flat on the table and leaned her body toward me between them. "Where are we going to get costumes, David?"

"You're not coming. Kardehay knows you."

"Exactly—as a correspondent of the Nord-Deutscher Agency. Remember? I told him I was that when he asked me to have a drink at that hotel in Milan. When I also told him I was on holiday he suggested the trip to his nice weekend place."

"No go, Romy."

"My turning up with you and Larry *will* startle him," she persisted. "That's what we're after, isn't it? To shake his nerve."

Larry intervened. "There may be something in what she says. I'd be willing. We'll be there to look after her."

"And," Romy pressed on, "I can tell him I've been to see Loeb about the bomb outrages. It will be interesting to see how he reacts."

Larry went on agreeing with her. "It all helps to build up the psychological pressure on Kardehay, and we need just about everything we can use at this stage. If anything breaks loose, it will be after we leave the Grand Canal, and I've got more men on the way. I'll load St. Mark's Square with them."

"Just because it wasn't your idea," Romy provoked me. "Where do we get costumes for tonight?"

"I've found a shop just the other side of the Rialto Bridge. You can come along with me, and I'll make sure you don't choose something obscene."

We went on working out the details, and at one stage Jeff Tarleton said he was short of men for watching Kardehay's place and following anyone who left it, so I offered to help before the party started. The session was just breaking up when Larry remarked that later I could mention to Kardehay that Sven Heim had also escaped the explosion at his villa.

"I won't do that," I said. "Else is safe and under guard outside Zurich now, but we've no idea where Sven is. I'd like to know that he was safe, too."

39: FREEZER

I met Jeff Tarleton at 7:00 P.M. in a bar called Angelo's on the Via Mazzini. In spite of Larry's reinforcements we were still short of men, and the new arrivals had now taken up positions in the area around St. Mark's. Larry was acting on a strong hunch that the trouble was likely to be in that district, and he wanted his men to familiarize themselves with their surroundings.

My assignment was simply to help out for a short time by acting as watching partner with Jeff Tarleton. So far I had no idea what we would be watching, because the Via Mazzini was some distance from Kardehay's *palazzo* on the Grand Canal. I had by now grasped the fact that it was a principle of Tarleton's that wherever possible two men went on watch duty—one to watch and the other to phone in an emergency.

When I entered Angelo's Jeff was sitting at a table drinking black coffee, which the waiter had just served. The bar was a long narrow place with the narrow side along the street. The floor was a dizzy pattern of colored mosaic, the walls made of glass brick, and a long way back was a chromium bar where the *espresso* machine hissed away merrily. I ordered black coffee, and the waiter hurried back to the bar to make it himself. From his young swarthy features and his accent I thought he might be Yugoslav. The bar was empty except for ourselves, which made talking easier. Jeff glanced toward the waiter's back.

"Normally there's a girl behind the bar. I suppose she's off duty tonight."

"You've used this same place since you arrived?" I asked in surprise.

182

"Since yesterday. I know that isn't a good idea, but it's the only place convenient to what we're watching. And I'd appreciate it if you drank your coffee quickly."

The waiter came back, and I paid the bill. He went off and disappeared behind a curtained doorway beyond the bar.

"Just what are we watching, Jeff?"

"I didn't mention it at the meeting because of Romy Silber. Sure, I know she's all right, but . . . Anyway, yesterday I followed Josip Riz from Kardehay's *palazzo* to this queer place around the corner, and we've watched it ever since. With no results so far. You'll see it for yourself in a minute."

The big Texan loosened his tie and collar. It wasn't hot inside the bar, so I decided he must be restless. My coffee was scalding hot. I took only sips.

"Where's the chap I'm relieving?" I asked.

"Sent him back a few minutes early to eat. He must be back to give you time to dress for your party." He grinned wryly. "Think of me standing in the alley when you're eating caviar. Still, you might have more fun than you think. You heard about the duplicate keys?"

"No."

"We've been busy. We managed to put one of our boys next to a chambermaid inside Kardehay's place. It cost us money, but we've made duplicates of the keys from the one's she loaned us—the keys to most of the doors."

"Isn't there a risk she may warn Kardehay?"

"That was what Larry liked about the idea. If she does, it puts more pressure on him to know we're closing in. If she doesn't, we might find those keys mighty useful." He mopped his forehead. "Hot in here. We'd better be going soon."

I swallowed one mouthful, and the coffee tasted funny, so I left the rest and followed him into the street.

183

"Down here."

We turned off the street into a narrow alley between walls. Under the lantern at the entrance I saw the words *Calle Garibaldi*. As I walked inside, the tips of my shoulders brushed both walls. The alley was cobbled, and at the end of the dark tunnel another lantern showed where the alley turned a corner. I hurried after Jeff and nearly fell over my own feet when I stumbled into something tall and heavy. Jeff. He was standing upright with his hand against the wall, and when he turned his face toward me the lantern glow showed sweat glistening on his forehead.

"Okay, David?" His voice was thick and slurred.

"No—and you aren't either. That coffee was . . . doped."

It was taking all my strength to remain upright. My legs were turning to jelly, and the lantern glow was on the move, coming forward and going away. I hit my knuckles hard against the stone wall, and the pain revived me.

"Jeff, we can expect company any time. Get back to the street, where . . ."

But he had stopped listening and now he was moving deeper into the alley, a gun waggling in his hand. I went after him, walking as though in a dream, feet stepping on clouds. Then I staggered, and Jeff's huge hand was pushing me backward inside a deep doorway, so my head banged the wood behind me. I wondered how he could stand up after drinking the whole cupful. His voice rasped.

"Stay there . . . moment . . . I'll see what they're . . ."

Then he was gone, and I was forcing myself to stay on my feet, fighting my sagging legs. I won the battle and keeled out into the alley, moving along its emptiness in a half-crouch, forcing my eyes away from the lantern, which seemed to be wobbling, concentrating on putting one foot in front of the other. I reached the corner. No sign of Jeff. Just

184

another stretch of bleak lonely alley. Venice is full of them. I had to reach that far corner. I kept moving, supporting myself with a hand on the wall. As I came close to the end of the alley I stumbled and sprawled flat, saving myself instinctively with my hands and never feeling them hit the cobbles.

The world was a daze, my head spinning around like a Ferris wheel. It wouldn't stop spinning. Round and round. What was it I had to see? What was it I had seen beyond that corner? I made my eyes open and realized I had fallen just clear of the corner. Painfully, I concentrated, and through the blur it all came into focus.

A narrow canal, perhaps twelve feet wide. A tiny humpbacked bridge. Steps leading down from the street-level walk to a ledge beside the canal. A long deserted stretch of canal, the walls high, walls without windows, warehouse walls. Four men carrying something. Jeff My head churned. A lantern came toward me, withdrew to a pinpoint, came back, enormous. I closed my eyes to blot out that awful moving lamp, felt a gentle sensation of relief, unconsciousness returning, and compelled my eyes to open again. Time had played a trick on me. The scene looked different. There were two men standing on a narrow barge now. Had it been there before? I couldn't remember. The packing case was climbing, being hauled up into the night on a pulley. The two men watched it go. I watched it go, unable to move, able only to keep my chin up off the cobbles. I watched the case stop, hover, then move inside an open gateway at first-floor level. Someone unseen closed the gate, and the two men left the barge and went inside the warehouse.

Very carefully I got my hands underneath my body and used them for leverage. I was halfway up when the elbows gave way. My chin hit the cobbles, bright light flashed, then darkness.

185

I woke up with a headache but my mind had cleared. I was still lying at the entrance to the alley. Keeping still for a moment I listened, but the only sound in the night was the lapping of canal water against stone. I opened my eyes and stood up groggily. My watch said 7:35 P.M. The scene had changed again, and there was no one in sight. In front of the barge, facing away from it, a motor launch was moored to the wall, while farther down the canal a small powerboat floated, its searchlight on and beamed away from me. The long stretch of canal looked like a backwater leading nowhere, but I knew that eventually it would emerge into the Grand Canal, a single link in the intricate network of waterways that honeycombed Venice.

For several minutes I stayed inside the alley, leaning against the wall and taking deep breaths. When I felt I could walk straight I took the revolver out of my pocket, went down a flight of steps under the humpbacked bridge, and crossed the canal by stepping on the barge. Under my weight it wobbled, and I noticed that my balance was steady. The handle of the door the two men had walked through stayed firm when I tried to turn it. I listened at the door, peered through a shuttered window. No sign or sound of life. I had a fixed obsession now that I must get inside this warehouse, whatever the consequences. Not caring about the noise, I fired two shots to smash the lock. When I tried the handle again it gave way, and I pushed the door open into darkness. I glanced along the canal, which was still deserted, and went in.

My pocket flashlight showed a large wooden platform inside the doorway and then a long drop. A railed stair ladder led down to my right, and its continuation went up to my left. The warehouse floor below was empty except for some piles of straw in the corners. I climbed the stair ladder up to the next floor. The door that barred my way was protected with a new heavy padlock. I fired one shot, and the lock was destroyed. While I reloaded the revolver, so that all chambers would be armed, I listened and watched the wooden platform. A wave of dizziness came and went. Then I pushed back the door, flashed my light about, and walked inside.

The room was high-ceilinged and large, the floor constructed of bare boards, and almost empty. I moved the light around and saw the terminus of the pulley projecting above the closed gate. Then my light beam returned to the object parked against the far wall. A huge refrigerator of the type used by wholesale meat merchants. I walked across, took a deep breath, opened the door.

Jeff was inside, cramped and coiled in a foetal position, the back of his head smashed in. His cheek felt colder than the waters of the Arctic.

40: WHY?

"The body had disappeared," Larry explained patiently. "By the time the police got there Jeff's body had gone."

"I was going back to wait for them," I said again. "I phoned you from the café, put the receiver down, and went out cold."

"It's probably a good thing you did—otherwise you might not be talking to me now."

I eased my back against the couch and looked around the room where we had all met in the afternoon, the room where Jeff Tarleton had sat farther down the table from me. The windows were closed now, the curtains drawn, the lights on, and the police had gone away. I looked at my watch. It was 9:00 P.M.

"How long does Kardehay's party last?" I asked.

"Till much later. I've phoned our apologies, and he said

come when we could—things were just warming up. I didn't like that last remark."

"That bar—Angelo's—where that waiter fed us dope. Have the police been there?"

"Yes, and found the girl who normally serves tied up in the back room. The till had been raided, so that made it look like a case of petty theft. Nothing there to give Captain Ferrano. He's arrived in Venice, by the way."

"What for?"

"Really to keep an eye on me. Some politician has told him nothing must happen that will upset Kardehay. But it doesn't matter—the main thing is he's here and he's prepared to attend that film show we're putting on for Kardehay later tonight. We're still going ahead with your plan, of course."

"When I saw Jeff's body I felt like murder, but it did flash across my mind that here we might have some positive evidence for Ferrano."

"Well, we've got to face it—the evidence is missing."

I stood up and started walking around the room to see what happened. I stayed on my feet.

"Larry—was the meat safe still there when the police arrived?"

"Yes, it was—full of frozen veal. That's something else we've got to face; these people are pretty well organized."

"What I can't understand is why they put him inside that refrigerator. They were going to take him away soon, so why not leave him under that straw on the lower floor. Why go to the trouble of hauling him up to the first floor? Why? That's what I'd like to know."

Larry looked at his watch. "David, I'd better get along to Kardehay's place with Romy. She's waiting downstairs. I haven't told her about Jeff yet, by the way."

"I'm coming with you. No, don't argue. I'm feeling much better." I waited while he poured neat whisky into a tumbler and then I drank it. "Now I'm feeling better still. What about costumes?"

"Yours is next door with mine. We'd better hustle it up. And when you see Romy the effect of drinking that whisky will seem like a glass of water."

"What's she going as?"

"You'd never guess. Incidentally, we're not watching that warehouse any longer. I'm concentrating everyone around St. Mark's." He paused. "There's something else you should know about, if you're feeling strong enough."

"What's that?"

"The police have had an anonymous tip—Bruno Fleischmann has been seen in Venice."

41: NEGRESS

I sat opposite the most exciting Negress east of Harlem. Romy had colored her skin, tied up her jet-black hair in a silver ribbon behind her neck, and she wore a sleeveless dress of silver which was cut very low over her breasts. She leaned well forward while I lit her cigarette.

"How far down does that black dye go?" I asked.

"All the way." She straightened up "When I do a thing I do it properly. Besides, I never know when I may have to take my dress off."

Kardehay's private party had reached the wild stage. The imported French jazz band was playing Basie, a heavy pounding beat, and on the floor couples were dancing with certain intimate abandon. It was a cosmopolitan crowd, and the fancy-dress costumes ranged across the centuries. I was dressed as an early pilot, complete with large goggles pushed up over the helmet. The costume had been chosen deliberately, because I could move about in it easily.

The room was vast, the floor marble, and long gilt wall mirrors reflected a drunken pageant of history. For a moment I watched Kardehay coming off the dance floor, his personality perfectly expressed in the costume he had chosen. With long jeweled cane and powdered wig he was impressive as Louis the Fourteenth, if a little too slim in the figure. The girl with him was tall and slim and her titian-colored hair was piled high in a Grecian style. She was wearing a short Grecian tunic, which revealed long slender legs. Romy watched her critically.

"Who is she?" I asked.

"His latest, I suppose. He'll bed her down before the night is out."

A masked George Washington asked Romy to dance just as Kardehay arrived. He sat down in the chair Romy had left vacant, and the titian-haired girl wandered off toward the bar. Lighting a cigar, Kardehay asked his question.

"We were interrupted when we were talking half an hour ago. I meant to ask you how you are getting on with your investigation?"

"We may soon have it all wrapped up."

"Really?" The eyebrow wedges shot up. "That is quite remarkable. I was fascinated to hear that the trail led to Venice."

"Well, the final answer may not be here, but some of the people involved certainly are."

The hooded eyes watched me. "So, you're as certain as all that. I take it that you are co-operating fully with the various international police forces?"

"This really is some party you've organized." I drank more whisky. "This gondola trip down the Grand Canal is the climax, I imagine?"

"Yes. The party disperses at St. Mark's. There's a whole fleet of motorboats waiting there already to take people home." He flicked cigar ash. "It's really most tiresome that the Venetians won't allow any cars inside the city."

"That regulation is the only thing that keeps the place afloat. So when we get to St. Mark's you'll be available to come and see that film I mentioned?"

"Of course. Although I can't see how I'm going to be able to help you."

"Wait till you've seen it. That's Josip Riz over there, isn't it? The one with a black patch, dressed like a pirate."

"Yes. He doesn't really enjoy this sort of thing much, but although I call him a chauffeur he's really a bodyguard."

"I didn't know that. Does he travel around Europe much?"

"Only when he comes with me. He's a countryman and prefers life up on the Brenner."

"I didn't see him around when you asked us up to the Torre."

"No. He'd come on ahead here to make certain arrangements. . . ."

He paused as the titian-haired girl came back and asked him to dance again. "All in good time," he told her. "I'm busy at the moment." She made a face and accepted an invitation to dance with George Washington. I saw Romy sitting on a bar stool talking to Larry and guessed that she was deliberately leaving us alone. Kardehay followed my glance.

"I was surprised to see Miss Silber with you, David."

"She's a reporter for the Nord-Deutscher Agency."

"I know that, but she told me in Milan that she was on holiday."

"Reporters will lose any holiday for really big news, and that's what she's expecting on these bomb outrages. I've promised her a scoop."

He sighed and reached for his jeweled cane. "I see she also knows Mr. Biggs."

"They're both reporters. These international-press people form a kind of club."

"I think I know why you're in Venice," he said quietly.

"Why?"

"That man in the turban"—he pointed with the cigar—"is an Italian policeman. He has just told me there is a report that Bruno Fleischmann has been seen near the Santa Lucia Station."

Before I could reply a gross fat man dressed like a caricature of a Spanish grandee arrived. He wore a monocle, and Kardehay introduced him ironically as Count Otto, his social secretary. Otto burbled in German, and as they went off Larry sat down and began talking urgently as soon as they were out of hearing. He was wearing Victorian evening dress and a black mask pushed up over his forehead.

"I'm getting worried," he began. "I brought Bob here with us to do a job, and now he's disappeared."

"Are you sure?"

"Quite sure, and I don't like the look of it. He was supposed to stay by the bar. I've spent the last half hour looking for him, and he's definitely not around."

"What was the job?"

"Kardehay's suite is on the next floor. It's the second door after you've turned right at the top of the staircase. I wanted Bob to try to get inside there to see what he could find. But now . . ."

"Give me the key," I said.

"You know . . ."

"Jeff told me. Slip the key in my outer pocket. That's right. Now, the only problem is to make sure that Kardehay doesn't come up there while I'm prowling around. I think Romy may help there."

I beckoned, and when she had sat down in the chair Larry vacated I told her what I wanted her to do. As I finished speaking she looked at me anxiously.

"You'd better be damned careful," she warned.

"And you'd better be damned good," I told her.

Fifteen minutes later I knew that she had taken my advice. I had to push my way through the crowd gathered around the floor to watch her performance. The band had returned to playing Basie, a hard thundering nonstop beat. And in the center Romy danced her Negress dance. The silver-skinned body shuddered and convoluted to the beat, erect as a totem pole, her expression oddly virginal. Kardehay danced with her, letting her go frequently to dance on her own, and she performed a coldly erotic movement. Her supple legs were splaying now, her face somehow suggesting that this was no part of her—her body was simply slipping out of control. When Kardehay came forward again she shook her head savagely, so savagely that the silver ribbon came away, and her hair fell loosely over bare shoulders. Her expression was full of arrogant contempt, a hint of growing wildness in her eyes. He stepped back, and she clamped her arms close against her sides, moving her hips so that her chest began to undulate. As I left, her body slithered into a particularly devastating cross-motion.

42: PLAYTIME

I leaned back against the inside of the door, eased my hand over the wall, and pressed the switch. I had expected a large room, but Kardehay's quarters were like a palace within a palace. The high ceiling was ornately decorated, and the lighting came from four giant chandeliers. Along the tapestry-covered wall at intervals alabaster pillars supported the roof. The furniture was late eighteenth century, richly upholstered in green cloth. Blue velvet curtains concealed the windows. I searched the room and found nothing interesting.

Switching off the lights, I used my flashlight to guide me along a wide passage into the interior of the suite. The first door I opened led into a bathroom where the bath was sunk into the marble floor. The next door opened onto the lavatory, but the room beyond was a bedroom. I shut the passage door and switched on lights. The main item of furniture here was a huge double bed under a gold canopy, and the walls were lined with long gilt mirrors. I searched this room rapidly and again found nothing. Switching off the lights, I went through an open door into a smaller bedroom.

The bed was smaller and without a canopy, but the walls were lined with gilt mirrors. Between two of them hung a single picture, a Manet print, close to another open door. I went through the doorway into a small dressing room. When I parted the curtains the pink lights of the Grand Canal landing stages glowed below. Closing the curtains, I searched both rooms quickly. I had been upstairs too long now. Behind the print I found a small wall safe, and then I heard a door bang. I switched off the light and slipped into the dressing room.

The door into the main bedroom opened. Light flooded into the smaller bedroom through the open doorway. I heard footsteps, which stayed in the main bedroom, then voices. Kardehay's voice, mocking, sardonic; a girl's voice, chuckling, protesting without anger, protesting playfully.

It didn't require much imagination to visualize the scene, and the voices were clearer now, so it was like being at the theater and listening with eyes closed. The script had been used before.

"Don't be in such a hurry." The girl.

"I have guests downstairs to keep happy and satisfied."

"There are other satisfactions to think of now."

I wondered who the girl was and when I leaned out of the dressing room I had a shock. In a mirror I could just see the edge of the bed, and over the edge sprawled a waterfall of titian hair, the face above it upside down, the eyes staring straight at me. I moved my head back inside the little room cautiously, but the next sounds told me she was too distracted to see me. I waited.

Five minutes later the voices had resumed normal conversation, and I gathered they were leaving. A door closed, but still I waited. Kardehay had left his light on. A few minutes later there were more voices, and two men came back. Kardehay and Count Otto, talking in German. Otto sounded undecided.

"We'll be going down the canal, Nikki. I'll be coming back, so I feel I ought to leave it here."

"Don't carry that around on you—put it in the safe."

The light came on in the smaller bedroom, and I pressed myself against the wall. Otto put an envelope down on a side table next to the dressing room, and then the phone rang in Kardehay's bedroom. He answered it and called Otto. I reached for the envelope and under cover of the sound of Otto's burbling voice opened the loose flap, expecting any moment that Kardehay would walk into the room. There was a photograph I recognized, a photoprint map of Bavaria, disfigured with a single cross north of Munich, and a hand-drawn map of a local area. A dotted line led to a house and was marked "van route." There was also tomorrow's date written in hand at the edge of the hand-drawn map. Grimly, I put the items back inside the envelope and left it on the table.

Several minutes later Otto put the phone down, came back into the room, and put the envelope in the safe. Then he switched off the lights and went out with Kardehay.

The suite was empty when I left it. Standing in the corridor I relocked the door with my duplicate key and went downstairs to find Larry. The tail end of a small procession of people was just leaving. Romy stood dressed in a topcoat and came running over, her voice a hurried whisper.

"Was it all right? I'm sorry—I couldn't hang on to him any longer."

"You did fine. Where's Larry?"

"With the party. They're just getting into the gondolas. I'm so relieved to see you. Josip Riz is in our gondola."

195

"In less than ten minutes now we reach St. Mark's," said Larry.

"You're sure everything's organized?" I asked.

"Up to the hilt. When we step off this boat I'll really feel I'm in control."

We occupied the rear vessel in the gondola fleet, and I sat next to Larry under a canopy. In the stern Romy had a compartment all to herself, and she sat facing us. The only thing that bothered me was that we had our backs to Josip Riz, who was now wearing a guerrilla outfit. He was standing in the bow of the large vessel several yards away, and as he stood he chatted with two gondoliers while they operated their long poles. Behind Romy's compartment a third gondolier guided the vessel.

When Larry whispered the only other sound was the swish of water lapping against the landing stages. At this time of year and night we had the canal to ourselves, and Romy kept changing position to look through porthole windows in the canvas awning.

"Those papers you sneaked a look at—were they important?"

"I think they showed the climax of the whole campaign of bomb outrages." I nodded my head in the direction of Josip Riz. "Tell you about them when we get to St. Mark's."

I peered out my own window. We were close to the Rialto Bridge now, and the magnificent *palazzi* of ancient Venice glided past, their color-washed walls like a stage setting in the moonlight, the ochers and greens and mellow reds glowing weirdly, seeming quite unreal. Above the palace walls ornate balustrades were silhouetted against the night sky.

For a brief moment I forgot about Josip Riz and our rendezvous at St. Mark's. Larry peered through his own window and absent-mindedly lit a cigarette.

"Where is Kardehay?" I asked.

"In the front gondola. There are six vessels in the convoy, and most of them are pretty big. Ours is the smallest. I'll say one thing for him—he knows how to finish a party. I'm going to remember this trip for a long time."

I stood up and stepped outside the canopy, straightening up to my full height, resting an arm on top of the canopy with my back to Romy. The advance guard of the convoy was already disappearing around a bend, and I saw that the other five vessels were all painted black, their only decoration multicolored canopies that enclosed the seating compartments. Our own gondola was a fancy gilt affair, which reminded me of a picture I had once seen of Cleopatra's barge. Above our own canopies gay flags embroidered with golden lions fluttered in the night breeze. I lit a cigarette, for the first time hearing the faint mutter of an engine behind me, and then Larry tapped my knee, so I crouched low and went inside again.

"When we get off at St. Mark's I'd like you to move along the landing stage to grab Kardehay. He's on the first boat, and we don't want to lose him." His lips hardly moved, and I cocked my head to catch what he was saying.

"He's accepted the invitation, so don't worry. But I'll run along and buttonhole him. What about . . . ?"

I gestured through my chest to where Josip was standing.

"He's my problem," replied Larry. "Three of the boys are waiting specially to meet me off this thing."

"And Ferrano?"

"He'll definitely attend the film show. He's much more cooperative than the local chap. In fact, he's waiting at St. Mark's now. I think I've sewed that one up."

"Don't get overconfident," I chaffed him.

"Less than five minutes to go now—and we are in the middle of the Grand Canal."

I began to feel restless, so I went outside again and leaned on the canopy. The sound of the approaching engine was much louder. When I looked over my shoulder a huge power barge was coming downstream behind us. The forepart of its deck was occupied by a long cabin, and there was no sign of life aboard. It appeared to be moving down the canal of its own volition. Ahead of the canopy Josip was still standing with his back to me while he talked.

"David!" Romy's voice.

I walked carefully to the stern, holding on to the side, and went into the compartment to sit beside her. In her voice there was a hint of strain.

"How much longer?"

"Five minutes, maybe less. Enjoying it?"

"I was, but now I'll be glad when we get there."

"Why?"

"I don't know—just a feeling. You've got it, too, haven't you?"

"I just want to get on with it, that's all. Larry has a small army stationed around St. Mark's—in no time at all you'll have plenty of company."

Her body stirred against mine, and she made no reply. In the circle of her porthole window I saw the nose of the power barge appear. It seemed to have moved closer to us. I was just getting up when her hand fell on my lap. Her voice was now harsh and alert.

"David, we've dropped behind the other gondolas."

"Be back in a minute. I'll just go and take a look."

As I emerged we passed under the large arch of the Rialto Bridge, so large that it accommodated three pedestrian walks and two lines of small shops. I made my way back to the second canopy and then stood upright.

The only sound now was the remorseless throb of the big

power barge, which was immensely long, its bulk effectively masking us from the left-hand side of the canal as it crept forward. On our right we were approaching the Rio Nuovo, a large side canal which came down from Santa Lucia Station. The power barge was alongside us, and still there seemed to be no one on board. Soon it crept forward no longer; it simply kept pace with us. Then a curtain over the cabin window was pulled half-aside, a face peered directly at me, and the curtain closed. Larry's voice called out quietly.

"Something wrong?"

I stood staring at the entrance to the Rio Nuovo, which had just come into view. From its mouth sailed a gondola, a gilt-painted gondola with golden lion flags mounted over its canopies, a gondola that in size and appearance duplicated our own vessel.

It was attended by a small fleet of one-man gondolas, which were unoccupied apart from the steersmen. As I bent down to warn Larry the one-man gondolas came up on the right-hand side. I stood up again, the revolver in my hand, watching Josip, who had turned around. Something heavy, a gondolier's pole, smashed down on my shoulder, and I dropped the gun over the side. Larry was halfway out of the compartment when a gondolier grabbed him from behind. Josip stood still, facing us, waiting. Swinging around, I grabbed the pole that had struck me, clasping it under my armpit. I pulled, suddenly pushed, and the man holding it lost balance and went over the edge, taking the pole with him.

The twin gilt-painted gondola was already sailing across our bows and heading downstream in the wake of the convoy. Our own gondola changed course and began to turn up inside the Rio Nuovo, surrounded by small black vessels. A gondolier aimed his pole. I saw it coming, seized the end, and pulled savagely. He came over the side of his gondola with the impetus and hit the water with a great splash. Holding the pole, I swung it around in a vicious arc, catching another attacker on the shoulder. He shrieked and dived headfirst overboard. The man I had taken the pole from was swimming toward me. I lowered the pole, aimed, and hit him in the face. The head went under. Larry was still struggling inside the compartment with his own gondolier, but now he was on top of the man, who lifted his head. Putting a hand under the chin, Larry smashed the head back on the boards. Josip moved forward.

Over my shoulder I saw another man about to jump on board from the power barge. I jabbed the rear end of the pole and caught him in the belly. He folded his body over the pole and crumpled into the canal. Our own vessel was continuing on course, and now I saw that it was heading in the direction of a huge water garage inside the Rio Nuovo. The garage occupied the ground-floor level, forming a man-made inlet from the canal. The doors were wide open. I felt a blow on the side and toppled forward, grabbing a strut for support. I hung there for a moment, half over the side, looking down the Grand Canal where the duplicate gondola was being poled by two men toward the stern of the convoy. Then it happened.

A muffled explosion swept the canal, and the gondola split in two sections. The two men disappeared, and debris rained skyward like a belching geyser. The vessel was beginning to sink rapidly as I recovered my balance and felt arms wrapping around me, locking my arms against my sides. I was kicking backward when the small gondola appeared in front of me. I saw the man hoist his pole and aim it like a battering ram. It sank into my stomach, and I jackknifed forward, still supported by the imprisoning arms. Ahead gaped the open maw of the water garage, and as we sailed inside a blow like an elephant's kick struck the back of my head. The dark cavern of garage filled with brilliant lights which rushed toward me and then went out as I went out.

44: ADRIATIC TAKE-OFF

Beyond the porthole the wooden triangle glided forward over the moonlit avenue. The bright light was there again. The vision went muzzy. It had to be a dream. Then my eyes cleared and I became aware of two things—the coolness of the glass against my cheek, the ache in my stomach.

The light was still there, a disclike glare at the far end of the avenue. I felt the vibrations of the engine and began to piece it together. I was aboard a power barge. The wooden triangle was the deck of the bows heading steadily along its course, and the stretch of water was not lit by the moon; it was lit by a searchlight that had been switched on to define our course.

I looked on each side of the avenue and saw there was moonlight also, fading moonlight, which showed the glassy calm of an open sea. When I turned my head I winced. I was inside a cabin, my body sprawled along a bunk, my head propped in the corner by the porthole. The cabin was in darkness, and I lay there in a daze, my wrists bound with rope, watching the light on the opposite wall grow brighter. The cabin was as bright as day when I heard footsteps and voices. The door opened, and Josip came in with another man. I was on my feet, held up on both sides, as the barge bumped gently into an obstacle and then stopped.

When we came out on deck the searchlight had been doused, but in its place men held lamps to show the way down the gangplank, which was railed and wide enough for a liner. Two more men were already carrying an unconscious Larry down the plank, and farther back stood Romy, wrists bound in front of her body, her face a mess of white skin and streaked dye. A man dressed in seaman's clothes held her arm, and she stood very still, watching them carry Larry to the shore. I went next.

The gangplank led over soft mud to a shore line fringed with shoulder-high reeds, so it was impossible to see inland. It was chilly, and a slight wind rustled the tall reeds, an eery sound, like whispering ghosts. A man with a lamp led the way along a path through the marshland, and Josip walked beside me, holding my arm. I was having a lot of trouble getting my legs to work, and twice I almost fell, but Josip's vicelike grip held me up. The ground was firmer now away from the sea, and we followed the moving lamp without really needing it any more because the moonlight showed the path.

"Where are we?" I asked.

"On the Adriatic."

His German pronunciation was so bad I only just grasped the word, but it gave me some rough idea of our probable location. It was still night, and the power barge was too slow to have crossed to Yugoslavia. So we must be somewhere on the desolate coast between Venice and Trieste at the head of the Adriatic, still in Italy. And I felt fairly sure we had traveled on the same power barge that had come alongside us in the Grand Canal. We walked for about ten minutes and then emerged into a clearing. The area was lit by hooded lamps mounted on collapsible tripods, and these showed the extraordinary scene clearly.

The clearing was no more than eighty feet in diameter and was surrounded with a dense wall of reeds. Even by moonlight, supplemented with the lamps, the ground had a hard sun-baked look, its surface crackled into hundreds of small irregular-shaped segments. Half a dozen men stood waiting, and one of them was Kardehay, dressed in his astrakhan coat but hatless. For once he wasn't smoking.

The Veetol stood in the center of the clearing on its four sets of wheels, two under its body and two more suspended from the wing tips at the end of slim metal legs. Waiting there in the glow of light it reminded me of an evil monstrous bird, a bird crouched and ready to attack. The impression was heightened by its vicious pointed nose. A metal ladder was propped against its body to give access to the interior, and I wondered how we were supposed to go up that with our hands tied.

Close by, Larry's inert body lay on the ground, and Josip left me to go over to him. Picking him up as though he were a feather pillow, Josip hoisted him over his huge back and took him up the ladder and inside the Veetol. He was coming down the ladder again when Romy arrived. This time Josip grinned and said something to one of the men in Serbo-Croatian. Picking her up in the same way he started to straighten up, but Romy arched herself above him, lifted her pinioned hands and brought them down like a club on the back of his neck. The blow hurt, and he put her down heavily on her feet. Then he raised the back of his hand. I took a step forward to kick him in the back of the knee and sprawled on the ground. Instead of the slap, I heard Kardehay's sharp word of command, and when I got to my knees Josip was carrying her into the machine. When he came back he undid the ropes around my wrists and shouted at me in his strange German.

"You go up under your own steam."

I nodded, and as he turned away I took three steps sideways toward the wall of reeds. I don't think anyone hit me. I simply knocked myself out again when I fell on the hard ground.

45: OVERFLIGHT

"Officially, you are now all dead, so don't think that anyone will come to look for you."

The voice was Kardehay's, sitting next to me. I opened my eyes again, saw the handcuffs around my wrists, and prepared to endure the vibrations of the Veetol in flight. The vibration was faint but constant, an oscillation that jarred my ragged nerve ends, and combined with the eternal hissing of the jets it demanded a major effort of will to think straight. Through a small window farther along the aircraft I saw that it was still night.

"Why officially dead?" I asked.

"Because the gondola you were all traveling aboard was blown to pieces. Just before we left Venice I heard that they were sending frogmen to search for the bodies."

"They'll think it funny when they don't find any."

"Not at all—they won't be too hopeful before they begin. You see, the current naturally flows out into the lagoon and to the Adriatic beyond."

I shifted position and made myself more uncomfortable. The small cabin had only improvised arrangements for passengers, and we all sat in canvas bucket seats with our backs to the fuselage and facing each other. Opposite me sat Romy, slumped in her place with her eyes half closed. I couldn't be sure whether she was listening to us or not. On my left Larry appeared to be unconscious, his head flopping sideways, and near to the door leading to the pilot's cabin Josip sat on a large wooden crate with an automatic weapon across his lap. I spoke to Kardehay without looking his way.

"The bomb explosion will cause a furore. You can't sit on that."

"I don't have to. There's an explanation for it, for the authorities, anyway. Earlier the police received a phone call reporting that Bruno Fleischmann had been seen near the Santa Lucia Station. The next thing that happens is a new bomb explosion. . . ."

"But not in Germany."

"We've recently had three outside Germany—in Switzerland. The impression has been created that the terrorist campaign is spreading, which at this stage is exactly what I need."

"You put a bomb on board that gondola—with two men inside?"

"This time, limpet mines were used—much more effective with a vessel. I'm afraid the two men were expendable. You see, the stakes now are rather enormous."

Asking questions was one way of keeping my mind above the surface. I asked another.

"Why pick us up?"

"Because the campaign is close to its climax, and I don't want any risk of a hitch. The best way to insure that is to cut off the head of the opposition—in this case yourself and Mr. Biggs."

"There'll be others. You'll trip yourself up somewhere along the line."

"But I have just told you—we are very close to the end of the line. After that there will be no more bomb outrages, so the trail will end in the middle of nowhere."

"This feels like the middle of nowhere. What country are we flying over now?"

"Let me explain." He stood up, took off his astrakhan coat, folded it, and put it in the seat beside Romy. When his back was turned as he sat down her eyes swiveled to it. "Now," he went on, "we left the Adriatic and flew due east, deep into Yugoslavia."

"The Italian radar will have picked you up."

"Possibly, but what will they have picked up? A brief tracking of an unknown aircraft flying east toward Belgrade. Then nothing. Once we were well beyond their range the pilot changed course to fly northwest over Yugoslavia and into Austria, where we are now."

"Over what area?"

"West of Vienna. Have you noticed anything happening?"

Just before he had spoken I had felt the angle of flight change, and now there was a sensation of losing height. I noticed that the muzzle of Josip's weapon pointed downward slightly. He looked at his watch, stood up to look out the window, and left the gun on his seat.

"We're going down," I said.

"That's right—a long way down for the last few minutes of flight. We fly along the Inn Valley below the mountain chain." He lit a cigar and smiled ironically. "This is the most dangerous part of our journey—if we die, we die in a flash. The best way to go, don't you think?"

I felt sure that Romy was listening now. I saw her lashes twitch briefly as I went on asking questions.

"At Innsbruck we turn south toward Italy, is that right?"

"You've worked it out well. Yes, and that's tricky, too. The pilot has to gain instant height to avoid the summit of Patscherkofel. Once beyond there, it is just a question of bringing her down at the Torre. Really, this is a most remarkable plane—I expect to make a fortune out of it." He corrected himself. "I am making a fortune out of it already —selling the machine to Egypt."

"Why Egypt?"

"Because the demand is there. The American and Russian governments have unofficially agreed not to flood the area with arms, so I supply their needs instead."

"Russia is supplying planes," I pointed out.

"Yes, on a small scale, but there are strings attached. The

Egyptians want a secret air force they can use as they like."

"You may have trouble getting your money."

"No. That's something I watch carefully. They pay me in gold—gold that comes from another Arab state. And the gold has to be on its way by air to Zurich before I supply the machines. Another advantage of dealing with a small state is that a smaller number of machines means more to them than they would to a big power."

"Where are you making the Veetols?"

"At a factory behind the Torre. The Brenner is in an excellent strategic position for my purpose." He paused. "You'll realize with my telling you all this that the future is rather bleak for all of you?"

I ignored his thrust and concentrated on obtaining as much information as possible.

"Why is the Brenner so convenient?"

"It's remote. So a secret factory is a feasible proposition. But the great thing is it helps delivery to Egypt. You see, David, the finished Veetols are flown one by one along this corridor we're passing over, then they fly over Yugoslavia to avoid the NATO radar. The final lap is risky but we've managed it so far. They cross Bulgaria and go down the Aegean before crossing the Mediterranean to land at desert airfields in Egypt."

"And you dare not manufacture openly?"

"No. You'll see why when we reach the Torre. We should be turning soon now."

Beyond the window there was a sea of frothy clouds, like the surface of some strange planet in the dying moonlight. At that moment we plunged into the sea, and the view vanished behind a wall of vapor. Kardehay stood up and went along to the pilot's cabin after a word with Josip. The huge Yugoslav sat down again and stared at the opposite side of the fuselage. Larry's head flopped on my shoulder, and his whisper could scarcely be heard above the hiss of the jets.

"I heard all that. Doesn't sound too healthy."

I put my hand over my mouth. "We'll have to wait till we reach the Torre."

"Is this the machine he's supplying Cairo with?"

"I'm sure it is. You missed something when you were carried unconscious aboard the Veetol."

"What's that?"

"The bomb-bay doors."

The mountain summit passed the window as we descended, too close for comfort, and then the endless snowbound slopes sheered past. I stood by the window next to Kardehay, and the Torre was a toy fortress far below. The Veetol continued its vertical fall, its rotating jets now pointed downward, controlling the fall. Farther along the aircraft Larry and Romy shared another window while Josip stood behind them. Everyone gazed downward, as though hypnotized by the phenomenon.

The Torre was much closer now, coming up to meet us, but our angle of fall was directed at a building I hadn't known existed. It lay behind the second hangar-like structure, and its roof was flat. As we drew closer, slowing down all the time, the flat roof began to slide open sideways, exposing a bar of light which steadily enlarged to reveal a huge empty chamber lit by green neon strips along the walls. I glanced along at Larry, and he looked back with an expressionless face.

Then we were moving down inside the walls, and the roar of the jets bouncing back off the cement floor was deafening. The Veetol landed gently, springily, and the motors were switched off. For a moment no one moved, still unaccustomed to the novel sense of stability. Kardehay came to life first and made his remark as he went forward to open the door.

"We'll have to hurry. This is the start of a very vital day."

His words emphasized something I had been thinking

about all during the flight from the Adriatic. It was already the day of the deadline, Friday, November 3. As we went down the steps of the mobile staircase armed men appeared at the foot. When I looked up I saw the power-operated roof shutting again, closing us off from the outside world.

46: WEAPON MAKER

Surrounded by guards, we walked up the concrete ramp and through the vast doorway from the shed we had landed inside. Beyond stretched a long concrete roadway, which was walled and roofed, so that it resembled a traffic tunnel. Overhead, green neon tubes illuminated it, and as we walked our feet thudded on the bare cement, echoing hollowly.

"This is the way the Veetols come on their way to Egypt," Kardehay explained.

We walked on in silence, and when I glanced at Romy I thought her face showed signs of strain. Larry looked around him with interest, his plump face betraying no emotion whatsoever. Then we reached the giant doors at the end of the tunnel. A guard pressed a switch, and the door slid aside with a purring noise. We stood staring without moving, and Kardehay watched us stare, a certain satisfaction in his smile.

We were looking inside the second hangar-like shed, which I had seen from the roof of its brother building close to the Torre. The walls were lined with Veetol bombers, squatting as though ready for take-off under the neon glow, an armory of warplanes and a sight to chill the blood. Romy shuddered, and Larry fingered his mustache.

Kardehay's tone of voice was matter-of-fact. "One strike by this force would wipe out Israel."

"Provided they didn't know they were coming," I said.

209

Kardehay said nothing and abruptly led the way down the center between the machines. The guards formed a file on each side, between us and the planes. When we reached the other end of the shed Kardehay had recovered his good humor and stood aside to let Romy pass through the doorway first. We walked out into the Alpine night.

Ahead lay the building I had looked down into through the ventilator fan. The trouble was I had looked down into the wrong building. As we crossed the snow I saw that the orange bulldozer was parked in a new position, and the bank of snow was intact. We entered the next building.

A dozen armed guards patrolled the interior of the factory, and at intervals men in white coats worked inside glass booths. I recognized Fritz Bauer at once and wondered what had happened to the police girl. As we passed the booths Kardehay pointed out their occupants.

"That's Arthur Riedel, from Regensburg, a leading German aircraft specialist . . . Theodor Bathe, from Münster, aerodynamics expert . . .

The roll call went on, the roll call of aeronautics men who the world thought had died in the bomb explosions. And the place was a hive of industry—men working at machine lathes, men calculating at drawing boards. . . .

"They are glad to work long hours," Kardehay explained. "They are naturally industrious men—leaders of their profession—and there is nothing else to do here."

"I'm surprised you get them to work at all," I said innocently.

"The hostages insure that. For each man we brought here we also brought an equivalent hostage—sometimes a daughter, or a wife, or a fiancée. You'll see. They are housed in this next section of the building. In the beginning I accommodated them in the Torre, but I found the technicians worked better if they knew their relatives were next door." He paused. "I didn't catch that, Mr. Biggs."

210

Larry looked at him and just shook his head, but I had heard the word he muttered under his breath. Bastard! I stood next to Kardehay while we surveyed the factory.

"What are they working on?" I asked. "The newcomers, I mean."

"The next generation of Veetol!" He smiled genially. "The mock-up is under that sheet over there."

"I don't quite follow that."

"To stay in business, you have to stay ahead. The new Veetol will be smaller and faster. Any nation equipped with the Veetol you traveled in would be wiped out when faced with an enemy equipped with Veetol Two, which at the moment is no more than that mock-up. That is why I need new top designers like Riedel and Bauer."

"Who designed the one we flew in?"

"The present model was based on plans stolen from the British and the Germans, with refinements added by designers kidnapped several years ago in the States. The men concerned were supposed to have died in an air crash in Utah, but we forced the plane to land, took off the team, took it up again, and crashed it. All a matter of organization."

"Where are they now?"

"I'm afraid they died later." Kardehay spoke quickly and said it was time we went up to his room in the Torre. There might be messages waiting for him.

We had been talking in the huge room with the plate-glass window for over half an hour. The window was now concealed behind a power-operated blind, and the four of us sat around a table. Only Kardehay and I had a drink in front of us. For the first time since I had known him, Larry had curtly refused the offer, and Romy hadn't answered at all. I had accepted my drink without thanks, because I knew the whisky would put new life into me.

"I'll drink with the devil, if necessary," I told him.

Drinking more whisky, I looked across at Kardehay and spoke again.

"You've admitted you planned the bomb outrages. What's the reason for them?"

"First, I needed these top aircraft men to work for me, and they wouldn't have because they prefer working in their own country, so I had to kidnap them. I would have done that in any case—the work is too secret for hired staff."

"Partly because now you pay no taxes?"

"That comes into it, of course. But there is a ban on selling arms to the Middle East, and I have other interests. Governments can exert pressure, if they know. . . . So, you see. . . . In any case, after leaving Hungary it became my life ambition to live in complete freedom, without interference from any government."

"Which is why you left the States?"

"Partly." Kardehay glanced at Larry. "Over there I supplied electronic equipment to the Defense Department, which involves fixed contracts, government auditors—that sort of life. Hungary is a completely state-controlled system, and once I left I decided I would be answerable to no one. I have only one life and I shall live it in my own way."

Near the door Josip sat on a couch, still clutching the Schmeisser machine pistol in his lap. Apart from our voices the only other sound was the low hum of the central heating system. Once, Romy looked bleakly across at Kardehay and then looked away. I went on talking.

"So no one really died in the bomb explosions, is that it?"

"You're wrong there, David. All the technicians were brought here, but the German political figures perished."

"Why?" I asked. "Why put bombs inside their homes at all?"

Kardehay preened himself. "It was a complicated plan, this terrorist campaign, with two objectives, one tactical and one strategic. The tactical objective was the capture of the technicians. Their disappearance had to be covered so that

212

there was no danger the international police forces would look for them. What better way than to make it seem they were dead? You're clear on that point now?"

"Quite clear."

"The strategic objective was more long-range, although we may expect to see the results shortly. It is no less than the expulsion of America's armed forces from Western Europe."

"Why? You don't like the Russian system."

"Do be patient, I'm coming to that. The main American force is now stationed in West Germany. I set out to make sure that the anti-American New People's Party will win the next election in Germany, because they will then call for the withdrawal of American troops. Once the rumor that the Central Intelligence Agency is behind the bomb outrages becomes public this will create a landslide vote for Langer."

"A little proof might help."

"Oh, that's all arranged—your friend Mr. Tarleton"—Kardehay turned to Larry—"or, rather, his body will help there."

"Why," I asked quickly, "do you want American troops out of Europe when you don't like the Russians?"

He looked surprised. "I thought you would have guessed that now. Once the American defense shield is withdrawn there will be a new armaments boom in Europe—every nation, especially Germany, will panic to increase its defense forces. I expect to make a hundred million riding on the wave of that boom."

"By supplying Veetols?"

"That's right—a revolutionary weapon because it needs no fixed airfield as a base and can operate from anywhere."

"And you've prepared for this by building shadow factories inside France, factories that will produce whole air fleets of Veetols?"

Kardehay looked surprised again and watched me

through half-closed eyes. "You're much better informed than I realized, David. What a good idea it was to take you out of circulation."

"Going back to the bomb outrages," I pressed, "there were bodies found inside the wrecked homes. . . ."

"There had to be, wouldn't you agree? Even with a huge bomb, relics of the inhabitants can often be found, so I provided them."

"How?"

Kardehay settled himself back in his chair. "The trouble with a plan like this is that no one appreciates the cleverness of it, so you provide me with an audience, an expendable audience. Let me explain. Whether it was a politician or an aircraft technician, the method was the same. He was invited to meet someone who would come to his house, and the invitation was phrased so that the hostage we needed—wife or daughter or fiancée—would also be present. I'm talking now of a case where the target was a technician. A little before the time of the appointment my men would arrive in a van with the time bomb. . . ." He paused. "Are you sure you wouldn't like a drink, Miss Silber?"

"No, thank you." She spoke without looking in his direction.

"They planted the bomb, preferably in the cellar, went into the house and kidnapped the two people concerned. It was really quite straightforward."

"But the relics of victims . . ."

"These were taken in with the bomb and deposited."

"Whose relics?"

"Don't be alarmed." He smiled sardonically. "We simply used people who were already dead, who had died naturally, and there's only one place to obtain them. . . ."

"From an undertaker," I said. "An Innsbruck undertaker named Egger?"

For the first time Kardehay looked disturbed, but his normal composure returned when I told him about Gustav Glincker, asking whether Glincker had worked for him.

"Yes. His main purpose was to organize that side of the system. He had the great advantage that he was dumb, so there was no danger of him letting anything slip in conversation. We installed a refrigerator inside his printing place—pathologists are so good these days that the relics had to be from men who were recently dead. Egger, the undertaker, provided what was needed, for generous payment, while Gustav kept what was needed until we were ready."

"So evidence of dead bodies was planted before all the bomb explosions?"

"No, and that helped to muddle the police, I'm sure. You see, we didn't need to plant any relics in the homes of the politicians. Our men simply planted the bombs and went away. In one case the politician's body survived the explosion intact."

"That was lucky," I commented grimly.

"Not at all—simply a matter of organization. We used *much smaller* bombs on the politicians. The big bombs were used in the houses of the technicians because they were being taken away and only relics would remain."

Romy reached for a box on the table, took out a cigarette, lit it, and puffed deeply. Kardehay looked at his watch, so I asked another question quickly.

"Manfred Klein, of Zurich, made the bombs, I suppose?"

"He made the time mechanisms, not quite the same thing. A watchmaker's craft is closely allied to the making of the mechanism controlling a time bomb."

"Why kill them all off—Klein, Glincker, and Egger?"

"Because, David, we are near the end of the campaign, and it's dangerous to leave loose ends lying about. It's also untidy—bad organization. Egger had no idea what he was supplying samples for, but he might have talked when Glincker was dead. And Klein became very nervous when a bomb exploded in his home town. Josip got the impression he might try to extract money from someone in return for information—to provide the funds for starting life elsewhere. And Josip"—Kardehay glanced toward the door— "is in charge of the bombs. We still have a large supply here in case we wish to repeat the campaign elsewhere later on."

"A large supply of high explosive?"

"Far too much, really. If you knew how much, you might not so happily have accepted my invitation up here the other day. You are now sitting over what is potentially the biggest bomb in Austria."

"We're in Italy," I pointed out.

"Here, we are, I agree, but along there—where my sleeping quarters are—is Austria. The border actually runs through the middle of the Torre, which is another reason why this place is so strategic."

"I don't quite follow that."

"Because the Torre is partly in Austria and partly in Italy neither government is sure who has jurisdiction over it. And"—he leaned forward—"because both governments hope I shall build industrial factories in their country they lean over backward not to offend me, which insures my privacy here."

"Why build a prison half in one country and half in another?"

"You're forgetting your history. This area once belonged to Austria, including well beyond Brennero. After the First World War the province was given to Italy, and the border drawn happened to go right through this prison."

"Very convenient for you." I helped myself to a fresh cigarette and gave one to Larry. "Why are all those Veetol bombers waiting in the shed? They're dead money here."

"Live money is on the way. They comprise the last consignment under the present contract. When those planes reach Cairo, Egypt will have air mastery over the Middle

216

East. I told you that I insist on cash in advance. At this moment a large delivery of gold bullion is flying toward Zurich. As soon as it arrives I start making delivery."

"All at once?"

"No. They will have to fly out singly over a period. It's not only a question of being seen on radar—we would send them one by one, anyway. In this area there is supposed to be a danger of avalanches."

"Avalanches? You mean on this mountain?"

"It hasn't happened for many years, but the Veetol does set up a lot of vibration. The last avalanche was twenty-five years ago, and it was supposed to have been started when a big Allied air fleet passed over on its way back from a bombing raid."

"It came down here?"

"No. It went down over that slope." He pointed toward the side window, where I had seen the watcher with the rifle. "And now, there are some questions I have to ask you and I am determined to have answers."

"I haven't quite finished. You said the bomb-outrage campaign was near its climax. What climax?"

He thought about it, looked at Josip, glanced at his watch, and started talking again.

"I don't suppose there's any harm in your knowing now. The terrorist bomb campaign will end with a bombshell—the death of the chairman of the New People's Party, Kurt Langer himself."

Larry looked up, and I saw Romy's fist tighten. The central heating system hummed away quietly. Kardehay took a case out of his pocket, extracted a cigar, and pretended to examine it, enjoying the effect of his announcement.

"What's the idea?" I asked.

"This evening Langer will make a speech. In that speech he will imply, so clearly that his meaning will be understood, that the Central Intelligence Agency is responsible

217

for the bomb outrages. He will then return home to die in the final bomb explosion. And Party Secretary Walther Loeb will take over control."

"The hard one," muttered Larry.

"The hard one," agreed Kardehay, "the man who will see that American troops *are* withdrawn from Germany."

"You said something about proof," I reminded Kardehay.

"Mr. Tarleton's body will be found in the grounds of Langer's house, only slightly damaged by the explosion, with his passport in his pocket."

"That may not prove a lot," said Larry heavily.

"He will also have a marked map of Langer's estate, a photoprint map on American copy paper, and nearby they will find the dead body of another American agent—Robert Stringer, the man Mr. Biggs brought to my party last night."

"You murdering bastard," said Larry quietly.

Kardehay ignored him. "And now, David, I have questions for you. They mainly concern Sven Heim."

"You wanted his miniaturized engine for the new Veetol?"

"That's right. When he refused to sell at the last minute I decided the only thing to do was to put into operation a new kidnapping plan. And it had come to the stage where I wanted him out of circulation for other reasons, too."

"What were they?"

"He had become suspicious of why I wanted the engine. I think he must have heard a rumor—he knows people in Beirut, I believe. He flew to Cairo and started making inquiries. Then he flew back via Beirut, and I think his contact there told him something about Egypt's Veetols. What I want to know is where Sven Heim is now."

"He's dead—you killed him."

"But you told me earlier in the evening at my party that Else Heim had survived."

"He sent her out of the house just before the bomb went up."

"In that case, why didn't my men find him inside the house when they arrived to take him away?"

"How should I know? Maybe he was hiding somewhere when he heard them come in. He must have heard them coming in order to send Else away."

He put his smoking cigar in an ash tray and watched me carefully; his voice was quite level.

"They went through the house looking for him, and the place was empty."

"They couldn't have looked for long, could they?" I asked. "From what I can gather, there isn't a lot of breathing space between the planting of the time bomb and its explosion."

"I'm afraid that's not good enough, not nearly good enough." His voice sharpened. "You see, I badly need Sven Heim's engine for the new generation of Vectols, and you're the only person who can tell me where he is. I'm convinced he's alive," he added.

"We all have our illusions," I said nastily.

His manner changed abruptly, his voice unpleasant now, as though I had caught him on the raw.

"And you seem to dwell under the illusion that I don't have the means to extract the information I want. I'm going to have to ask Josip to keep you company."

"We won't have anything to talk about," I assured him, "and I doubt if we'd understand each other. Your nonworking chauffeur speaks lousy German, you know."

Josip stood up, the Schmeisser held loosely across his body. Instead of watching me, he watched Kardehay, whose face was flushed with annoyance. But he spoke calmly as he picked up his cigar.

"It may help if I explain the psychological approach we shall use. One reason you are still alive is there are a lot more questions I want to ask—when you are in a more pliant mood. And if you aren't co-operative I may decide to leave Mr. Biggs's body near Tarleton's in Munich."

"Ask your questions now," I said. "Sven Heim's dead so far as I know, so you'd better accept the fact that your miniaturized jet engine isn't available any more."

"I have an idea that you're hoping to play for time—you were always a great talker, even during our negotiations."

"I'm just trying to save us all a lot of trouble."

Kardehay smoked the cigar and looked at me directly as I stared at him. An air of tension was rising in the room, and I was careful not to look at Romy or Larry. By the door Josip shuffled his large feet impatiently and then stopped shuffling when Kardehay frowned in his direction. When I stubbed out my cigarette and reached for a fresh one Kardehay's slim hand hauled the box away from me. He shook his head.

"I don't think I want to listen to your lawyer's tongue any longer. I'll explain the method, and then Josip can take over. It's simply a question of reducing your moral and physical resistance—bringing on such a state of fatigue that another part of you answers the questions, a part of you that is only concerned with your survival. The next step will be to bring all of you back up here."

He deliberately stopped speaking and waited. So I asked him about the next stage, hoping to prolong the conversation a little longer.

"What does happen when we come back here?"

"Then I ask the questions."

"And hope we'll answer them?"

"Oh, you'll answer them—because if you don't, the next stage will be a certain manipulation of Miss Silber's naked body."

He was close enough, and my gorge rose high enough. I leaned forward and hit him with my knuckled fist on the cheekbone. He rocked sideways and went over, taking the

220

chair with him. I was standing up when I heard Josip cock his weapon, but Kardehay shouted from the floor. When he stood up his face was cut over the bone, and he mopped the blood with his handkerchief, speaking rather breathlessly.

"That was really rather foolish of you. I simply wanted to make sure that you weren't indifferent to Miss Silber's fate. We'll proceed with the first stage right away. Josip, take them down."

47: BRUNO

It was a long way down into the bowels of the Torre, and I was surprised when Kardehay came with us. We were taken out of his living room and down a corridor. At the end we waited while Josip pressed a button. The metal concertina door slid back to reveal a large freight lift, and inside stood six men armed with Sten guns looped over their shoulders. They formed a circle around us as the door closed and the lift creaked its way down to the lowest rampart level, an area that had not been shown to us during the visit.

When the lift door opened we emerged into another huge cell block, similar to the one we had seen on the floor above. As we walked along it I noticed that all the cells were empty; it was a part of the Torre that was never used. Josip opened a door at the far end, and we entered a large stone chamber lit by orange lanterns. The room was laid out like a dining hall, and behind the tables three or four dozen men sat eating breakfast. Their tough weather-beaten faces reminded me of pictures I had seen of mercenaries, and along one wall hung a rack full of rifles and Sten guns. On the opposite wall Alpine winter clothing hung suspended from hooks, a pair of skis and poles leaned between each outfit. The equipment was beautifully maintained, and in the lantern light I saw the gleam of newly applied oil on the steel edges.

We left the dining room through another doorway and walked down a long stone passage lit by more orange lanterns. Kardehay led the way, his back protected by a guard, and I walked behind the guard. Romy came next in the column, and a guard separated her from Larry. As we passed a corridor going off to the right I saw through an open doorway the lights of the snowplow focused on the main gates leading into a building, the building where they worked on the Veetol mock-up.

Then we turned a corner and started to descend a spiral staircase. The lanterns threw shadows over the steps, and we had to walk carefully. As we went down, a smell of dank fungus began to pollute the air, and the ancient stone wall sweated oily moisture. I noticed that the mortisework between the stone blocks had crumbled in places. When we reached the bottom another stone passage faced us, and in the flickering lantern light I could see grilled cell doors at regular intervals. We were now well below the surface of the earth.

"Punishment cells," explained Kardehay as we waited for the tail end of the column. "Who knows how many despairing wretches lived and died down here?"

"Get on with it," I said abruptly.

"You'll wish you hadn't been in such a hurry when you reach your destination. But first there's someone I wanted you to meet. I'm sure you are going to find it an interesting experience."

We walked halfway along the gloomy passage, and then Kardehay stopped outside a cell. I looked inside the locked door. High up on the cell wall, far too high for a man to reach, hung an oil lamp. In the glow beneath it a man sat on an iron bedstead, his brown hair neatly brushed back over his head. He was tieless and wore a blue denim suit. As I

222

looked through the grille door he stared back at me, his face lean and bony like his long hands, his face expressionless.

"Bruno Fleischmann," said Kardehay.

"So it was you who took him out of Bremen?"

I moved farther down the passage away from the cell door so that Fleischmann couldn't hear me. Behind me, I felt Romy tread on my heels.

"Yes, that was the beginning of the whole operation."

"Why release a criminal lunatic?"

"It gave the police a fixed idea as to who was behind the outrages. You might say he acted as perfect camouflage for several months. I realized that as more and more bombs went off the suspicion would grow that there was an organization behind them, and this I wanted at a later stage—to point the finger of suspicion in a new direction, toward the Central Intelligence Agency. You see, most of the technicians were kidnapped in the early stages. At that period Fleischmann was a perfect scapegoat. The fact that he is an expert with high explosives helped to substantiate the smoke screen."

"You don't give a damn for anyone, do you?"

A guard lifted his Sten gun, and Kardehay smiled. "Don't worry about Fleischmann—he's probably better fed here than he was in Bremen. The strange thing is he seems to be perfectly harmless. Now, some accommodation for Miss Silber."

We waited while Josip produced a large ring of keys from his jacket pocket. He unlocked the cell door next to Fleischmann's, waited until she had walked inside, and then locked it again as I protested to Kardehay.

"For God's sake, man—if you have to lock her up, put her in a cell farther away from Fleischmann."

"I think this will do nicely. It will give you something to think about during the hours of waiting."

48: PIT

"Take a good look down, Martini—that's where you're going."

We had descended another spiral staircase, Larry and I alone with Josip and two guards. At the bottom we had entered a large stone-flagged chamber. It was cold as a tomb and empty except for a curious stone structure which rose three feet above the floor in the center of the chamber. It was a round structure, hollow inside, measuring about five feet in diameter. As he spoke, Josip prodded me with the muzzle of the Sten.

Resting my hands on the cold rim, I peered over the edge and clenched my teeth. I was looking down inside a vertical chimney, and I saw the faraway bottom where a lantern flickered dimly. At a rough guess I estimated the drop at thirty feet. No one could possibly survive such a fall. Although vertical, the chimney was not a perfect cylinder; it appeared to narrow as it went down, although that might be a trick of light. I felt a movement behind me, and Larry shouted, but my reaction was too late as Josip grabbed my arms from behind. His voice warned me.

"Keep still, Martini. We shall lower you down—unless you resist. Then the guard will shoot."

I looked sideways and saw a Sten gun aimed at me. The other guard covered Larry. Behind me Josip dropped a loop of rope over my head, fed it under my armpits, and pulled it tight.

"Climb over the edge," he ordered.

I hesitated, wondering whether I was going to be shot as I balanced on the rim, but if I stayed there I was going to be shot anyway. So I eased my legs over the top and sat on the brink, keeping both hands on the rim to preserve my balance. I glanced at Larry. He watched grimly, his face as moist as the staircase walls. Then Josip punched me in the back, and I went over.

He let the rope go slack, and I went down ten feet in a shock of horror, thinking he had let the rope go altogether. Then it jerked tight under my arms and nearly tore my body off my shoulders. For a moment I expected to be ill. I hung dangling over the sheer drop, folding my arms to stop the rope slipping up over them. My feet flopped helplessly in space, and only the enormous strength of Josip's grip was saving me from the death plunge. He held me there for half a minute, and I guessed he was recovering his strength from the jerk his body had taken when he broke my fall. Then I began to go down again, my heart thumping with the effort of breathing against the vicelike grip of the rope. The flickering light of the lantern rose to meet me slowly, and I began to think I had miscalculated the depth badly. I also began to prepare for the muscular reaction I felt sure I was going to need—letting my legs relax and twisting my hands so that the palms faced outward. As the lantern came closer I had the strong impression that the chimney was closing in on me, and when the light was strong enough I saw that I was right. The base of the chimney was about four feet in diameter. As the light came up to meet me a strong musty smell filled my nostrils, and I saw fungi growing on the slimy circular wall. I was about ten feet from the lantern when it happened, as I expected. Josip let go of his end of the rope, and I crashed down the final drop, legs still relaxed, missing the lantern by inches, hands flying out to hit the wall first— to protect my face and head. Then I lay there on my knees, looking up.

The mouth of the chimney was vaguely illuminated by the oil lamps in the chamber, and the disc of light seemed as far away as the stars. Then the yellow disc was broken by a head leaning into it, and Josip's voice echoed eerily down to me like the voice of a disembodied soul.

"Comfortable, Martini?"

"You twisted my bloody ankle with that drop."

His laughter was a disjointed rumble, and then the disc cleared as he withdrew his head. I scrambled to my feet and found I was intact. No twisted ankle, no broken bones. But my knees were bruised, my hands grazed. Reaching out my hands I measured the diameter. Yes, four feet. About. I had expected the base to be earth, but it was stone-paved. I had just completed my check when I looked up and saw the disc of light half-obscured by a bulky shape masking the light on one side of the chimney. They were lowering Larry. If they dropped him he would flatten me like a sledge hammer.

He seemed to come down even more slowly than my own descent, and I watched him come as I stood with back flat against the wall, the lantern shielded behind my legs. At each stage I tried to gauge how far down he had come, but it was difficult because now his body was obscuring most of the light. When I judged that he would be only about fifteen feet above me I shouted as loud as I could, hoping my voice would carry up to Josip.

"Watch it, Larry, when you're much lower he'll let go suddenly."

I may have fooled Josip into thinking that Larry was much higher up the chimney, but Larry's feet were within three feet of the floor when the rope was released, its end slashing my face and then withdrawing up the chimney. Larry fell heavily but stayed on his feet and grunted.

"Make out he hurt you," I whispered.

Larry sank into a sitting position and began groaning, moving himself as though in agony. I shifted so the lantern shone on him. I was looking up the hole now, and suddenly my blood chilled. The barrel of a Sten was pointing downward as Josip's head appeared, his voice distant and harsh.

"Here it comes—the full magazine."

We froze and waited. The sweat from my hand mingled with the slime on the wall. The silhouette against the disc of light remained very still, and the world was more silent than I had ever known it. Behind my jacket my heartbeats thumped, and Larry's breathing was strangely hoarse. Then Josip's voice came down to us, a weird echo.

"Not now, but next time it may be different."

The disc of light reappeared emptily, but still we didn't move. I strained my ears to hear any sound that might indicate they had left the chamber, but the silence was unbroken. I told Larry to keep quiet and counted up to six hundred. Ten minutes. As far as I could hope that indicated they had left the chamber, otherwise our silence and their own curiosity should have tempted someone to peer down the chimney.

"I think they've gone," I whispered.

"God, I'm stiff. I can hardly move."

I helped him up, and he stood against the wall, working the cramps out of his muscles. My own body was stiff with tension, and for several minutes more we said nothing. Larry began feeling around the wall. When he had completed his circuit around me he spoke softly and grimly.

"No way out, pal."

"Only up."

"You'd never make it."

"I'm not so sure. It means going up the center of the chimney in a crouch—bottom against one side, hands against the other, feet splayed, everything holding on. Bottom, feet, hands, shoulders—the lot. Like a cork pushing itself out of the neck of a bottle. I once saw an acrobat in a circus pull a similar trick."

"But this bottle gradually gets wider, so about two-thirds of the way up, if you ever get that far, you run out of body to jam yourself in. Then you just come all the way down again."

"We'll have to risk that."

"Forget it—it was a brave thought."

We were just able to stand in the pit without leaning on each other. When I asked him, he leaned flat against the wall, and I bent down to adjust the lamp wick, which was beginning to smell, wondering how they'd got it down here, and then I saw the large ring bolted to the canopy. The oil smell was beginning to foul the bottom of the pit.

"What do you think this place was in the old days?" asked Larry.

"Punishment pit—their idea of solitary confinement. We've progressed in some ways, I suppose." I reached out to check the diameter. "I still think I can make it—even allowing for a wider hole higher up."

We both looked up, and I thought about it carefully. Now I thought the diameter at the top might be less than five feet, a few inches less. Yes, there was a chance. If I had the muscle power. If I had the luck. I said again that I might just manage it.

"You'll get high enough to break your neck when you come down. Mine, too," he added. "Forget about my neck," he said a moment later. "But remember your own."

"It's worth a try. Don't look so grim about it."

"I was thinking about Josip. I've got just one idea at the moment—to kill Josip with my bare hands."

I estimated that I was halfway up now, my body athwart the chimney, like a man crouched on his haunches on the floor, but the floor wasn't there.

I was wriggling my way up inch by inch, doing two things at once—levering up my crouched body and trying to make sure it stayed stuffed across the chimney. The skin was coming off my hands now, but I hardly noticed this, since my brain could only feel the incredible strain along my back. Pressing the flat of my hands into the stone like suckers, I held them there and eased my bottom a few inches higher.

Holding it there, I moved the pressure against it and pushed one hand up a few inches, then followed it with the other. I still sloped downward a fraction, my bottom higher than my shoulders, because the greatest danger was that I would start sliding feet first, and once that movement began I would never arrest it.

My eyes never left the wall, never looked down, although vaguely I was aware that the lantern glow was a long way below me. Taking a deep, careful breath, I started the same maneuver again, for the thousandth time. Up with the stern a few inches—*not too far,* otherwise I would upset the balance the other way, end up plunging headfirst down into the pit. Now the hands. Left one first, hard against the stone and up. Hold it! Check the position of the back. Raise the right one, keeping up the pressure on the left. Steady! Back to square one. Pause for a breather. I was thankful that ever since I had started the ascent Larry had not said one word, not even a word of encouragement. He just let me get on with it. I guessed his nerves were close to breaking point. It's always worse for the one who watches. The thought made me want to giggle. I checked the impulse quickly. Now, again—up with the stern . . .

I was much higher up, so the drop below was much greater, when I found I had two other things to worry about. The chimney hole was now wider—I could *feel* that it was wider, feel it because my body was a little less crouched, a little farther extended. And the air was fresher. I welcomed that because it gave me the illusion of new-found energy. The second thing I worried about was the pain in my back, which had now lost its sharpness, deteriorating into an aching daze. The trouble was I now found it more difficult to judge the angle of my back, the height of my bottom above the shoulder level. The dazed effect was distorting my judgment. This worried me more than anything and made me move up a shorter distance over each

229

lap than before, which slowed down progress when I knew my reserves were running out.

Try it again, same maneuver. Risk it, hoist the back a shade higher. That's it. Now the hands again. Left up, check position, right up . . . It was becoming a reflex action, and there was danger in that, the danger of a moment's inattention which would be my last. There was too bloody much to think about. I stayed still for a moment, stuck inside the chimney, swearing softly to myself, feeling sure that Larry would hear something, would feel compelled to call up, but he kept his mouth shut. He must have practically bitten his tongue clean through. No point in hanging about in midair . . . The giggle started to come again, so I wiped the thought out of my mind and began a fresh wave of hoisting. . . .

I was pretty close to the top now. The width I had to span told me that. The strong light told me it as well. And *I knew I wasn't going to make it.* I was fully stretched, out as far as I could go without the whole complicated muscular mechanism collapsing into a pile of death at the pit base. And I still had a little way to go. I hadn't looked, but I felt sure of it. Keeping my head down was an essential key to keeping my body rigid across the chimney. Long ago I had become soft pulp, pulp beaten with iron hammers. At times I no longer cared whether I got there or not, but some mechanical instinct urged me to repeat the movements, so I repeated them. Once more . . .

Then I did lift my head a fraction, and saw the rim just above me. I froze, locking everything rigid, and waited. I waited to draw out of myself some hidden last reserve. There had to be one. The last maneuver would be the most dangerous of all. It might well be my last maneuver, my last attempted maneuver. I may have stayed still a minute, but all sense of time eluded me now. The thought that I was waiting because I wanted to put off the last gamble spurred me into action. I hoisted myself higher and then fumbled the fingers of my right hand over the rim, feeling the enormous strain grow in my left wrist. I was sure it must be a hallucination when my fingers felt the iron ring stapled into the outer side of the funnel. Then I grasped it, wrapping my hand around inside the metal, let go with my left hand and whipped it up over the rim. It scrabbled over the stone and began to come over the top. I would have gone down but for the iron ring. I managed to hang on, to haul myself higher, my shoulders well above the rim, until I levered my body forward and fell on the stone floor.

I lay there for ages before I wondered whether the chamber was empty, but it had to be empty or else they would have come to me by now. Then my brain began to function again. The iron ring—I should have realized its purpose as soon as I felt it. The rope that had lowered us into the pit had been inserted through it after I had gone over the top and Josip had enjoyed his joke. It had probably been there for years—perhaps since the time when the pit had been originally used. They had needed some method to lower people into it.

When I stood up I saw that the door was closed. It was also locked, and when I peered through the small grille window all I could see were the lower steps of the spiral staircase. The rope they had used hung from a hook on the wall. I took it down, looped one end through the iron staple, and pushed it down over the edge, feeding more rope down as I called out.

"Larry, the rope's coming down."

"Okay."

His reply might have come from the center of the earth. I went on feeding down rope until I felt a tug. Then I fed out a few more feet and waited, listening for any sounds of someone coming down the staircase. Larry's voice spiraled up to me.

"Rope fixed. Can you make it?"

I stood well back from the chimney mouth and began

hauling, being careful not to trip over the growing coil of used rope behind me. Sooner than I expected, his head appeared above the rim, then his hands grasping over the stonework. This was the difficult part—I couldn't let go, I couldn't help him, and his body was plumper than mine. I waited with anxiety as he fought to get a leg over the top. Once he slipped and had to start all over again. Then he managed to hoist his right leg over and simply fell beyond the chimney onto the floor. I let go and went to unfasten the loop around his chest. He managed to sit up with his back against the round of stone and then he stayed there, temporarily exhausted.

"Good job . . . David."

"Don't talk—get your wind back. We're locked in here anyway."

"Don't mind me . . . mind door."

He must have been clairvoyant, because when I listened at the grille someone was coming, one pair of steps, I thought—heavy steps which moved ponderously. I heard the key rattle in the lock as I pressed myself against the wall on the opening side of the door, and it opened with a rush, the key ring still dangling in the lock. Josip walked in confidently, the Sten gun held loosely by his side, and then saw Larry. At that moment I bent down and tore the gun out of his hand.

He reacted quickly for such a big man, clenching his hands together, lifting them, and bringing them down over my exposed neck as I stood half-crouched. To avoid the clubbing blow, I lunged straight in at him, and instead of hitting my neck he chopped me on the back, but it still winded me. I dropped the gun and fell on my knees, seeing a blurred vision of him stepping back from me. He lifted his right foot and drove the boot straight at my head. Hate killed fatigue and gave me the reflex to jerk sideways, still on my knees. As the foot came forward I grabbed it, twist-

232

ing the boot savagely and pushed. He had expected me to pull, so I caught him off balance, but he slapped a hand against the wall and steadied himself, still on his feet, as strong as an ox. I knew I had to take him myself, because Larry couldn't take a kitten at the moment.

While he recovered his balance I hauled myself up on my feet, appalled to find I could hardly stay on them. I had my back to the stone wall now, only vaguely aware of what I was doing. Even more vaguely I saw him coming for me, and I hadn't the reflex left to move out of his way, so instead I tried to butt him in the stomach. Something went wrong, and I felt the huge hands closing quickly around my neck. Instinctively I went limp, as though I was done for. His grip began to tighten as I kept myself limp, summoning up the energy in my leg. I hit him feebly in the side and then drove my knee hard up into his groin. Through the mists I heard a grunt, then his hands relaxed, left my neck, and he stooped forward, still close to me. Using the wall for leverage, I lifted my knee again, into his stomach this time, and heaved. He lost his balance and began to stumble backward, still on his feet, doubling up over his middle, shaking his head from side to side.

I leaned against the wall, thinking about the gun on the floor, powerless for the moment to pick it up. Josip was still on his feet, but the effort to keep his balance took him farther into the center of the room, and his lower legs came up against the chimney face, which acted as a trip wire. Still half-crouched, he fell over backward and began to go down the chimney. His broad span and the reflex of fear saved him. Shooting his arms out sideways he clamped his hands down over the rim and hung in mid-air, his feet still on the floor. Then he began to lever himself upright so that he would automatically slither back onto the floor. I was still half-dizzy when Larry climbed to his knees, grabbed Josip's nearest leg, and lifted, thrusting the leg away from him.

233

Josip screamed, lost his grip with one hand, his own weight tearing the other loose. Then he disappeared, traveling down headfirst with a frightful wail.

49: TIME BOMB

I led the way up the spiral staircase armed with Josip's Sten gun, and Larry followed behind with the key ring. At the top I paused. The short passage was empty, and I heard nothing beyond it. Around the next corner led into the corridor of cells, so as I reached it I listened carefully again. Peering around the corner I saw the guard.

I thought he had probably come down with Josip and was waiting here for the Yugoslav's return. He stood with his back to me outside one of the cells, and across his back was looped a Sten gun. I crept very quietly toward him, and he seemed to be dreaming while he smoked his cigarette.

A few yards from him, I called out quietly. He turned, startled, saw the gun, took a step sideways, and raised his hands. Larry slipped past me to relieve him of the weapon, and a bony hand shot out from between the grille bars. The hand grasped the Sten and literally tore it off the guard's shoulder, ripping the cord and withdrawing the gun inside the cell. Bruno.

The guard looked terrified, and I knew he was waiting for the bullets to hit him. Walking along until I could just see inside, I found Bruno sitting on his bed. The Sten was propped harmlessly against the wall. He nodded to me as I took the guard by the arm and led him back to where Larry was releasing Romy.

"Josip's somewhere along there," she whispered.

"It's all right. He won't worry us."

As the guard walked into the cell I used the butt of the Sten gun to knock him out. We locked the cell again and left him sprawled across the floor.

234

"Bruno's got a gun, although he's still locked in," I warned Romy, "and the way out is past his cell. I'll go first, then you, then Larry."

Bruno nodded again as I walked slowly past his bars. Romy began to walk past, and then I heard Bruno's shout. She froze, and when I walked back Bruno was standing up, the gun in his hands, pointed at Romy.

"Let me out. I know you have the keys—I heard you let her out. If you don't, I'll fire." His voice changed. "You don't have to worry—I've nothing against you people. It's the others. . . ."

He stopped and shoved the muzzle at Romy, so I told Larry to unlock the door. Romy put her hand to her mouth quickly and then recovered her composure. When Bruno emerged he nodded again and told us to go in front of him. He repeated that we had nothing to worry about. I looked at him closely and his manner seemed perfectly normal, but I wasn't happy as we went along the corridor and started to climb the second spiral staircase, myself in the lead, Romy and Larry behind me, while Bruno brought up the rear.

At the top of the staircase I paused. We were approaching the corridor that led to the dining room where the guards had eaten their meal. No sound came from beyond the corner. Creeping along the short passage, I paused again. There were still lights on inside the distant doorway, but the part of the room I could see was empty. Quietly, I began to walk toward the doorway, my gun aimed at the archway of light.

I remembered that midway along the corridor another passage ran off to the side, a passage that emerged outside the Torre close to the first hangar-like building, but I wanted to supply Larry with a weapon. I also wondered what time it was. Our watches had been taken while I lay unconscious in the Veetol, but I estimated that it was early morning, probably close to daybreak. When I looked down the side passage it was deserted, and the door at the end was shut. Leading them inside the passage, I whispered across Romy's shoulder to Larry.

"See if that door is locked—if it is, try to find a key on that ring that fits."

"I can't—Bruno took the keys from me coming up the spiral."

I looked at Bruno. "You go then."

To my relief, he went past us to the end of the passage and then came running back, his voice urgent.

"Someone's coming."

And as he spoke we heard the rattle of a key being pushed into the outer door. Running to the corner, I turned left and waited. Romy and Larry moved past me as Bruno took up his ambush position behind the opposite corner.

The door opened, footsteps shuffled, and the door closed and was locked again from the inside. I glanced back over my shoulder and saw Larry watching the doorway behind us. In this position we stood a good chance of being caught between two fires. The footsteps echoed again, coming along toward us. Behind the corner wall Bruno stood crouched, holding the Sten gun in front of his body like a bayonet. I tried to separate the footsteps, but they were a muddle. More than two men, I felt sure. Three or possibly four. A man came around the corner, walking toward the guardroom. Fritz Bauer.

He saw me immediately and continued walking without breaking step. Behind him followed Arthur Riedel. He almost gave us away, but I nodded my head savagely and he went on past us. The first guard came quickly after him and stopped dead when he saw my gun. His own Sten was looped over his shoulder. As the second guard appeared Bruno sprang forward, jabbing the gun muzzle into his stomach with tremendous force. The guard gasped, choked, gurgled, doubled up. He was still bent over when Bruno brought his gun butt down on the man's exposed head. I heard the crack as the first guard raised his hands. Before I

236

could react, Bruno shifted his grip on the Sten and smashed the guard's head with the edge of the butt. I bent down and pulled the Sten off the crumpled guard, giving the weapon to Larry.

Fritz Bauer had come back along the corridor and now he bent down and took something out of the first guard's side pocket. He looked up at me.

"Key to the outer door."

"Get moving," snapped Bruno. "Through the guard-room."

Bauer stood up, looking at Bruno. "Who's this?"

"Another prisoner," I said shortly, but by this time Riedel had joined us. He stared at Bruno and his mouth tightened.

"He's helped us so far," I said quickly. "We'll need every bit of help we can muster to get out of here."

"I think the guardroom's empty," whispered Larry. "There were more Stens on the wall. . . ."

"I can use one," Bauer said quickly, but I grabbed his arm to hold him back.

From where I stood now I could see farther inside the dining room, and there were at least two Stens hanging on the wall. There didn't appear to be anyone inside, but I couldn't imagine them leaving the place without any protection. Motioning to the others to stay inside the corridor, I moved forward cautiously. Bruno followed at my heels.

I was standing in the entrance now, next to the half-open door, and I could see over a dozen weapons slung on the wall. Close by, canvas satchels were hanging from other hooks. The room seemed quite deserted, and then I heard the scrape of a shoe behind the door. Stepping back against the far wall, I took a deep breath and then hurled my body against the door, following through with the impetus. The door smashed back, trapping the man behind it. I heard a groan of surprise and pain, then a clatter as the Sten hit the stone floor. Behind me Bruno ran past and around the end of the door. Struggling hands came out from behind the

237

door, and Bruno grabbed the hands with his own, the gun tucked under his arm. As I pulled my weight off the door the guard emerged, hauled forward by Bruno, who then twisted his body suddenly, jerking the man around in a wild arc, suddenly letting go. The guard was thrown several feet before he tripped over a bench and sprawled on his face. He tried to get up as Bruno's gun butt flailed down twice. He was killing the guards one by one.

"For God's sake, man . . ."

I stopped as he swung around, pointing the gun directly at me for a moment, then turning to stare along the room to the door leading into the Torre. The others ran into the room, and we headed for the weapon rack.

I was filling my pockets with spare magazines when Romy took down a Sten from its hook.

"Ever used one before?" I asked.

In reply she loaded a magazine into it and cocked the weapon. "Only a six-hour course," she said, "but these things are easy to use. You just aim and fire." Adjusting it to single-shot fire, she collected spare magazines from my satchel. Farther along the wall, Bauer was telling Riedel how to use his weapon, and behind a table Larry was trying to watch both entrances at once. I opened the flaps of the other satchels, and the last one contained lethal equipment of a different kind—hand grenades. I slung the whole satchel-load over my shoulder, feeling Romy's shoulder touch mine.

"Bruno's behaving oddly."

I turned around. He was moving slowly in a crouch, the gun held at stomach level, backing away from us toward the inner door, sweeping the muzzle vaguely across the room. For one horrible second I thought he was going to empty the magazine. By the table Larry stood very still, his gun covering Bruno now. Bauer moved close to me, and I kept my voice down.

"You said you've got the key to the outer door . . . ?"

238

"Yes. It's the only way out—Riedel says so. We've got to get the women out of the hangar."

"We've got to do a lot of things—and quickly."

I was watching Bruno. Casually, Romy's gun turned until it also faced Bruno, who was still retreating backward, still sweeping the Sten in its menacing arc.

"Your friend's pretty savage," Bauer observed quietly. "I heard the guard's skull split back in the corridor."

"He was in the Bremen asylum."

Riedel was standing with his back pressed against the wall, the Sten held clumsily across him, the muzzle aimed at the roof. He stood as though transfixed, unable to take his eyes off Bruno. No one dared move, because no one was sure what Bruno was going to do. The scene was taking on a macabre touch—the crouched man moving backward toward his own destruction, threatening us with his weapon if we attempted to interfere. At any second I expected the door behind him to open, but he moved closer and closer and it stayed closed. Then he reached it, held the gun in one hand, opened the door with the other, and vanished. At that moment Riedel found his voice, and as the door closed he shrieked his warning.

"He's heading for the explosives store—he knows where it is—he once fixed a defective mechanism for them. He'll blow us all up."

"Where is it?"

I ran along the room and Riedel followed me, but he let me go through first. Running into the huge cell block, I saw Bruno near the far end, running at incredible speed, the gun held loosely in his hand. I ran after him, hearing Riedel's panting voice behind me.

"It's all right, it's all right! I must have been mad—he can't get inside. They keep it locked. . . ."

"He's got the keys. Where's he gone now?"

"Door on the left—down there."

At the end of the block, close to the lift gate, a small pas-

239

sage ended at a metal door. I opened it, caught a glimpse, and jumped aside, pushing Riedel out of the way with my arm.

In the brief glimpse I had seen Bruno standing in front of a large steel door. The door was open, and he stood facing me, his gun aimed. As we jumped back a fusillade of bullets came down the passage and then cut off. When I looked again the steel door was closed.

"Does it lock from the inside?" I asked Riedel.

"There's a bolt. You'll never get in now. . . ." He was almost incoherent with fear. "I had to go inside myself once to . . ."

"Come on—we must get back."

"The amount of explosive stored . . ."

"Come on."

We were halfway back along the hall when I heard something like the clang of a door high up in the cell block. I was hoisting my Sten as a guard appeared on the catwalk over our heads. A second before I squeezed the trigger a burst of fire echoed through the desolate hall, and the guard dropped his weapon. A moment later he fell over the rail and landed with a dull thud. In the open doorway leading to the dining room Romy lowered the muzzle and waited. She had even remembered to switch to continuous fire.

"Thanks," I told her. "I gather you passed that course."

"The others have gone out to the building."

"We *must* hurry," begged Riedel. "All that explosive . . ."

"We are hurrying."

We rushed through the dining room and along the corridor, avoiding the first guard's body, and then ran down the passage. The outer door was open, and Bauer had left the key in the lock. While Riedel waited in a fever of impatience I transferred the key to the outside, turned it, and then broke off the end with my gun butt. Riedel burst out.

"He may blow the place sky-high."

"There'll be a small army of guards inside the Torre, and I'll be surprised if those shots weren't heard."

It was chilly in the open, but dawn was already on the way. From behind the mountain a faint glow of pale light was creeping over the white landscape as we hurried through the snow. It was soft fresh snow.

"When did this lot come down?" I asked Riedel.

"During the past hour. It snowed very heavily—like a blizzard—and then stopped just before we came over here."

"Where were they taking you?"

We were moving rapidly across the snow now, our feet sinking in deeply, and the early light was weird and somehow disturbing. Romy shivered, pulling up her coat collar.

"They were taking us to see Kardehay," said Riedel.

"That means they'll soon wonder what's happened to you. We can expect trouble. Is there a tap to that thing?"

I pointed toward a huge oil-storage tank that lay half-concealed inside a giant alcove cut out of the mountain. It stood at the top of a steep slope close to the exit from the Torre.

"Yes, it's behind a flap painted red. You just lift the flap. . . ."

"Wait for me outside the building."

In spite of Riedel's protests I ran back and started up the slope, the satchel of grenades banging against my side. The flap stood about four feet above the ground, and when I lifted it the metal sheet slid back inside the top of the compartment, revealing a huge copper tap. I turned it full on and left gallons of oil gushing over the crest of the slope. When I reached the door where Riedel waited with Romy I was out of breath. Riedel was almost going mad with anxiety.

"Any moment now . . ." he warned me.

"We still mustn't forget the guards. If we get caught now, we'll go up anyway. What's happening inside?"

We found a strange atmosphere inside the living quarters,

which were constructed on three levels inside the building, rather like a block of flats without windows. I imagined the absence of windows was to prevent signaling at night. Several women, their hair awry, hastily dressed, were coming down a staircase, carrying things in their hands. Bauer appeared at the top and ran down the steps past them to reach me.

"This is going to take some time, you know—they have to get dressed. I've warned them. . . ."

"Tell them just to pile clothes on—anything to keep out the cold. And boots—don't forget that. They must be ready in five minutes. No hanging about to collect personal things. How many are there?"

"Ten of them, including Anna, the police girl who came with me. She's trying to hurry them."

"Where's Larry?"

"Along there waiting by the door into the factory. There are six guards inside having breakfast. No," he forestalled me, "there's not much danger of them hearing this commotion—the wall in between is soundproofed to keep out the noise of the machines."

"Tell them to hurry. Riedel . . ."

But Riedel had caught sight of his wife at the top of the staircase and he ran up to meet her, the Sten gun held stiffly and pointed downward, as though he were afraid it might fire all by itself. It was getting to be a muddle. God knew how we'd get this lot away. I turned to Romy.

"Watch that door—leave it open a fraction so you can see. I'm worried about the guards inside the Torre. If you see them coming out, fire a burst to warn me."

Then I ran toward the interior of the shed, seeing a woman and wondering where I had seen her before. Probably in a newspaper. I found Larry waiting outside the heavy door that led into the factory section. He gestured toward the window with his Sten.

242

"You can see them eating over there. Bauer says the whole lot are around the table."

I looked through the small square window, and beyond the profile of a machine some distance away I counted six heads. When I checked the door it had no locking device on our side. Looking through the window again, I saw that one man was standing up now, smoking a cigarette as though he had finished breakfast.

"We're going to have to put that lot out of action," I told Larry. "Any minute now and some of them will be wandering along here."

He nodded as I opened the door carefully. We had come through this same doorway earlier after landing in the Veetol. And I remembered that it had been opened without making a sound. Now I hoped and prayed for a repeat performance. I waited until Larry had slipped through the gap and then I followed him, closing the door behind me. It closed with a loud sharp click—a click we hadn't heard last time because we had been on the other side when it shut. Larry pointed to the left, stooped low, and disappeared behind some machinery. I moved over to the right, listening for a reaction from the table, hearing only silence.

Then I knew something was wrong because they had been talking when we came in. A minute later when I peered between two machines everything appeared to be normal. They were sitting at the table and they were talking. Five men. There had been six before. From that moment only my eyes moved. I scanned the floor below girder level inch by inch, but nothing moved. The precious minutes ticked past; the men at the table talked on. Was it imagination or was there an element of falsity in their conversation, even though I couldn't hear what they were saying? Then something did move—Larry's body flitted past between two machines as he moved in closer to the table. And a second later, out of the corner of my eye I saw a further movement, high up among the girders.

The sixth man stood on an inspection platform next to a huge overhead crane which slid along the girder. I was shielded from him by the tall machine I crouched next to, but I realized that Larry had exposed himself by moving to a new position. The figure in the girders lifted his Sten slowly and squinted down the barrel. I fired. One long burst. He fell over backward, and then his body hung fixed at a grotesque angle, trapped between the meeting point of two girders. I heard a rattle of gunfire and saw the table was empty. Larry's voice called out quickly.

"Two down—three more behind big red . . ."

His voice broke off as a Sten stuttered, and I saw where they were. Diving my hand inside the satchel, I waited until the gun had stopped and then shouted.

"Head down—*keep* it down."

Taking out the pin, I counted and then lobbed the grenade from my crouched position. It curved through the air and vanished behind the big red machine. I was sure I had let go too soon. *They would have time to throw it back.* Then a ripping, cracking sound murdered the silence. As the echo died I threw another. When I lifted my head cautiously Larry was on his feet, gun held forward, walking around the side of the red machine. He reappeared.

"On target. The lot."

"Let's get back—Riedel is worried the whole prison will go up."

"I doubt that—those walls . . ."

We met Bauer in the open doorway. He had come to look for us.

"Did you get them?" he asked.

"The lot," I said. "Are they all ready in there?"

"Yes." He sniffed. "Smells like a war in here."

"You volunteered—remember? I still think that was a crazy risk, staying in your house." We were walking back

244

along the passage into the living-quarters area. "Rudi takes chances he shouldn't."

"He was beginning to suspect people were being kidnapped. He explained that, and I offered to act as bait to see who was behind it. That was the arrangement. He had men in the house directly opposite, and they saw us being brought out to the van. If that hadn't happened, they'd have come inside to see what was happening. And half those houses were empty. Dorf had evacuated the area."

"Nobody tells me anything," I said.

And then I heard the first burst of Romy's warning gunfire.

She was standing just inside the open door, emptying the whole magazine. As I came up she reloaded and opened fire again. When I looked out I saw why.

They had forced open the door from the Torre, and men were spilling out across the snow, a small horde of hooded men wearing Alpine winter clothing. Riedel grasped my arm.

"We'd better go back through the shed. That lunatic inside the explosives store . . ."

"If we do that, they'll be all around us."

I fired a burst over Romy's barrel and caught two men running along the ridge of the higher slope to get behind cover of the shed wall. They dropped and lay still. Apart from Bauer and Riedel, the technicians and their relatives were huddled against a wall out of the range of fire. A fairhaired girl who was completely dressed shepherded them briskly. I assumed she was Anna, the police girl from Mannheim. The rest of her party looked like refugees from a disaster, which in a way they were.

Larry was firing through the door now, and the combined barrage of three guns momentarily drove the hooded guards back close to the Torre wall. One of them slipped and fell, but not from Sten bullets—his feet had overbalanced in the chocolate fudge of oil and snow that led from the silver tank, down the slope, and over a wide area in front of the doorway. I gave Riedel my Sten to hold and told Larry and Romy what to do. Then I put my hand inside the satchel again.

They had been reloading alternately, to keep up the barrage, but now Romy waited while Larry reloaded. Then they opened fire together and kept it up until both magazines were empty. The moment they ceased firing I took out the pin, counted, threw.

It was a long throw, and my arm nearly came out of its socket and followed the grenade. Against all the laws of sanity I watched the first climb of its trajectory. As it reached an apex and began to fall I dodged behind the wall and waited. There was an agonizing pause, time enough for me to tell myself it was a dud, and then it exploded. We looked out. The explosion had ignited the oil, and a sea of flames roared up in front of the Torre doorway and along the wall. Inside the oil-smoky flames hooded men struggled, squirmed, and fell. The flames were rising higher now, and even at that distance I felt a breath of warmth. I looked over my shoulder.

"Time to go. Anna, the iron posts we're coming to mark the way through a mine field. Get everyone to walk so close to a post they touch it."

The predawn light was growing stronger now as we made our way from the building and across the snow. We moved more quickly than I had dared hope, and then I heard that everyone knew that Bruno Fleischmann had locked himself inside the explosives store. Larry and I stayed by the post line until the whole procession passed safely beyond the mine-field zone. In the distance Bauer and Romy led the advance guard, which had reached the alarm-bell fence. I had told them about this, and told them to get through it and keep moving. When the bells started ringing I knew they were on their way beyond the obstacle. I wondered what had happened to the Torre warning horn and looked back.

The flames in front of the entrance to the Torre were dying down now, but farther up the slope they burned furiously close to the huge oil tank. Without waiting any longer we headed for the wire fence. I was climbing through it when I heard the sound of the plane, a steady beating noise. As we moved across the snow it worried me. We still had a long way to go down to the covered bridge over the abyss. I forced myself to move faster and caught up to Riedel.

"Has Kardehay any helicopters?"

"No—I'm sure he hasn't."

"Well, there's one up there now in the mist."

"They're starting to come after us," said Larry quietly.

I kept walking as I looked back. In front of the doorway the fire had died down to a flicker. Men began to fan out near the area of the doorway, and from their ease of movement I guessed they were on skis. They would overtake us in a matter of minutes, and as I watched they moved into formation. I checked the magazine in my gun, and Larry repeated my action at the same moment. Then he looked over his shoulder, so I glanced back also, and we both saw it happen.

The flames at the crest of the slope were burning vigorously, and suddenly the oil tank blew. The sound was like the firing of a giant gun, and the shock wave swept down the slope and buffeted our bodies. Ahead of us the procession stopped, gazed back. We shouted and waved them on. I looked back again immediately, and the hooded men had vanished behind a vast pall of evil black smoke. The smoke rolled, congealed, and then spurted fresh clouds which climbed toward the sky. When I turned around again the helicopter was in view, flying very low now as it passed over the heads of the trudging procession. It was still not clear enough to see the machine properly, and we couldn't make out the symbol painted on its side. When it reached a position close to the Torre it circled once, giving the huge smoke cloud a wide berth, and then returned to pass over our heads, continuing on toward the covered bridge.

"There's something coming," I said.

"I heard it, too—from down there."

From the area where the helicopter had vanished a bank of white mist was coming up to meet us. I thought I saw something move inside it, and Larry was peering fixedly, as though hoping to penetrate what lay beyond. In the half-light of predawn the mist looked sinister, as though it might conceal some strange monster. Then they came through it, straight up the slope, the noise of their engines suddenly loud and distinct.

They were large motorized sledges, and their lamps glowed eerily in the mixture of half-light and mist. I began to run down toward the advancing vehicles like a madman, no longer concerned about acting as rear defense, running past Riedel, past women with woolen scarves around their heads like peasants, past a man I now knew to be Theodor Bathe, and Larry ran close behind me. He shouted something, and I looked up to my right. The high ridge where the sniper had stood was coming into view, and along its crest an endless line of men skied through the predawn, skied *toward* the Torre. Italian mountain ski troops! Then the helicopter came back, followed by another, and another. Somewhere above them planes droned, like night fighter planes patrolling in a circle over the mountain. When I reached Bauer and Romy I stopped. And the leading motor sledge blinded me with its beams as the voice spoke. Sven Heim. Rudi Dorf sat behind him.

We stood waiting, beyond the covered bridge, our eyes on the dim shape of the distant Torre as the dawn grew. The technicians and their relatives warmed themselves in front of fires recently lit by the patrol of ski troops, while beside

248

me stood Sven and Rudi. Then Riedel came up, smiling for the first time.

"It must have been a small explosion."

"You think it's gone off already?" I asked.

"I'm sure it has."

He was full of optimism now that he was no longer near the place. He went off smiling to find his wife. I looked at Sven.

"You're responsible for this small war then?"

"I spent more time up here than you did. I managed to see inside the shed full of Veetol bombers. When I found that, I went down to Brennero and contacted the authorities. I wondered if it was you that night I shot those three skiers—something about the way you trudged through the snow."

"You've sent a message warning Langer?" I asked Rudi.

"Yes. There's a radio unit down the valley. He won't be giving that speech tonight about the CIA—and when the van arrives at his house with the bomb and Tarleton's body we'll be waiting for them. Romy has already sent a news flash—Sven took a photograph of the bombers lined up, you know. That will be sent out later."

"Those ski troops have been recalled from the Torre for the moment, I hope."

"Yes," said Rudi, "although it's far too late for an explosion now."

"You've got a watch, Bauer," I called out. "How long since we left the place?"

"Less than you might think—twenty-seven minutes."

"Look!" Larry grabbed my arm.

And as dawn came, the Torre died. The sound of the explosion rolled down toward us, a steady rolling boom, far louder than I would ever have anticipated at that distance, and the boom went on reverberating among the Alpine peaks. In the center, the highest rampart of the ancient prison had suddenly gone wild. Pushing itself outward and upward, it burst into the air, sending out a vast dust cloud which rivaled the oil-smoke cloud still rising by the northern wall. Just before the dust cloud billowed, I saw the hairline of the monorail flake off into the abyss. Then a crack appeared left of center, and huge chunks of the second and third rampart walls left the face of the Torre and slid downward, disappearing into the abyss, leaving behind them a scarred mountain face. We were standing there, silent and still, when Sven lifted his head and turned it to listen.

"It's coming," he said quietly. "What I was afraid of."

"What?"

"Avalanche—listen. The fresh fall of snow . . . this explosion . . ."

I listened, but what I heard was a familiar sound, an unexpected sound—faintly, I caught the roar and hiss of jet motors starting up. Kardehay was leaving in the Veetol. Then I heard Sven's sound, too, a long way up the mountain. A sinister rumbling sound like the distant advance of tanks over a rock desert. I looked up toward the peak, and the mountain was coming alive, a small wave of snow sweeping down, growing larger, longer, gathering up more snow as it gained momentum. The sound wave was increasing now, too—a fearful low growl of immeasurable forces on the move, downward, toward the Torre. For a second, because the noise was obliterated, I forgot the Veetol, and then I saw it emerging, coming up out of the earth—a slim torpedo-like shadow against the white slope. It began to ascend vertically, as though drawn up by an invisible cable, and I thought Kardehay would just make it, to fly away to Egypt. Up on the mountain the downward movement had now become a tidal wave at least half a mile wide, the slope writhing as the crest leaped forward, crashed down, sheered forward over a bluff, met the Veetol emerging from behind the steep face, caught it like a paper plane, and thundered over it and downward.

250